P9-BIW-456

A Nest of Singing Birds

A Nest of Singing Birds

Susan Charlotte Haley

NeWest Press
Edmonton

Copyright ©1984 Susan Charlotte Haley

All rights reserved. No part of this book may be reproduced in any form without the written permission of the publisher.

First edition

Canadian Cataloguing in Publication Data

Haley, Susan Charlotte, 1949—
A Nest of Singing Birds

ISBN 0-920316-63-8 (bound). — ISBN 0-920316-61-1 (pbk.)

I. Title.
PS8565.A44N4 1984   C813′.54   C84-091342-7
PR9199.3.H344N4 1984

48, 408

Credits
Cover and book design: S. Colberg
Typesetting: T. Marx
Printing and binding: Friesen Printers Limited

Financial Assistance
Alberta Culture
The Canada Council

NeWest Publishers Limited
Suite 204, 8631 - 109 Street
Edmonton, Alberta
Canada T6G 1E8

We are a nest of singing birds.

Dr. Johnson
of Pembroke College
Oxford

CAMROSE LUTHERAN COLLEGE
LIBRARY

Chapter 1

And so the winter began to close in. The signs were not ominous at first; indeed, there was an almost welcome series of meteorological changes, beginning with the early morning beauty of the city cloaked in hoar frost and the first really satisfactory snowfall.

Anna pushed a clumsy black English bicycle through a crackling puddle to the street. The grease in the wheels was stiff with cold. Anna was a small pale woman on the verge of thirty, with long black hair that fell below her shoulders. She was wearing a wide woolen skirt, tied up in knots to prevent entanglement in the bicycle chain, and two sweaters under an inadequately warm winter overcoat. She kept her hands doubled for warmth in gloves chewed stealthily at night by the cat, steering with her fists except at difficult corners.

The university was only ten minutes from her apartment. Anna taught philosophy in a little western city at the provincial university, the third little western city and the third little provincial university since the inception of her career. During this ten minute ride, or twenty minute walk, as it was shortly to become, Anna usually experienced that freedom of thought enjoyed by someone putting off a task, not necessarily unpleasant, but to be endured. She had an 8:30 class.

As there were no clocks on her road, and her watch had recently given up the ghost after too many baths, Anna was relying on her estimation of how far they had got into the 8:00 news when she left the house. It was in fact slightly earlier than she believed.

She had been hired for this job in the preceding spring. The age of university prosperity had terminated at about the time of Anna's entry into graduate school, so although she had been teaching for four years, she had never had a job which held any promise of permanence. Anna was currently replacing someone away on sabbatical leave, which meant that her appointment would come to an end in the spring.

Her interview with the Philosophy Department, to which she

had been flown at the university's expense, had been conducted in the falsely hilarious atmosphere of an end of the year party. The chairman, Peter O'Toole, was a slight, weedy man who had managed to gain his position after eight years of insecure lectureship. His fondness for punning variations on song lyrics and literary impersonation had only become apparent at the party. He blossomed into a gravelly-voiced baritone, popping up unexpectedly with the rye bottle, a song on his lips, and his arm around her waist. Several other members of the department had also been present; a light-footed fat man from a Welsh university, a logician who played classical guitar, and briefly, the tight-lipped ex-chairman of the department. As an interviewee, Anna's adrenalin was propelling her toward discussions about the outward reaches of the philosophy of science. Her hopes of discussing anything at all were blighted by the drunken exuberance of the party. Carried forward by the rye, the conviviality of a couple of students and the blandishments of the leprechaun, O'Toole, at her elbow, in the end she forgot it was an interview altogether. The next day, after a shaky meeting with the Vice-president and a pre-noon double rye in the Faculty Club with O'Toole, she was ready to see the job as a possibility.

And now, brushing her bicycle through the shrubbery towards the rack in front of the Arts Building, she had a library card, half an office, and an 8:30 class coming up.

The main lobby of the Arts Building was crowded with students making their way to and from the cafeteria, holding sticky styrofoam cups slopping with coffee. The clock beside the elevator gave her more than ten minutes until her class, and as she devotedly pushed her key into the office door, slinging her coat off her shoulders, she was thinking of her lecture.

The office was darkened, but inhabited as usual by the historian, Mr. Michie, a thin young man with thick glasses, who read there from his arrival at 6:00 until hers at 8:30. He stood up hastily behind his desk, which was placed squarely before the shrouded windows. A faint ray of light fell across the book in front of him.

"Morning," said Anna, cheerily.

He seized his teapot from the top of a filing cabinet and edged around her to the door, murmuring: "I'll just . . ."

Anna sat down at her cluttered desk behind the door, simultaneously pulling a sweater over her head and clearing a space on her blotter. His exits for tea were always timed for her arrival. She had no need to wonder what he had been doing there before she came in. A well-filled wastebasket revealed an insatiable lust to get something published. He was a little older than she, and had almost achieved tenure, now quite difficult to attain with excellent people going begging on the job markets. Publication was a *sine qua non.*

For three minutes Anna read over her lecture notes. These were jotted on the back of an envelope from the telephone company and appended at the bottom was a grocery list and one or two reminders of trivial errands. Having finished her reading, Anna took up the textbook and jammed the envelope into it as a bookmark. As an afterthought, she picked up a handful of old examination booklets and combined them with the book under her arm. Her kind of lecture notes had already caused comment in the few weeks she had been there. She shared an elevator ride with several colleagues, whose well-worn, yellowed folders were much in evidence.

Two of these colleagues were now pacing in the hallway in front of the elevator outside her door. Professor James, a Marxist who lived in the suburbs, had published thirty articles in the previous year. This information had been passed on as a shameful secret by O'Toole prior to Anna's first meeting with James. He was a short, thickset man, who always wore a bow tie. He usually said little, and Anna found this appropriate in a person whose every waking thought was committed to paper.

The other was one of her favourites, Eddy Wiebe, the department's nineteenth-century specialist, a man in his middle forties who exuded an aura of uxorious, family-loving, bourgeois comfort. Their first meeting had not been propitious. He had given Anna what seemed a two-hour harangue on the inferiority of Canadian universities, the other two at which she had taught and the one at which she had studied being singled out for particular disfavour. It appeared that this conversation was by way of being an initiation, for Wiebe treated her thereafter with jocular friendliness, and Anna had begun lately to take secret pleasure in his discourses, which involved an enthusiastic display of hyperbole accompanied by body English. Right now he was shouting at James about the findings of the Committee on Teaching Improvement and Evaluation, and his forefinger was much in play. James was holding his ground in silent displeasure.

". . . and so now that bunch of jackasses comes down with a report like this! Are we going to permit them to invade our classrooms? Next they'll be taking a look at my tax form, and then —"

"Hello Anna," said James stoically.

"Hello Jim. Hello Eddy."

Michie emerged from the elevator, the teapot steaming in his hand. He got his hot water from the cafeteria on the main floor. He passed by silently and closed the office door behind him with a click. James was already looking over his notes as they entered the elevator, and Eddy gave Anna a paternal wink.

Anna made her way through the now almost deserted corridor towards her classroom, doors closing up the hall ahead of her. A slight sinking feeling in her stomach reminded her of breakfast, but there was no time even for coffee now. Absently she untied the knots in her skirt. The usual burst of energy that got her started was coming.

"Good morning all," she said, entering. She put down her book on the table at the top of the room and picked up the blackboard eraser. Her 8:30 class had begun.

Chapter 2

Fifty minutes later, Anna was in the faculty coffee room with a styrofoam cup of black coffee on the table in front of her. The room was still deserted. Other victims of an 8:30 class paused to refile their notes, she supposed.

The room where she sat was a very large one, filled to overflowing with old-fashioned, overstuffed furniture. This was arranged every night by the janitors to facilitate their naps at coffee-break time. Several sofas in remote corners were turned towards the wall so that the occupant could remain entirely out of sight from the doorway. Anna, who preferred to read lying on her stomach, occasionally took advantage of this herself. At the moment she was sitting on a sofa beside the coffee urn at the end of an elliptical arrangement of chairs.

Since she was still alone, Anna made shift to glance at her textbook. The next lecture was going to be a very easy one, she observed. They were dealing with the classical proofs of God's existence, a topic introduced into the curriculum to draw students into Philosophy 1, especially the many in Western Canada who had had fundamentalist upbringings. Anna's class had two major factions,—those who believed that God was an omnipotent father, and those who believed God was a piece of green slime at the beginning of the evolutionary process. Under these circumstances teaching was reduced to adjudication except in the case of her early afternoon class, which was listlessly disinclined to discuss anything.

Michael Jimson entered the room, as he usually did at this hour. He was a young man, close to Anna's age, a political scientist with an Ivy League background. His wife was a civil servant in Washington who refused to follow him into the wilderness. Jimson was in his second year there as a sabbatical replacement and a deadly enemy of Michie's; both were trying for a permanent job in the History department, which included the small coterie of political scientists.

"How goes it, Anna?"

"Mm . . . Too early to tell."

"Michie there as usual?" Anna had confided her views on Michie's habits to Jimson earlier in the term.

"There's evidence to that effect, yes."

Jimson sipped his coffee reflectively. Anna decided that he was not really torn between a desire to take over Michie's job and a desire to return to the center of things in Washington. He spoke rarely of his wife, an assistant to some under-secretary, but warmly and frequently of Michie, whose progress he liked to follow closely.

"Defenestration?"

"No good. His desk blocks the window. Besides, why should I do the dirty work?"

"Ah, then we shall just have to fall back on the department review, for what it's worth."

"When is your reviewer coming?"

"A team of them. We managed to sneak in a political scientist. What a victory, considering that the live half of the department is all on that side. They come next week. Yours?"

"The week after."

"Eddy should be at his best."

"He was warming up this morning in front of the elevators."

Jimson began to describe in vituperative terms the history member of the reviewing team. The political scientist was a "pal" of his, or so he said. Anna looked covertly at his impeccable university professor costume—a tie with a crest, grey trousers, dark blue blazer, and shirt with a detachable collar. No concessions were made to Western winters even in the matter of footwear, and she knew he had a handkerchief in his sleeve.

The room began to fill up. The psychologists arrived as a group at 10:00 on the dot, leaving punctually at 10:15 all at once. They congregated in a corner by themselves on one of the turned-around sofas, talking of second mortgages. O'Toole wandered in as Anna was leaving, hitting her in a comradely way on the shoulder.

"Keep your chin up, Anna. Only four more days in this week."

"After today, of course."

"Of course." O'Toole's suede ankle boots were very down at the heel. He was wearing the almost regulation drill of the sixties, a sergeant's fatigue blouse from U.S. Army surplus.

Anna resisted the desire to get another cup of coffee and go back to her chair. O'Toole's approach to the coffee room was instructive to watch. He instantly drove away all undesirable elements and held the remainder spellbound with a line of patter, a technique which he claimed derived from his "roots." Only a hangover or the vice-president's freezing glare got O'Toole down, and not for long.

Dropping her book off in her office, Anna discouraged Michie in his attempts to leave by telling him that she was going to work in the Library. She snatched a sheet of paper covered on one side with some admonitory chicken scratching from O'Toole about fire drill, and left the room.

The stacks were deserted. The Library was often Anna's haunt in the mornings. Today she was going to the Russian section to a special carrel where she had left *Swann's Way* the previous Friday. Frequently varying her routine, she read novels in the medical library, in the mathematics section, and in amongst the literary P's. She was not without conscience about this and sometimes spent a penitential hour poring over *The World as Will and Idea* in her own domain to partially make up for the morning's escape.

Settling herself in the carrel as comfortably as possible, with one knee up on the sharp edge of the desk in front of her, she roughed out a timetable on a sheet of paper backed up against an open page of *Swann's Way*. The morning she did not bother to fill in. It was already decided what she should do this morning.

"12:00," she wrote, " — Lunch; 12:30 — bookstore for India ink; 1:00 — thesis emendation; 1:30 — class . . ."

An odour of Scotch whisky passing like a zephyr made her look up. The chairman of the English Department, a tall, sandy, middle-aged Scotsman wearing a shabby tweed jacket was walking by with some care. She gestured faintly, uncertain whether he wanted to greet her or not, and he stopped short, gazing at her palely. Anna sat up and smiled.

"Such a large Russian literature section this university has."

"Yes indeed." He leaned his elbow on the carrel partition ahead of her and looked down at the timetable. "Getting away from your office?"

Anna was relieved to see that her book was well covered by the paper. "I share with Michie, you see. I think he likes to be alone."

"Undoubtedly he does." The English professor, whose name was MacGregor, had a pronounced Scottish accent, ameliorated by the whisky fumes which reached her nose as he leaned against the carrel.

"Is that a novel you're reading?" He seemed interested.

"Well, yes, actually it is." Anna blushed and showed him the title. At least it was a respectable novel to be reading. "I don't work very well in the morning." She had gone too far, she realized, implying that she frequently did this in the morning. She blushed again.

"I haven't looked at that for thirty years," he said thoughtfully.

"Oh come. Did you read it when you were ten?"

"Fourteen. I read it at school. I don't think I understood a word of it at the time."

"Oh." Anna couldn't think of anything to say, but she found herself liking him. Their previous meeting had been at the President's wine and cheese party, a stiff little reception she had attended with O'Toole, a guiding sprite at her elbow.

"Would you like a drink?" he asked. She recalled hearing that he drank a lot, "one of the half-dead" from Jimson.

"Well—yes. Why not? At the Faculty Club?" She half rose.

"No. I've got the stuff here." He drew out a pocket flask. "These Russian stacks have more uses than one, you ought to know."

"Thanks," said Anna, accepting a capful of whisky, poured with a very steady hand. A moment later she was choking on the swallow. It was malt. He surveyed her with a faint smile and took a delicate swig from the flask. The pale look had vanished.

"What do you think of the university?"

"Well, I'm enjoying myself here. It's difficult to find anyone to talk to, but I've only been here a few months, so I suppose . . ."

"Yes, you'll find that problem intensifies as time goes on. I've been here for twelve years and I notice it getting worse."

"But it's better to be here than . . . I mean, I was lucky to get a job here. It's hard to get even a temporary position now." She spoke reprovingly, with a touch of Jimson's self-righteousness.

"Here today, gone tomorrow. I could do with a bit of that myself. Here, have some more. You get to like it."

He poured her another slug.

"I don't do this very often, as I'm sure you were going to say about that." He gestured toward her novel. "But we've got the reviewer coming in a few hours and it seemed like the time for it if there was going to be a time."

"Well, it is an unexpected pleasure."

"You get along well enough with O'Toole? He's a sound man in his own peculiar way."

"Yes, I like him."

"As for the rest—you're better off here." He indicated the novel.

Anna swallowed the burning brew in her mouth and held on to the half-filled cap firmly. Her eyes were swimming.

"I don't know any of the people in the English Department," she contributed. "They seem to keep pretty much away."

"Pretty much." He took a taciturn swig. "Do you like Fichte?"

"I don't know Fichte very well. It's true that they hired me to teach aesthetics . . ." Anna wondered, not for the first time, why they had done this.

"You ought to try him out. I used to make something of Fichte."

"You read him when you were fourteen, I suppose."

"No, sixteen."

"And you understood him?"

"I thought I did," he said, rather shyly.

"It's very hard."

"It is. Would you like some more of this stuff? I've got to stop, I'm afraid." He looked at his watch. "I have to meet a child."

Anna shook her head, and he took the empty cap out of her hand. She watched him screwing it back onto the neck of the flask. He had wide-knuckled hands with a few straw-coloured hairs on the back, a sprinkling of freckles. He took his elbow off the carrel partition.

"It was nice," said Anna, searching for another word, but fearing to laugh.

"Yes."

"Will you be all right—for the review this afternoon, I mean?" Anna asked tentatively. He seemed quite steady.

"Oh yes. Lots of time. Do you read here often?"

"Lately."

"I'll probably be seeing you again, then. Goodbye."

"Goodbye."

Anna looked down at her timetable after he had passed out of sight. Absently, she crossed out the entries with an elaborate series of X's. A vision of what it would be like to go to bed with MacGregor was passing unstoppably through her mind. He had nice, curly, fair hair, quite thick. He probably had a paunch from drinking too much, although this was concealed by his loose-fitting tweed jacket. MacGregor seemed to be sitting on the edge of her bed in the half dark leaning over her. She was calling him "Ian" and he was caressing her softly with his sandy-haired hands.

Anna pulled herself together. She wondered feebly whether she had been thinking any of this before he had left. Did it show? I'm getting desperate, she thought. The man is probably happily married, too, or at least married, and he's quite middle-aged. Think about someone like Jimson, if you must.

Mechanically, bored at once by the thought of Jimson, she rose and took her book back to French Literature-in-Translation.

There was no hope for it. It was barely 11:30 and she was on her way back to the office.

Chapter 3

On Thursday afternoons they had departmental meetings—
not every week, but scarcely less often than once a month. O'Toole
clung tenaciously to ideals of democracy nurtured in the sixties.
Aside from Anna, there was no agreement on this point from the
department, but as each thought himself best suited to be autocrat,
the meetings were always well attended.

On this particular Thursday the subject under discussion was
what O'Toole liked to refer to as "the game plan" for the
forthcoming departmental review. All the Arts departments were
being evaluated. All six members of the regular department and
Anna were tensely present. Toying with a piece of chalk (she was
trying to give up smoking), she looked around the table at the
yellowed slatches of old departmental minutes in front of
everyone. Eddy beside her was riffling through a thick pile of
notes. Even James, who was deftly transcribing a few references
from a professional journal into his pocketbook, seemed
preternaturally alert.

"Who is the reviewer?" Anna asked her neighbour, a tall,
thin, clean-shaven man named Peterson, who when excited was
inclined to talk in a very fast and sibilant whisper with his eyes
closed. Anna presumed that this was so that he would not be able
to notice any frantic attempts at interruption.

"Thor Andersen from Toronto," he replied, blinking his eyes
very fast, but not yet closing them. "A very able man, very able."
On the last words he cast his eyelashes down on his cheeks for
emphasis, but opened them up wide again at once.

"I've heard of him. A medievalist, isn't he?"

Across the table, ffrench, the logician, had been telling Gore, a
Leibniz specialist, a private joke, and they both burst out
simultaneously into baying laughter. Peterson cast a glance of
contempt across the table at them, and once more closed his eyes.
He had been head of the department until displaced by a coup.
ffrench and Gore were the two youngest men in the department,
although their appointments had been made several years in

advance of O'Toole, who had had difficulties in completing his dissertation.

O'Toole now came bustling in, several minutes late, with a sheaf of handwritten timetables in his hands. The academic vice-president was very stingy about secretarial help; the Arts faculty shared five secretaries and one photocopy machine. O'Toole had solved this problem by writing out all notes, letters, and memos in longhand. He was presently engaged in a long campaign to capture a typewriter for the department, but everyone recognized that this would take months and perhaps years of persistent memo-writing, as the same object was coveted by History, a slightly larger department.

O'Toole busied himself in spreading around the schedules and a two-page document explaining and justifying the time divisions as laid out. Everyone was to have fifteen minutes in private with the reviewer, Anna noted, and stopped reading.

"Where are you going, Anna?" inquired O'Toole. "We're just about to begin."

"I won't be a moment. I have to get a cigarette from my office."

"Smoke it in the hall, then, will you. We'll leave the door open." The seminar room was a tiny, windowless cell lined with bookshelves.

"Can't do that," said Peterson at once. "Confidential business of the department is being discussed. I, for one . . ."

"Never mind. I'll just smoke this chalk here. Sorry. Go ahead."

"Just a point, by the way, O'Toole," said Gore in the high voice he affected when he was being offensive. "There are one or two errors here. I wonder if you missed . . . Did a secretary do this? Page two, you see: 'one' is usually picked up by 'one', or if you must, 'he', never 'you', you know. And here, too, bottom of the page, there should be commas around 'if you want', otherwise it's ambiguous."

"Ah, thank you, David," said O'Toole, making emendations.

"Just a minute, David," said ffrench. "Putting commas around doesn't make any difference to 'if you want'; it's the placement in the sentence that makes it ambiguous."

"Cut the cackle," said Eddy, who had been reading profoundly through all this. "The thing is that the whole idea is no good. Sorry, Peter, but I won't put up with this. Either we meet him or we don't meet him, that's what I say." He folded his hands and glared around.

"What do you have in mind?" O'Toole was being patient.

"I won't sit in my office waiting my turn to see anyone—even if he's world famous, which this guy Andersen certainly is not—while I know that he's going the rounds getting fifteen minutes of slander from everybody else before I get my crack at him. And furthermore—"

"There's no question of slander—" Peterson began, ignoring Eddy as usual and addressing the chairman.

"Do you want to have an open meeting and all let our hair down together?" inquired Gore, leaning across the table.

"Why not just let in the dean in the first place. He can decide whom he's going to fire," snarled ffrench.

"Perhaps Eddy has a point," said O'Toole reasonably. "They haven't left him much time with us. Two cocktail luncheons with the deans and a dinner with the president cuts a lot out of two days. I couldn't see how to make the private meetings last more than a few minutes."

"Open meeting, it's the only way," murmured James, lifting his eyes momentarily from a lengthy bibliography.

"That's not a good idea, Peter," said Peterson, drawing his long fingers over closed eyelids. "I'm sure I have a few things to say to him that I couldn't talk about publicly, and . . ."

"That's exactly what I mean!" shouted Eddy, half rising and thumping down his notes.

". . . and so do some of the rest of you," went on Peterson imperturbably.

Anna was having a hard time to keep from laughing. She crunched her teeth down on the chalk and took a deep breath.

"I don't think fifteen minutes is really long enough, Peter," she said. "Most of us like to talk in paragraphs or chapters. There won't be time to get through anything but the preliminaries."

"There's an atmosphere of poison in this department," thundered Eddy, "and I don't want it spewed out all over this guy. Secret meetings—we've got to avoid any of that. I know all about the kind of forked-tongued gossip that—"

"What about a general meeting, though, Wiebe. You ought to attend to what could happen there." Gore's high-pitched voice cut through Eddy's shouts like a saw. "Look at this meeting. And what about the one last year when Isaacson threw a chair." Anna was replacing Isaacson, the aesthetician now on sabbatical leave.

"Isaacson was off his nut," said Eddy, suddenly calm—the eye of the storm, Anna presumed.

"Well, let's see," said O'Toole, taking up a pencil and emending busily. "We could take this block of time and do something less formal with it. We could put him in here with a coffee urn and just have people drop by and chat, or . . ."

"Not good enough, Peter," said Peterson. "It's not a chatting matter—what I have to say to him, at any rate."

"What do you have to say to him, anyhow, Willy?" inquired Gore, suddenly hostile.

"That's the point, that's the point!" cried Eddy. "He won't tell us!"

"Well, I think we've had quite a useful discussion of this. Unless anyone comes up with some more suggestions, I think we should . . ." O'Toole smiled slyly at Anna.

"Not so fast, Peter," said Eddy. "There's something else that should be raised. This whole business of departmental review is a mug's game! What right has the administration got . . . ?"

"Look Eddy," said O'Toole patiently. "There's nothing we can do about it. The whole Arts Faculty . . ."

"Eddy has a point," said James, stopping his bibliographic work on a semi-colon. "They're probably trying to figure out how they can cut down on the faculty."

"Well, so what if they are?" screamed Gore, suddenly. "It would be a good thing if . . ."

"Don't say that word. Don't say that word," said Anna in an undertone. Instantly everyone was looking at her.

"What word, Anna?" sawed Gore.

"Deadwood," said Anna, taken aback.

"I should think that a person in your position of all . . ."

"Look," she went on, trying to keep her voice down. "Probably this is an act of aggression by the administration. I think we should stick together, if so. Philosophy, of nearly all the Arts departments, has the most tenuous hold on funds. There won't be any department at all, perhaps, if there isn't some sort of positive united front—"

"Be realistic, Anna. We all know—"

"Anna's right," said Eddy tightly. "I agree."

"You're exaggerating the degree to which there is divisiveness here," she went on.

"Here! Here!" said O'Toole.

Anna began to laugh.

"There should definitely be a committee struck to look into this whole business," said Eddy.

"What business, Eddy?" asked O'Toole.

"Departmental reviews in general and the review of this department in particular. I, for one, am in favor of telling this guy where to get off."

"Tell it to the Dean, then!" shouted Peterson suddenly, clenching his eyes tightly.

"I think I'll have to go back to the drawing board with this," remarked O'Toole in a conversational voice. "I'll try consulting each of you about it tomorrow, and I ought to be able to get out a new proposal by early next week."

"Mail ballot, then," said Peterson.

"Oh, I hope we won't have to vote on it at all. Consensus is what I'll be trying for."

"Are we finished with this?" asked Eddy, rising. "I didn't think you fellows would be courageous enough to talk about the real issues involved."

"Anything else on the agenda, O'Toole?" asked Peterson with a frown.

"Just a few little administrative matters."

The meeting droned on about work loads for next year, division of secretarial time, a possible change in the position of mailboxes. At 5:30, Anna looked in on Michie.

"Just going home," she said encouragingly. He looked down at his typewriter. He usually had a sandwich at 6:00 and returned to work for a few hours before going over to the bachelor faculty residence.

Anna went out, shutting the door carefully behind her. "Nice day, isn't it," she remarked, pulling on one of her sweaters. "Really quite warm for November." She opened the door to the staircase and descended three flights to the floor with the women's bathroom, murmuring pleasantries to herself as she put on her coat. Coming off the staircase through the door onto the fourth floor, she bumped into MacGregor, overcoated and wearing rubbers, standing before the bulletin board patiently waiting for the elevator. She had just been remarking: "A good day for birdwatching" to herself.

"Oh, hello," she said, blindly plunging into the alcove where the door to the women's toilet was placed.

When she came out he was still standing before the bulletin board, apparently reading a long notice about a new anthropology journal.

"Do you birdwatch?" he asked.

"Well, not really. I like birds," she said lamely.

"So do I." There was a pause. Anna found herself completely at a loss. Unusual for her, she couldn't think of anything to say.

"I was pretending to talk to Michie," she remarked at last.

He raised his eyebrows. "I see."

"I'm not really out of my mind. It's just a private joke."

"I can appreciate that."

"We had a departmental meeting this afternoon. About the department review." Anna wondered whether she should tell him more. "Everyone's ruffled, one way or another."

"A bit wild? Someone told me something about Isaacson throwing a chair last year."

"I'm sorry I wasn't here." Anna was laughing. "It's a legend."

"You like that kind of thing, do you?" He spoke austerely.

"It's an acquired taste," said Anna, uncertain of his attitude. She went over to the elevator and pressed the button. What had he been waiting for?

"How did your review go?" she asked, recalling the conversation in the library.

"As well as could be expected. Not having Gore or Wiebe in the Department, it was rather quiet." His smile was dour.

"Eddy was certainly raving this afternoon," said Anna, smothering another laugh.

"Mm. I can imagine."

The elevator doors opened. They both moved simultaneously. He was apparently trying to hold the door for her, but misunderstanding, Anna dropped back a pace to let him on first. In the resultant collision, she banged her wrist against the door jamb. The elevator doors clanked shut and a rushing noise portended its upward progress. They were left standing in the hall.

"Sorry," said Anna. "I'm very clumsy." She nursed her wrist.

"My fault. Does it hurt much?"

"One of those horrid tinglings. It'll pass in a minute."

He looked out the window at the end of the hall in silence until the elevator returned. It was empty. He stood back. Anna entered and held the door. As they started their descent, she said, "I had a look at a secondary source on Fichte. I think I'll use it in the second term. It's a good idea for my aesthetics class."

"You haven't been in the Russian section lately," he said to the air above her head.

"No. Have you?" she asked, wanting to tease him.

"No," he said in melancholy.

The elevator doors opened. He paused, his finger on the "open" button, until Anna had fully debarked.

"I have a bicycle out this way."

"Oh, I see. Well—goodbye."

"Goodbye."

Cursing to herself, Anna mounted her bicycle and pushed off. Instantly her skirt became entangled in the chain. Cursing now aloud, she got off and tugged at the material. There was a slight tearing noise. With an effort involving the use of unknown back and shoulder muscles, she turned the machine upside down on its handle bars and moved the chain backwards. The skirt came away, leaving a few blackened tooth marks at the hem.

As Anna tied up the knots in her skirt, she glanced back at the foyer of the building. Out of the corner of her eye she had a fleeting impression of grey tweed overcoat, which passed immediately, as though retreating from the window.

Turning the bicycle right side up, she rode off, moaning low, like Dr. Johnson, to take her mind off things. She had forgotten her gloves in the bathroom on the fourth floor.

Chapter 4

Anna was in the Russian section again. The previous weekend had been a particularly bad one. Saturday afternoon she had filled up with cooking, Saturday evening with a long walk in the crackling, frosty weather, looking around at the large city mansions close to her neighbourhood. But Sunday had been by all accounts a disaster, beginning with doing the dishes from the previous day's cooking. The afternoon was spent tangling with the final edition of her dissertation, long accepted and still to be made worthy of the printer and the library. The beginning of the evening was desperate: she had written a letter to a friend which contained no news at all and then burned it in the ash tray. She had ended up finally in the Public Library watching a free Chaplin movie. After the movie, she had put herself to sleep with the Scotch bottle, crying a little out of sheer exasperation.

It was Tuesday. On Monday, she had spent her morning with Michie, varying him a little with episodes of Jimson in the coffee lounge. But certainly she was curious about what could happen in the Russian section, and even though Anna breathed in and out rapidly, crossing and uncrossing the first two fingers of her left hand every time she thought of her last meeting with MacGregor, she felt a curious attraction.

"After all, he mentioned it himself," she muttered, raising her head from her book, a philosophy text.

"Some human contact is necessary." And then, "What an idiot I am!"

Sensing the presence of some seeker nearby in the stacks, Anna strove to suppress her muttering by singing: "Scotch Whisky, Scotch Whisky, Scotch Whisky" rapidly over and over under her breath.

It was in fact MacGregor, who leaned at once against her carrel, smiling slightly but not looking at her directly.

"Nice day for birdwatching," he remarked.

"Not so very nice," said Anna literally, and they both gazed out the window at the falling flakes. He had not been drinking.

There was an awkward pause. Anna was canvassing her thoughts wildly for something to say and had just thought of reintroducing the subject of Michie, which he seemed to understand so well, when he spoke.

"How did you like that Chaplin film? It's one of my favourites."

"I'd seen it before," she said. "I like it a lot too. Were you there?"

"No. I was taking a child to the library. I looked in."

"I was rather lonely," she said, looking at her hands and trying to say something honest. "So I thought I'd go."

"I see."

"Weekends are the worst." She glanced up. He was looking at her kindly, rather like Eddy in his paternal pose. "Although, it's hard to choose. Weekdays . . ." She wanted to indicate that it was a joke.

"You don't have a family. I would have thought it would be rather a gay life—being a bachelor."

"Oh yes. It takes a while to get to know people and—where to go and so on, in a new place. I do like it here."

"I wouldn't know about that. My social life tends to run in the four- to six-year-old range." She realized that he, too, was trying to say something honest. "Your department is full of gay blades, isn't it?"

"They decided to hire me at a wild party—yes," she said, laughing. "I don't know when I've ever met anyone as bizarre as Peter."

"He's a sound man, O'Toole," MacGregor repeated thoughtfully.

"His wife is nice, too. I see her every once in a while, usually dashing off to some political meeting or other."

"Very beautiful woman." He pondered this.

"Yes, I know," she said, laughing. "While Peter—he makes her laugh."

"You spend a lot of time talking to Jimson, don't you?"

Anna herself was dubious about her relation with Jimson. His malice was never directed against her, but she had the feeling that this was possibly because he regarded her as a rather malleable, stupid, or at least simple, ally in his social and political machinations. Short of saying that she had no one else to talk to, she didn't see how to answer this query.

"What do you think of him?" She decided that he might give an opinion.

"I really couldn't say."

"He's certainly smart," she suggested. "He's ambitious, though."

"Oh?"

"I used to see you sometimes in the coffee room talking to Helen Bertelsmann." The Bertelsmann was in the German Department, and on first meeting Anna had listed every single one of the ways in which living in Germany was superior to living in Canada. Anna wished she had not made this remark sound so much like an accusation.

"Helen is a very interesting woman." He stated this simply.

"I've just talked to her once. She seemed to rather hate living here."

"Well, so do we all."

Anna took a deep breath. It was no time to get into an acrimonious dispute about nationalism.

"What are you reading today?" he asked abruptly, as though aware of her thought.

Silently she showed him the volume of philosophy.

"Why here? That's all right, isn't it? You could do it safely enough even in your office."

"True." Anna began to hate him. Why was she here, after all?

"You haven't been here for a while, have you?" He seemed to be speaking to someone in the stacks. His voice reached her as from a distance.

"I really don't read novels every morning."

"I suppose not."

There was another awkward pause. He glanced at his watch.

"You have an appointment with a child?"

"Yes."

"How many children do you have?"

"Three."

"Oh."

"Goodbye," he said abruptly.

Before Anna had time to reply, he was walking briskly down a stack corridor.

Anna examined this conversation from every possible angle. It seemed to her that she had offended him in some subtle way. Always ready to believe that she had made some error due entirely to stupidity, she raised the question cautiously with Jimson the next afternoon.

"I keep running into Professor MacGregor lately." This was the literal truth.

"Oh yes?"

"He seems interesting." Anna realized this was too tepid a beginning to capture Jimson's attention. "He has flocks of children, I gather." It occurred to her that the thought of her having this conversation about him with Jimson might have been what made MacGregor leave so abruptly. Anna flagellated herself briefly. Why had she asked how many children he had? Why had she raised this precise point with Jimson?

Jimson seemed to have been giving her remark lengthy attention, for when Anna began to listen again, he was saying:

". . . and so the poor little things are left to his tender care. How many there are, no one knows, of course. You always see him leading a different one around by the hand."

"Why is this? I missed the first part."

"My dear Anna, you must listen more closely. You're so vague." Jimson leaned forward and patted her knee. "His wife was a scandal once upon a time. The scarlet woman of this dim little academic grove, in fact. She went off to Harvard with Bateson, in Religious Studies. Didn't you ever hear about all that?"

"How long ago was this?"

"Three years. Our Ian has been drowning his sorrows ever since, although a good deal more over not going to Harvard himself than over losing his wife, I daresay."

"He drinks, does he?" Anna suppressed a giggle.

"Drinks is not the word. He's always turning up pissed at this or that. There's another fine example of deadwood for you. He saves himself from the pruning fork by being the only person in his department who can teach at all. What with poor Emily and doddering Dodgson . . ."

"Pruning fork?"

"Well, whatever you prune with."

"Tuning fork. Pruning knife."

"Thanks a lot. I must write that down."

Anna was now anxious to get off the topic of MacGregor, feeling extremely guilty at initiating it with Jimson whose malice with the faction known to him as deadwood was boundless, but Jimson, apparently sensing her reluctant interest, was unwilling to be budged. He speculated on the true parentage of the children, dwelling on various points of gossip that made MacGregor out to be many times a cuckold. He also questioned MacGregor's relation with several middle-aged women, among them his colleague in English, Emily Dowell, and making Anna extremely uncomfortable, Helen Bertelsmann. At last Anna stood up.

"I really must go."

"What about a spot of dinner at the Faculty Club?"

"Don't belong. No money."

"It's on me."

"Well . . ." Anna deliberated. The alternative was a bleak bite of cold fried eggplant at home. Her half-edited dissertation was spread out over the living room floor.

"All right."

"Get your duds, then. I'll meet you in the hall."

As they walked across the leafless campus to the Faculty Club, it was snowing rather hard. Anna decided to leave her bicycle overnight in the rack and get a ride home with Jimson after the meal. He had a small sportscar. A faint melancholy began to steal over her. Jimson was chatting on gaily.

". . . she's been sleeping with Spong, if you really want to know."

Anna analyzed her depression. She would just have some sort of sandwich and go straight home. The company of Jimson, even though it pandered to the worst side of her character, was better than no company at all. She thought again of the eggplant, congealed and curling in the frying pan, and shuddered.

". . . strange couple. But you know more about that than I do, I expect."

"Who's this?" asked Anna, coming out of a vague attempt to calculate her bank balance. Perhaps she could pay Jimson back for her share of the meal.

"The O'Tooles—your beloved chairman and his wife."

"She hasn't been sleeping with Spong?" Anna was alarmed.

"Not as far as I know. Although his groping fingers close around anything warm that breathes." Spong was a vague-looking, thin man with glasses. He taught seventeenth-century poetry.

They were approaching the Faculty Club. "You haven't been paying attention again," he said. He put his right arm suavely around her shoulders, simultaneously opening the glass door to the Faculty Club with his left. "I was just saying that the O'Tooles don't have much in common. I wondered whether you knew what it is?"

"What what is?"

"What they do have in common." He spoke patiently. Anna had the feeling that he was reading her mind. She had been wondering whether there was any graceful way of backing out of this dinner.

Dinner in the Faculty Club could be either off the steam table in the hall below, or the expensive gourmet meal offered above. Jimson unerringly led the way upstairs and settled them at a small, white-clad table, romantically overlooking the river.

"Now, young Anna, what will you have? Not one of these lollipop drinks, I hope." He took the liquor list out of her hands. "I prescribe a very dry martini."

"Boodles gin only," he told the waiter. Humming to himself, he began to dissect the wine list.

"Can't I have something to read too?" complained Anna, the martini beginning to left her spirits.

"Just let me finish with this and then I'll entertain you all you like." He ordered a very good wine, the merit of which he explained in detail to Anna.

"That's better," he said as they received their second martinis. "This is really very adequate. Now, where was I? Ah, yes, the O'Tooles."

"I like them." Anna tried to head him off.

"Women have strange tastes. Melissa O'Toole, now—I can see that. You go very well together. Same sort of colouring. Black hair—not blue eyes in your case, but one can't have everything. O'Toole, himself, though —"

"Peter is very funny." said Anna.

"He's a funny sort, yes. I knew that already, however."

"Who is this who's sleeping with Spong, then?" Anna made a feint. She didn't want to discuss O'Toole in these terms.

"Ah, I'm so glad you've got back to that. Our little Francoise . . ." He went on to detail the sexual adventures of Francoise Hibert in the French Department, whose notorious promiscuity extended to a large proportion of the male faculty, according to Jimson. She seemed to have committed some nameless crime in connection with Jimson himself at the beginning of the previous academic year.

When they reached the dessert course, he looked across at her with a tender expression. "And now, tell me about yourself."

"Can't we talk about classical philology or something?"

"I'll order some cognac. This coffee is not particularly good. Where did you grow up?"

"I forget." Anna sat up straight. She was feeling drunk. "Drinking gives me amnesia."

"Well, you should definitely have some cognac. It's very good for you in other ways."

As he talked on, helping her to several more glasses of cognac, Anna began to focus drunkenly on his detachable shirt collar. She ondered whether it came off with the shirt, or whether he took them off separately, and if so, which one first. The thought of Jimson wearing the collar but not the shirt made Anna laugh.

"What are you laughing at? Oh, I think I see. Time to go home now." He began signalling for the bill.

"This has been very nice, Michael. But you must let me —"

"No, no. Entirely my pleasure. I assure you, Anna, this place would be a desert without you."

They made their way to Jimson's car. There was a lot of snow in the parking lot and Anna found herself falling down repeatedly. Jimson's brushings-off became more and more perfunctory as he noticed that she really was drunk.

"What you need is a hot shower and some coffee to sober you up," he said cheerily as they got into the car.

"What I need is four aspirins and bed," said Anna, as firmly she could manage.

Jimson turned around in the bucket seat of the car and put his arm casually about her shoulders. "Yes. Bed—with me, darling," he said, investing the last word with deep drama.

"No, no. You've got that wrong. Not 'darling'—'pal'.

"Yes, dear Anna. We really are friends, aren't we?"

"Friends? Oh yes—friends. Pals." Anna folded her arms and closed her eyes.

"Oh all right." He took his arm away and started up the car.

"You're sure about pals?" he asked when they reached her house. "Dear Anna." He put his hand on her knee. "Shouldn't I come in?"

"I want to go to bed."

"That's what I mean."

"My cat wouldn't like it."

"Cats like me."

"All very well in an armchair. He likes lots of space in bed."

"Whatever you say. Can you make it to the door?"

"Naturally," said Anna, trying to disentangle the seat belt.

"Let me help."

Anna opened the car door and began to back out through it, jackknifing forward to draw herself under the shoulder belt. Jimson, meanwhile, was trying to reach around her to pull the whole apparatus back over her head. Anna gave a hasty backwards wriggle and found herself sitting in the snow on the curb outside the low door of the car.

"Can you walk?" he asked, raising his eyebrows.

"Thank you for a lovely evening," said Anna with dignity, trying to stand up and bend over at the same time so that she could still see his expression.

"Yes, well, I'll see you tomorrow," he said ominously.

Anna shut the car door, then quickly opened it again to

retrieve her shoulder bag. Wordlessly, he helped her disentangle it from the seat belt. She slammed the door again.

With extreme care, she marched up the frozen path to her fire escape. The car started and roared off as she put her key into the lock of the kitchen door.

"Pals," said Anna somewhat later, waking up in her dark bedroom. "Real pals."

Chapter 5

Anna, walking in the next morning, very hung over, was reflecting on her reasons for turning Jimson down. She realized that it would have been easier to have accepted him, at least from the purely social point of view. Now she was going to have to go through days or weeks of tortuous explanations and avoidances, possibly culminating in accepting him anyhow. For Jimson, she knew, would not let a blow to his *amour propre* pass without a spirited struggle. She speculated that she had committed the same crime as Francoise Hibert to whom Jimson had not spoken in more than a year.

She prepared to use her hangover as a weapon of self-defense.

"I can't talk now, Michael; I have a hangover," she said experimentally, glancing through the shrubbery at her bicycle, still there, forlorn in the snow. "As you should know, Michael, I'm hung over."

Should she offer again to pay for her share of the extravagant dinner? The vision of her half-eaten filet passed sickeningly through her memory. Perhaps it would help to pretend that nothing serious had been broached between them. "I'm afraid I drank too much last night, Michael. Did I make a fool of myself?"

In her office, once Michie had fled, she tacked a number of vital items onto an old list. Must go to the BANK. Must buy some GLOVES. Get an ALARM CLOCK.

The class was by any standards a disaster. A student of the God-is-a-piece-of-green-slime school succeeded in grossly insulting both the radical atheistic wing of his own party and the religious believers on the other side. From the resultant brawl, Anna was able to save almost nothing of remote philosophical interest. *Ad hominem* and *ad baculum* flew through the air too swiftly for her educational rebound.

Hunched over her plastic cup in the coffee room with a cigarette burning in the ashtray beside her, she waited for nemesis. There was no point putting it off. Avoidance at this stage would reveal a fatal weakness in her defensive posture.

MacGregor sat down beside her, heralded by a slight reek of whisky which made Anna's stomach churn.

"I thought I should find you here at this hour." Was he making a study of her work habits, Anna wondered irritably. "Here, I've brought this." He passed her a weathered volume, Fichte's *Science of Knowledge*. "I don't know whether you've looked at it."

"I have, as a matter of fact. Long since, though. Thank you very much." She examined the flyleaf which revealed it to have been a prize book from some Scottish educational foundation.

"Sorry," Anna added hastily, as a gloomy silence began to prolong itself. "I'm a little the worse for wear this morning. Awful class."

Jimson swung himself gracefully into his usual chair. "Hello, Anna. Hung over?"

"Very."

MacGregor sighed slightly, and settled himself deeper into the couch at her side. Anna's carefully planned defense was totally destroyed by this unexpected action. She gave a weak smile to no one in particular and drank deeply of her coffee.

"Look here, MacGregor," said Jimson, taking in the situation, "you're on the Library Committee. Can't you do anything about Politics? There's nothing in the Library later than Adam Smith."

"Disbursal comes from individual departments. We just arrange for budgeting." MacGregor was laconic.

"Yes, yes, I know that. But we're nearly enough men—pardon me, Anna—persons, to form a department on our own. Only the antiquated structure of this university subordinates us to History. That should be taken into account."

"Undoubtedly. Still, that's not up to the Library Committee, is it?"

"Everyone stands together on this one, don't they? Tradition, even wrong-headed . . . Pardon me, Anna?" Jimson flashed her a tender smile.

"I said, 'doesn't he'."

"What did you mean by that, if I may ask?"

" 'Everyone stands together on this, doesn't he?' " Anna groaned to herself. MacGregor was gazing at her in silent approval.

"Ah. I see. A point of grammar." Jimson took out his cigarette case and elegantly extracted a handmade cigarette—his special blend of tobacco. "So you're not a feminist, Anna?"

"I would have accepted 'doesn't she'."

"You must really watch that, you know," said Jimson venomously. "I realize that philosophy is a funny kind of discipline at best, and you should try hard not to let it rot your brain. Your colleague Gore, for instance, appears to have this kind of thing . . ."

Gore now entered the coffee room in his cat-footed way.

"Did I hear someone mention philosophy, linking it with my name?" he said genially, spilling an immense quantity of sugar into a cup before adding the coffee.

"Your name came up, yes," said Jimson. Anna saw that he was sulking.

"Michael thinks we philosophers are too involved with language," she said, suddenly deciding to go on taking the high road.

"Not so," said Gore, sitting down. "Impossible. One cannot be too involved with language."

As Jimson began laying out his battle plan, leaving his flanks exposed for subtle infiltration from Gore, Anna closed her eyes briefly. This was possibly the moment for escape, if she could gather her wits together sufficiently to set in motion the muscles usually used for standing up. When she opened her eyes again the head of a moose shot many autumns ago by the academic vice-president seemed to be coming down off the wall toward her.

Apparently seeing the direction of her eyes, MacGregor remarked in an undertone, "One reason why I rarely come in here is the decorations. I find them oppressive."

"Yes," said Anna weakly. "I really must go now. It was nice of you to bring the book." She got up.

"Going so soon?" Jimson looked up. "Too bad. I was looking forward to a chat."

"Perhaps later," replied Anna, and made blindly for the door.

Before she had time to consider her plans, she found herself on her bicycle pedalling rapidly home. Her next class was at 1:30. Time for a bath, a nap, a good lunch.

After her 1:30 class she went downtown and wandered through the stores aimlessly, realizing that in her current malaise she would not be able to buy anything she could like later on.

Just before supper, as Anna was doing the dishes, the telephone rang.

"Hi, Anna." It was Jimson.

"Hullo Michael." Anna extended the full length of her body across the living room rug, arm at the stretch for the cigarette package. It remained out of reach.

"You've been avoiding me all day. Or is that just my paranoia?"

"I've been feeling sick. I had a lot of naps."

"You were drunk last night, weren't you? I only realized it in the car." This was Anna's opening.

"I expect I made a fool of myself."

"Not at all, I like that kind of foolery...." Anna made a lunge for the cigarettes, putting the receiver on the carpet. When she picked it up again he was saying: "... but I value our friendship too much."

"Me too." Anna spoke around the filter of the cigarette she was holding in her teeth and struck a match against the box clenched between her knees. She wondered whether there was any truth in this.

"It's difficult in a place like this to find anyone who's even close to sane." Anna nodded. So that was it. "That fellow Gore, for instance. I don't know how you tolerate it. Between Eddy and Gore, you've got quite a department there, Anna. Not up to the standard of History, of course, but then . . ."

"Gore's not so bad. He's very erudite in his field."

"And what might that be? Comma placement and the use of the semi-colon?"

Anna laughed to avoid pursuing the matter.

"You're getting pretty chummy with MacGregor, I gather."

"I keep running . . . meeting him."

"They do all hang together, you know, just as I was saying. Mass mediocrity doesn't need defense, apparently."

"I like him, I think," said Anna. "He's kind." She was groping for another word.

"Kind of what?" He allowed himself an elegant chuckle. "Well, I collect specimens myself. It passes the time."

"Michael," said Anna urgently, "you must let me pay for part of that dinner."

"Oh, come now. We're not poor graduate students any more."

"Well, but it was simply a waste of good cognac." She realized how this might be taken. "I mean, I just got drunk. It might have been beer."

"Not as far as I was concerned. And I like company on these occasional trips back to civilization."

"Well—it was really delicious."

"Did you think so? Monosodium whatever it is. The watercress was parsley."

"You're so critical. It was very good parsley. We peons aren't supposed to notice things like that."

"Peons is right. I hear that Pinch-penny Pigeon is going yachting in Bermuda this Christmas."

"Christmas. When will that be, I wonder?"

"Just wait till the spring term, my girl. March is a month of eighty days in these parts."

"One hundred and eight days in February."

"All the rest have twenty-two, except August which has fourteen."

Anna stubbed out her cigarette on the back of the cigarette package and stowed the butt carefully in her pocket. "I must get back to my muttons. A pot of thin gruel is boiling over on the stove."

"Well—do get better."

"It's coming along."

"We're still pals?"

"Absolutely."

My weakness, Anna thought, is for chatting. For a chat I will do anything, sell out on my cat, give up good health. Even go to bed with Jimson, although we hope it won't come to that. The more superficial forms of friendship attract me like a moth to a flame. The emptier it is the better. A couple of witty remarks sets me up for a whole day. A bit of gossip of the right sort and I'm on for a week. I must do something serious about this.

She sat down at the kitchen table and pulled a pile of unpaid bills over in front of her. Using the cigarette pack as a straight edge, she carefully ruled out a checkerboard of blocks on the back of an envelope and began labelling them down the left side: "8:30-9:30; 9:30-10:30 . . ."

Chapter 6

Standing at the mail boxes the next morning beside ffrench as they waited for the sorting to be completed, Anna remarked, "What came of that dispute over the external review?"

ffrench, a tall, cavernous, young man with long blond hair which was a constant source of offense to his older colleagues, scowled briefly and shrugged.

"Peter has worked out the ideal compromise. He's given everyone twenty minutes in private and we're going to have a general meeting in the evening before Andersen catches the plane."

"How did he make the extra time?"

"Well, for one thing, only tenured staff will be meeting him."

"But I'm the only untenured one."

"True. I'm just telling you how he made the extra time."

"I see."

ffrench snatched a sheaf of mail and shuffled through it briskly. A letter captured his attention and he broke into it with a long, yellow fingernail. He grew his fingernails for the guitar. Anna turned her attention sadly to a single large envelope with the university crest on the back. It contained an invitation to the faculty Christmas reception: "Wives are invited."

ffrench gave a crow of laughter over his letter, then allowed his features to slip back into his habitual angry intensity.

"Bateson has got his come-uppance," he remarked to no one in particular. Anna glanced around. They were alone together in the mail room.

"Bateson?" she inquired, assuming that he wanted to convey this news to somebody.

"Yes—Bateson. This is from a friend at Harvard. Lucky devil to be there and not here. Bateson—well, well. Might have expected something like this." He unfolded the letter again, gloating over the page of typescript.

"What happened?"

"He's being fired. Out on his ear before Christmas."

"How awful. What for?" Anna recalled Jimson's gossip. Bateson was the man who had run off with MacGregor's wife.

"Turpitude—or incompetence. Can't be that; must be the former. There's nothing really *incompetent* about plagiarism on that scale, I suppose."

"Good heavens. But Bateson is famous around here as a scholar."

"Well, as I say, it was a pretty competent job of work." He began to ease himself out the door, apparently eager to find a more knowledgeable ear.

Anna, still gazing stupidly at her invitation, thought briefly about how MacGregor would find this news. His feelings about Bateson could hardly be very positive. On the other hand, his wife was with Bateson, and the old scandal about this would be resurrected with the addition of a new element, the taint of Bateson's disgrace. Anna gave herself a mental shake. MacGregor could probably look after himself perfectly well. Why should she take Jimson's view that he was a loser? His main problem in life was people like Jimson—and herself, she reflected, sadly— working him over behind his back.

The party (R.S.V.P.) was scheduled for the last day of classes before the Christmas break. This was the Friday of the coming week. The Dean extended his invitation to the Arts and Science Faculties. To be held at the Faculty Club. Members and non-members alike.

Half an hour later in her office, Michie silently passed her the phone on his way out the door. It was Jimson.

"Anna." His tone was gleeful. "Have you heard all about Bateson yet?"

"Yes," said Anna, warily.

"Oh." He seemed disappointed.

"I was in the mailroom when ffrench got the letter."

"ffrench? Oh, I see. I got it from Speer—my esteemed colleague, Speer." Speer was a historian whom Jimson cultivated rather along the same lines as he attended to Michie. "Quite a story, don't you agree?"

"Rather Scrooge-like of Harvard to throw him out before Christmas, I thought," said Anna, trying to keep to non-essentials.

"Throw him out? That's not the half of it. Perhaps they'll take him to court."

"Whatever for? Not plagiarism? It's not an indictable offense, is it?" asked Anna. She lit a cigarette and then hastily put it out. Michie hated smoking.

"Fraud. Forged credentials. It seems our little Geoffrey was weaving his deceitful webs way back in the less distinguished phase of his career when he was here. One did hear the occasional story about unpaid debts and so on, but we tend to discount such things in the presence of genius, don't we? I mean, Einstein had trouble remembering about the water bill and so on."

"I see."

"No you don't, you don't see at all! He doesn't even have a Ph.D., according to Speer. And the funniest part of it is that all these old fogies here who were virtually bowing down, kissing the hem of his robe. . . ." He began snorting with laughter.

"You're in your office, are you, Michael?"

"Yes, Why? Oh, I see. Nothing to worry about. As I was about to say, they'll all be onto him like a pack of wolves now." A new thought seemed to occur to him. "Maybe MacGregor's wife will come trailing back."

"For Christ's sake, Michael."

"Oh all right. Below the belt, I see that. You're right. Restraint, social code, stiff upper lip."

Michie slid uneasily through the door and coughed his way toward his desk. Still coughing, he slid a package of throat lozenges out of his desk drawer.

Anna glued the receiver to her ear.

". . . kneeling beside his pillow as he expires of cirrhosis . . ."

She began clicking the receiver buttons up and down.

"Is that you still, Michael? I can hardly hear you. There seems to be an interruption in the line."

Michie was feebly trying to open the window, pausing to cough into his fist.

"Perhaps the lines are crossed," remarked Anna. "I got in on one of the assistant deans having a chat with one of the other assistant deans last week."

"Oh yes? Well, we must have coffee together this afternoon, eh? Oh, by the way, Anna, about this shindig of the Dean's: want a drive?"

"All right, that's kind of you."

"Very well. I'll come by to get you in a taxi, honey," he sang. "Half past eight?"

"Well—nineish. I like to make something of an entrance, you know."

"My lords and ladies: Mary Anna and Mr. Jimsonweed."

"The Earl of Jimson and Lady Anne."

"Sister Anne."

"Good-oh, then."

"Right."

"Oh, yes. P.S. Wear that dark red dress of yours, will you? It's just the right sort of thing."

"Do you have a tie to match or something?"

"Try to be graceful, dear. A lady says thank you."

"Thanks awfully."

"Not at all."

Michie had succeeded in opening the window when Anna rang off, and he was now trying to prop it open with a book.

"Sorry about that," she said casually. "I forgot. I just had a gasp or two and then I remembered."

He gave up on the window and took up his teapot defensively.

"Leave the door open," she called after him. "The smoke will be clear by the time you get back."

A moment later a shadow fell over her shoulder from the door. Anna, who was writing, "Yes, thank you. I'll be sure to be there," on the back of the invitation, looked up. It was MacGregor, leaning against the door frame. He always seemed to be leaning against something.

"I see you are alone," he said pensively. He came further in in a tentative way and leaned against her filing cabinet. She saw that he was smoking a cigarette.

"How do you answer these damn things, anyhow?" asked Anna, holding up her card. "I was writing on the back of it. A bit graceless, do you think, or is that offset by the saving in paper?"

"You're going, are you?"

"Are you?" Anna recalled her recent talk with Jimson with shame.

"I don't usually."

"Please sit down," she said, pointing out a chair beside the filing cabinet.

"Shall I shut the door? Michie isn't here, I see."

"I drove him out by smoking. That's why I had the door open, actually." MacGregor glanced at his cigarette, then shut the door efficiently and sat down, blowing smoke through his nostrils.

"Do you think he drinks?"

"Michie? I don't suppose he does."

"Too bad. Would you like one yourself now?" Again recalling her conversation with Jimson, Anna nodded slowly. Taking out his flask, he deftly poured a capful for her, then removed a sardine tin from his coat pocket and set it on the floor between them.

"I usually carry my own ashtray. No one in my department smokes." Anna took two cigarette butts out of her pocket, the one from yesterday's telephone conversation with Jimson and the one from today's, and deposited them under the rolled-up lid. At this moment Michie opened the door a crack and began to slide through, then changed his mind and backed out coughing and pawing the air. MacGregor kicked the door shut again.

Anna put her head down on the crook of her arm.

"Don't take on so. He can go to the Library himself once in a while."

"Not with his teapot."

"Well you can't smoke there either, can you?"

"I suppose that's true."

"Don't let me destroy all your domestic arrangements, however," he said, addressing himself liberally to the flask. "I wanted to ask you a private question, that's all." She realized he was well into his flask, and took a quick swallow herself. Nervously she lit a cigarette.

"There seems to be some story going the rounds this morning about Bateson. Have you heard it?"

"Yes," said Anna, feeling sick.

"Well, I haven't. What is it?"

"ffrench got a letter this morning from some friend of his at Harvard," she said. "I was there when he opened it." Better to leave Jimson out of it altogether.

"Here, have some more."

"ffrench said that Harvard was going to fire him—for plagiarism." She swallowed another mouthful.

"Anything else?" He was looking at her attentively, no sign of emotion on his face.

"Well, he didn't tell me anything more. I wasn't much of an audience, though, not having known Bateson."

"Well, thanks." He fell into a brown study, looking at his shoe. At last he said: "Nice of you to tell me. No one else would. I expect you know that my wife went off with Bateson."

"Yes."

"Jimson told you, probably." He smiled slightly. "So there's no need to embarrass you with any more about that, then."

"I'm terribly sorry. Is there anything I can do?"

"Not at all. You've been very nice. Just remain sitting there, possibly with some more Scotch in hand."

He poured out another capful and put the flask down with a frown on Michie's desk some distance away from his chair. Anna noticed that her hand was shaking as she lifted the cap to her lips.

"I expect you realize I think they're all bastards," he said, laughing shortly. "Not necessarily my wife and Bateson, although Bateson—well, anything I think about Bateson has an interpretation one way or the other, doesn't it, so what's the point of that? No, I mean the rest of them. If they had the guts, they'd have plagiarized themselves to Harvard, but since they haven't they can hardly contain their spleen." He lit another cigarette, the flame of his match unwavering in his fingers.

"Perhaps you should go home for the afternoon or something. This is going to be ghastly all day."

"I'm all right." He glanced at his watch. "I have an appointment with a child as usual. Just sit still for a few minutes and relax."

She smiled at him. "I'm not the patient here."

He smoked silently for a short while, glancing around the office, which was largely decorated with Michie's books, and returning to scrutinize her minutely at intervals. At length he got his flask from Michie's desk and, taking the empty cap out of her fingers, began to screw it down tightly.

"You're all right, are you?" he asked, standing by the door. "Don't feel badly about this."

She smiled again, and he paused, then went out without saying anything.

Anna got up and went over behind Michie's desk to open the window.

Chapter 7

Anna, wearing her dark red dress, was drinking a small glass of sherry at the kitchen window of her apartment. It was 9:15 on the Friday of the Dean's party. Classes were over, and to celebrate she had bought a winter chrysanthemum which was now decking the windowsill in her otherwise barren kitchen. Jimson was fifteen minutes late.

There are two classes of party-goers: those who arrive early and sit uncomfortably together until everyone else comes, by which time they are thoroughly ill-at-ease and want to go home; and those who come late and go late and have a wonderful time in between. Anna, usually of the former class, had the comfortable sensation that Jimson was looking after her interests.

Someone was knocking on the window. Peering through the glass, she called, "Just a minute!" and started to pull on her sweaters. He began rattling at the kitchen door from the fire escape. She let him in reluctantly. Having Jimson too familiar with her amenities was not a plan she favoured, especially after the events of the previous week.

"I brought something," he said cheerily, getting a wine bottle out of a paper bag and following this up by withdrawing a corkscrew from the pocket of his overcoat. Did he think she lacked a corkscrew, then?

"We're already late, Michael."

"The later the better as far as I'm concerned. Do you really want to attend this bash? We could have quite a good time by ourselves here. I've got some more in the car."

"Each with its own corkscrew?" asked Anna. He was going through her cupboards for wine glasses.

"Thank God for that too. Don't you have any hock glasses? I use this kind for orange juice."

"Sorry about that. I have mugs. Would you rather?" Anna put her sherry glass, a cream cheese jar, unobtrusively behind the chrysanthemum.

"It spoils the wine, that's all," he said, giving up the search.

"We could drink out of the bottle."

"You like that, do you?"

"It's the way I was brought up."

"All right—here goes. Anything but mugs."

"I would like to go to the party, though. What about our entrance?"

"I was thinking about that. John Thomas and Lady Jane."

"No, I'd rather not. I've been thinking about it too. I'm not really your type."

"Now what do you mean by that? What do you think my type is?" He was delighted.

Anna had been expecting to get into this, but not so early in the evening. She tried to think what she meant.

"Someone with wine glasses."

"And a corkscrew."

"I have a corkscrew, damn it!"

"I bet it's on a Swiss army knife."

"Well, that's just what I mean."

She could see that he was enchanted with this and began to pour on more of it. An unsophisticated country girl and an Ivy League-educated city boy were like oil and water. He thought this was good, but when she began to enlarge upon his elegant habits, he showed signs of discomfort.

"Someone who spurns Webster, does not have to use a magnifying glass on his Oxford."

"Well . . ."

"Who owns an M.G. of vintage make—wire wheels . . ."

"Oh really, Anna!"

"Wears a tie with a crest."

"Don't be absurd."

"Drinks only Indian tea."

"You're making fun of me."

"Not at all. Oxford marmalade, imported tobacco, French cigarettes, wine cellar, Châteauneuf du Pape—what was that thing we ate the other day?"

"Crème brulée."

"Right: crème brulée, rimless glasses, Perrier water, ski stockings, Boodles' gin, steak and kidney pie —"

"Are you drunk already?"

"A tiny bit, yes. What is this? It's very good."

"Not very. A passable Moselle."

"Right. That's what I mean." A—passable —"

"Okay, Anna. Calm down. I think you're being silly."

"It's a tragedy, really," she said sadly. "The poor girl was in love, but hopelessly, and he had a perfectly good wife."

"Oh, that's it, is it?" He was thoughtful. "You have a point."

"Are you giving any exams?"

"Not me. You?"

"No. So you'll be seeing her—when, exactly?"

"The day after tomorrow." He looked at his watch. "My flight gets in at 8:05 in the evening."

"So . . ."

"Well, perhaps you're right. At least we'll postpone this discussion. So now—what about going to this bash? You're ready, are you?" He cast a censorious glance at her sweaters.

"Under this I am wearing a red dress. Let me look closely at your tie." She peered at it.

"Okay, Anna. Let's go."

The party was being held downstairs at the Faculty Club. The rather shabby downstairs was unrecognizable. The steam tables had been pushed aside and several room partitions opened up to create a dance floor. Some of the furniture and plants from above had been moved down, and a band was playing loudly at the end of the largest of the rooms.

Standing guardedly beside a potted palm, Anna watched Jimson guide his partner, Francoise Hibert, with whom he had achieved an unexpected rapprochement just lately, across the dance floor in an expert waltz. At her own elbow was Professor Frame, a timid geologist, who was the French woman's escort.

"I think I'll get myself a stronger drink," she remarked crossly, putting her empty beer bottle down beside the stems of the plant. He made a faint gesture of assent, his eyes not leaving the couple on the dance floor.

She made her way through several well-lit rooms to the bar. This party, so well attended, unlike the President's reception, gave off a buzz of enjoyment. Beside her at the bar O'Toole tapped her on the arm.

"What vision is this?"

"Hullo, Peter."

O'Toole's wife gave her a nod and went on talking animatedly of Margaret Atwood and Margaret Laurence to Spong of the English Department. She was dressed carelessly in a pink *peau de soie* ballgown dating from her undergraduate days, and she had never looked more black-hairedly and blue-eyedly beautiful.

"Glad you made it," said O'Toole, taking Anna's elbow.

"Much better come over here." He led her to a cloakroom. "Over here, we mix three-ounce drinks." He took a paper bag-cloaked bottle out of the pocket of one of the coats hanging on the hooks and poured a large dollop into Anna's pallid glass.

"Now do tell?" he went on. "You came with Jimson doubtless. Not a hint of scandal about you and Jimson though, little Anna." O'Toole was slightly shorter than Anna, which made him about five feet two. "What do you have to say for yourself?"

"Was I too early? It's a fault of mine."

"Not of his, though, you see?" He stuffed the bottle back into the pocket.

"Does this belong to you?" She sniffed her glass suspiciously. It was, as she had feared, rye.

O'Toole put his finger beside his nose in reply.

"I bet it is yours."

"Anna," he sighed, changing characters, and taking her free hand, "What can I do about you? I . . . you see . . ." He gestured in a way that indicated public censure from the world outside the cloakroom.

"You could have given me fifteen minutes with the external reviewer," said Anna suddenly, withdrawing her hand.

"Why?" He was alert at once, his day-to-day self, the chairman.

"Damn it, Peter. I thought it was pretty underhanded of you to take away my chance to talk to him."

"Want a job at Toronto? I'll get you a job at Toronto. Anything else?" Putting his finger beside his nose again, he grabbed her hand.

"Let's see. I want a raise in pay, a pink ribbon, and three lollipops," said Anna, coldly. "You're a pig, Peter."

"I've always been of that opinion," came the adenoidal voice of Gore over her shoulder. "Mind if I horn in on this?"

"Philosophers always talk to philosophers at parties," said Gore's estranged wife, Emmy. She was clinging to his arm, smiling, but her eyes rested on Anna with hostility.

"Where's Eddy?" asked Anna, looking around in paranoia.

"He never comes to these affairs," said Gore. "Stays home with his family and the pet rabbit."

By virtue of twisting her wrist against his thumb Anna had succeeded in releasing her hand from O'Toole's grasp. She said to Gore now, "I like Eddy's rabbit, though we have never met," and moved away.

Later, as she was pouring the last of her rye into the beer bottle she had left in the plant pot, she became aware of an emanation at her elbow. She knew who it was before she turned around because of the faint breath of Scotch whisky conveyed to her nose by some dancer's passage.

"You came with Jimson, I gather." He was looking pessimistically at the dance floor.

"I did. Who did you gather it from?"

"O'Toole, more than elsewhere. Do you like to dance?" he asked abruptly.

"No, I never do, or at least, I told Michael that." She shrugged. "What are you doing here?" Instantly she regretted asking. It must be some form of self-punishment.

"I thought I'd see how you were getting on." Was this 'you' a personal 'you'?

"I was pouring out some rye that Peter gave me. Rye makes me horribly sick."

"Oh? Well. Would you like some Scotch now?" His hand was halfway to his lapel when Jimson appeared around the verge of the plant pot.

"How are you getting on, Anna?" His tone was as of a doctor to a patient now possibly on the mend.

She put on a death's head grin. "I'm having a remarkably good time, Michael. I've quarreled with all the philosophers I could find, and now I'm chatting with Professor MacGregor here, as you see."

"Are you sure you don't want to dance? It's a reasonably good band, you know."

"No, no. I really don't. Especially now. I'd break your leg, probably." The band was starting to play a polka.

"Can I get you a drink?"

"No. For heaven's sake, find yourself a partner, Michael. I'm quite all right," she said irritably.

Jimson disappeared, wraith-like in the gloom, with a hollow, parting "very well." It was hard to hear anyone against the music.

"Ian," he said.

"What did you say?"

"Ian," he bellowed. "Come back here behind this tree."

"Ian," she repeated.

"Yes," he said in a lower voice. "That's my name. Stop calling me Professor MacGregor."

"What was this about Scotch?" Anna realized that she was already drunk.

"I have some." He took out his flask. The band was very loud in the background. Anna, who was finding it difficult to attend to anything in her fury, reached out and took his hand.

"For heaven's sake, let's get out of this!" she cried against a spirited outburst from the band and led him into refuge in the outer hall.

"Not good enough," she remarked, noting a cache of overshoes by the front door and the straggler taking his ease on the rubber runner which covered the floor. "Where do we go now? Are we driven into the outer air?"

"The Art Gallery," he said, retaining her hand in a warm, dry grip.

"Should I get some ice?" Anna began to worry about this.

"Ice is a waste with malt." He continued to hold her hand.

As they made their way to the Art Gallery, Anna was feeling extremely uncomfortable. She was making a fool of herself. After a good deal of surreptitious wriggling, she managed to free her hand.

The Art Gallery was open, but deserted. They sat down on a fake leather chaise in the centre. The frigid room reduced Anna to a state of neutrality. Her eagerness to get away from the party had evaporated.

He passed her a capful of whisky without any comment whatsoever.

"What are you going to do for Christmas?" asked Anna helplessly. She already knew the answer. He would stay at home with his children.

He took a swig from the flask and then removed the untasted capful of whisky from her hand, setting it down on the floor with his flask. Anna's mind was working slowly as she watched him do this.

A moment later, she found that she was staring straight into his eyes, head on, from very close up. He was inspecting her face attentively, in the same way he had done before in her office. She did not avert her eyes, although an argument of the 'you're not my type' type flitted through her head. Why had she agreed to go to the Art Gallery?

"Are you sure you should have left Jimson like that?" he asked, apparently curious.

"No," said Anna dolefully.

"I don't like him."

"He has some good points," replied Anna, trying to be fair. What were they? She was not thinking clearly.

"Definitely not," he added, putting both arms very slowly around her bare shoulders.

The words "I don't . . ." were almost at lip level when she realized that she did, she certainly did want him to.

The room began to feel a good deal warmer. Anna found that if she kept her eyes closed she was concentrating better. A warm, orange core like that found inside a carrot seemed to be growing up to the level of her throat, inside her thorax.

"You're not drinking anything," he said, not letting go.

"Oddly enough." She opened her eyes and laughed. Instantly he began to kiss her again.

There was a burst of band music behind them and a cold draught heralded the voice of O'Toole saying, "Let's go in here."

O'Toole, Gore, and—could she believe her eyes?—ffrench, burst into the room with party hats and noisemakers. Was it some kind of trap? She focussed her eyes on MacGregor, whom she had been privately addressing for some time as "Ian" and noticed that he was screwing down the cap on the flask in such a way as to attract a minimum amount of attention. They were now sitting three feet apart.

"Having a good time, Anna?" called O'Toole satirically as the room began to fill with merry-makers.

"Not at all!" cried Anna, rising, her heart full of rage, and stalking out of the room. In the cloakroom she pulled on her two sweaters, the inadequate leather coat and a headscarf. She was looking for her gloves when Jimson grasped her sympathetically by the arm.

"Not having a good time, Anna?"

"Not at all," she agreed. "See you next term."

She left the building at a half run and was two blocks on towards home before she realized that there was someone behind her. It was MacGregor.

"What now?" She stopped in her tracks.

"You haven't any gloves," he said, taking both her hands.

"I'm used to it. I'm in a rage, Ian. I'm going home."

He did not let go of her hands. He had no gloves, either, and no overcoat.

"Just let me go home."

"Are you all right?"

"Fine."

"Ah."

She turned on her heel, withdrawing her hands and marched steadily towards the river, not looking back.

Chapter 8

During the first week after the Christmas holidays were over, Anna saw a lot of Michie. She talked briefly several times with Jimson, still full of the "political reality" of Washington. He had been to the big Christmas conference of his professional association.

"Don't you feel like a prostitute at those things?" said Anns, sympathetically. They were chatting in the coffee room. "Hawking your body in hotel rooms and bars." These conferences were the market places for people wanting jobs.

"I saw a lot of my old pals," said Jimson with satisfaction. "They think my having a job here is very quaint."

"Living in the backwoods like this, with your bean rows and your beehive."

"I have hopes for better things to come." He was now smoking a new kind of cigarette. He selected one carefully from his case, tapping its filterless end lightly on the table. "Did you have a good time, yourself? What did you do?"

"A quiet time," said Anna cautiously. "I went home to my parents.

"Oh, you have some of those, do you? You've been very reticent on that point, if I may say so."

Anna came from a small town on the prairies. She wondered whether she had been hiding this fact, feeling ashamed.

"How's your wife?" she asked, parrying. She had not really been hiding her background. It was the sort of thing it would be impossible to talk to Jimson about, that was all.

"In good health," he replied coolly, directing his glance toward the coffee room door. Francoise Hibert entered the room and sat down on the arm of a chair. "Hello, Francoise. What brings you to these parts?"

"It is necessary to go away from the French Department. Pouf!" She waved her hand in front of her face. "What an atmosphere there is in that place."

"Yes, well, you must tell me all about it." Jimson got to his feet. "Ta, Anna." Anna nodded vaguely. Not very interested in this turn of events, she went back to Michie.

She was avoiding the English department by never going to the lavatory on the fourth floor.

Now walking in the morning darkness to her 8:30 classes, she sang or whistled "Yankee Doodle" or blew out through her nostrils when the thought of MacGregor came up. She also changed her novel-reading perch to the Chinese section, not so near the Russian section as to be easily located, but near enough to make it the last place he would look.

On January 21st there was a footstep in the deserted stack corridor behind her. It was late in the afternoon. Anna's aesthetics classes now took up her mornings.

He leaned against the stack column and gazed at her austerely.

"Hello," she said, looking up, her heart sinking.

"Are you hiding?" He came straight to the point.

"Yes," replied Anna.

"Ah. I'll go then."

Anna stood up reluctantly. "No, don't go," she said slowly.

He seemed about to say something but remained silent. This left Anna standing in front of him rather foolishly. He was doing his usual minute inspection of her face.

"Come with me," he said suddenly, and without uttering anything further led her through a maze of stack corridors, glancing over his shoulder occasionally to make sure that she was following. He came to a halt in front of a baize door with a brass plaque on it: The Henry Williams Woods Memorial Collection. This door he unlocked from a key ring which, she had time to notice, also had a plastic effigy of Mickey Mouse dangling from it. He entered first and turned to press the door to behind her. There was a muffled click as the lock came home. He put his hand at once on the small of her back and began very firmly to kiss her on the mouth.

After a time, Anna started to laugh. She was feeling the same warmth as in the Art Gallery, accompanied this time by a drowsy security which derived, as she knew, from the lock on the door.

"Why are you laughing?" he inquired, trying to look at her face. She pressed her nose further into his lapel.

"You have a way with you," she said, noticing with pleasure how her voice reverberated through the tweed. "None of this wrangling for hours in bars and parked cars, bars and cars..." she repeated dreamily.

"I got the impression at that dread Christmas party—" he began, clearing his throat.

"By the way—" A thought had struck Anna and she leaned back against his arm to look into his face. "Do you think O'Toole has a key to this place?"

Without bothering either to finish his sentence or answer the question, he began to kiss her in a more leisurely and sensuous way than before.

"Let's go somewhere and have tea or something," said Anna urgently, after a time. She did not want to finish a seduction scene half-dressed on a library table.

"Must we?" he asked sadly, unbuttoning the lowest button of her blouse.

"Yes," said Anna, letting her arms drop to her sides. "I don't know you very well . . ."

"Oh." He put the button slowly back into the buttonhole. "That's probably a good thing, actually."

"For heaven's sake, Ian. Don't start this self-hatred nonsense. I just think it's much better in bed, that's all."

He glanced down at her, smiling. "Is that the kind of thing that all young women say these days?" He did up the top button of the blouse and put both hands into the gap in between.

"There, you see." She did up the buttons around his wrists. "You don't even know how old I am."

"Yes I do. You're twenty-nine."

"How did you know that?"

"O'Toole passed it on in a friendly way after you left the party. I was just going myself."

"What else did he say?"

"Oh, for heaven's sake." She pinched his arm. "Out with it. I like to keep abreast of O'Toole's thinking."

"It was his opinion that you were not a virgin," he said, looking across the room at a full length portrait of Henry W. Woods. "Although . . ."

"Go on."

"You are renowned among his colleagues for your chastity."

"Vicious pig!"

"He meant well."

"All right. Here—take your hands out. Let's go somewhere else while you tell about yourself. I don't have any sources like that."

"Half a minute." He withdrew his hands from the front of her blouse and put his arms around her again. The Scotch scent seemed to come from his pores. Anna was beginning to like his mouth in a familiar way.

Somewhat later, walking across the winter lawn outside the Library, she said, "Go on about yourself."

"Ian Charles MacGregor."

"Yes?"

"Forty-five—no, actually forty-six."

"Born in Scotland?"

"Yes."

"Educated?"

"At Edinburgh."

"Divorced?"

"No," he said shortly.

There was a pause.

"Well?"

"What?"

"What else do you want to know?" They were nearly at the entrance to the Arts Building.

"Are you . . . ?" she tried to put this well. Pausing with her hand on the door, she glanced at him. He was studying her outstretched hand and arm. "Are you involved with anyone—sexually, I mean?"

"Yes."

"Oh."

"Well, go on. Don't stop there," he said.

"Who, then?"

"You."

"Oh." Anna began to laugh. "Why are we going in here, by the way?"

"I haven't the faintest idea." He looked around vaguely. "Do you know the time?"

"It's 5:30," said Anna, catching sight of the clock beside the elevator.

"Oh Christ," he said. "I have to meet a child."

"Oh dear."

He began to walk away very fast down the corridor towards the east door of the building. Suddenly he swung around and walked back. Grasping the lapels of her coat, he said quietly: "I'll call you when I get the chance."

"Do you know my number?"

"I've looked it up from time to time." He let go of her lapels and walked away rapidly, breaking into an awkward run as he rounded the corner.

Well, well, thought Anna to herself, and followed this up by thinking: yes indeed, yes indeed. She remained standing quietly by the elevator looking into space for a short while. Then she started to walk home very slowly, thinking over the events of the afternoon with surprisingly intense pleasure.

As she was doing the dishes she had a pleasant hazy feeling of anticipation. She made her bed with some care, putting away no fewer than fourteen books and some stray underclothes which had become entangled in the sheets and blankets. A sticky saucer containing a piece of chocolate halvah was removed from the orange crate beside the bed and rinsed under the faucet. At 8:00 she decided to take off her clothes from the day, and changed into a rather pretty nightgown with flowers embroidered on the low neckline. At 8:30 she bethought herself and began running a bath pensively, fingering a dusty bottle of Chanel, but deciding against it in the end. At 9:00, as she was dreamily washing herself, after twenty minutes of reading in the bath, the telephone rang. Anna seized a towel and ran dripping into the living room.

"Hello, Anna. What have you been doing with yourself these days?" It was Jimson.

"Oh, Michael. Well—I was just in the bath."

"Dripping all over the carpet?"

"Yes."

"Well, put on something warmer and get your cigarettes. It's time for a nice long chat."

"I really can't talk for long. I'm expecting a call."

"Anything important? Your parents are all right, I hope?"

"No, no. It's—just a friend."

"Well, so am I a friend, and that's why I called. I haven't seen much of you lately, young Anna, and so I feel that you must be bursting with news which I haven't heard yet."

"No, not really. I've been trying to work somewhat. I haven't seen much of anyone lately."

"Well—tell me about this friend. Is it anyone I know?"

"Oh no. You don't know him."

"Aha. 'Him.' Name, please."

"He lives in Regina," said Anna desperately. "He and his wife were my best friends for a while."

"Oh. Well, do let me tell you some gossip. It's about Spong... Got your cigarettes? I don't suppose you ever have anything on hand to drink at times like this?"

"I have some Scotch," said Anna, smiling to herself.

"Okay, let's part briefly and I'll look up something similar for myself while you get organized."

"No, really Michael, I must get off the line. He—they said they'd phone about now."

"All right." He sounded annoyed. "Don't you want to hear about Spong, then? I suppose I could call later."

"No, no, I'll hear now," said Anna nervously.

"Well, in brief . . ."

Jimson gave her a very detailed account of the Spong divorce, including as appendices his own view of Spong's character, the character of Spong's wife, and the characters of several minor personae in the affair.

His informant had clearly been Francoise, athough he did not mention this.

Anna, who was really shivering, allowed her teeth to chatter audibly.

"For God's sake, woman, are you freezing to death? Why didn't you take my advice about clothing yourself?"

"Look Michael, I really must hang up now. It's not just that I'm cold. I'm nervous about staying on the line for so long."

"Nervous? What is it, Anna? Why don't you tell me all about it?"

"You see, she's going to have a baby and—it's long overdue, so they wanted to induce labour this evening."

"Good heavens, you should have said so at once. I'll ring you up later and you can tell me what happened."

"No, no, I'll tell you about it tomorrow—if anything happens, that is."

"Well, if anything particularly ghastly happens, ring up, all right? I have a sympathetic ear."

"Thanks, then."

"Bye, Anna."

Anna put down the receiver with a sigh. It was 9:35. She got her book and sat down on the rug with a cigarette. Five minutes later she got out a pair of scissors and carefully trimmed the deadheads off her winter chrysanthemum. She went into the bathroom and brushed her hair. She peered out the kitchen window, then rummaged in her purse for the powder compact. The cat was behaving oddly. Did he want food? There was food in the dish. Anna changed his water. It was 10:03. She sat down again with the novel.

At 11:00 she switched off the lights and lay down on her bed. After a time, she switched on the bedroom light again and wound the alarm clock. She piled up one pillow on the other, and went out to the kitchen for a cigarette, turning off the bedroom light.

There was some sort of knocking on the kitchen door leading onto the fire escape. She went over and parted the curtains on the window. Someone was standing on the landing with his back to the door. A match flared and she recognized the back as MacGregor's.

She opened the door and he swung around tensely.

"Thank God it's you," he said with a smothered laugh. "I've been waking people up all over the building. I couldn't get in the front."

Dropping his cigarette underfoot, he grasped her bare shoulders as she stood in the doorway and hugged gently. "You're so warm."

"Why didn't you call?" Anna backed into the kitchen and he followed, bringing in a lot of snow on his rubbers.

"I did call, actually; several times, in fact, but the line was busy."

"Oh, around 9:00?"

"Yes. Then I thought perhaps you'd taken the phone off the hook, so I had a bit to drink." He sat down on a kitchen chair rather heavily. "Then I decided to see you instead."

"It was that pig Jimson," said Anna, going over to stand up against his chair. "He chatted and chatted."

"Jimson? Oh. Does he call you up in the evening?"

"Sometimes. I told him I was expecting a call, but he wouldn't get off the line." She put her hand timidly on his opposite shoulder, and he reciprocated by swinging her down not too skillfully until she was lying across his lap, hanging onto his neck.

After an interval he said, "I cannot stay very long."

"Who is looking after your children?"

"No one. That's the trouble."

"Would you like a drink?"

"I've had a drink. Do you know how to make tea?"

"Of course not," said Anna. She struggled into an upright position.

"Don't go."

"What about the tea?"

"Do you mind if I take this off?" He picked up a fold of her nightdress.

"How about you? You're still wearing your overcoat?"

"Oh, yes. I'd forgotten." Anna got up. He began to take off his coat. A moment of constraint fell upon them. He took off his rubbers and his tweed jacket, revealing a clean white shirt with the sleeves rolled up. Anna had retreated to the living room door. He looked around him, taking in the kitchen facilities. "This is nice," he said shyly, pointing to the potted plant. He came towards her, switching off the kitchen light apparently as a reflex. The apartment was left in total darkness.

About an hour later, Anna came out of a doze as she felt the bed rebounding slightly under her.

"Don't wake up. I've got to go," he whispered, sitting down again and pressing her back against the piled-up pillows. She could dimly see that he was buttoning his shirt with the other hand. A moment later he stood up and began tucking it into his trousers in a characteristically male way.

"What a failure," he said, sitting down again and groping for his socks. He didn't seem to be addressing this remark to anyone in particular, but Anna came to grips with it immediately, in the same way as she had done on past occasions with its big brother: "I'm never any good the first time."

"Why doesn't this question come up for women, I wonder?" she said, laying her hand on his arm. "Surely I can be a failure just as well as you."

"You were most emphatically not a failure," he said, putting his forehead down hard against her shoulder. Anna already knew this, so she merely stroked his hair in silence.

"It's the drink, you realize," he said, pinning her arms against the pillow above her head. "I knew what I was doing when I had those drinks tonight. I knew I'd want to be coming over here, and I was just making sure it wouldn't be any good."

"I liked it anyway," she announced, using his technique of addressing the whole room.

He began to kiss her, holding her wrists crossed above her head with one hand and pulling down the blankets with the other.

"You can't stay," she whispered after a while. "Come another time."

"Tomorrow?"

"Won't you come to tea?"

"Yes, I can arrange that. I'll see you in the morning." He got up reluctantly and went to the bedroom door.

"What time is it?"

"Only 12:30," she said, turning the alarm clock around.

"Oh hell!" he said violently, and a moment later she heard him shutting the outer door.

As Anna was finally drifting off, after a short period of repeating the words: "you were most emphatically not . . ." over and over with various different intonations, the telephone rang. It was Jimson.

"Did she have it?"

Chapter 9

Anna was in a state the next day. She was late for her 8:30 class, which had nevertheless gone fairly well, after getting off to a bad start. She was avoiding Jimson, which meant not having a cup of coffee, and Michie had a student in the office when she came back from the mail room. She crossly tapped her foot up and down, three taps at a time, folding her arms and looking down with a frown.

"Oh, Anna?" said O'Toole, coming up the hall. "Can I have a word with you?"

This request, even from the relaxed O'Toole, always sent shivers up and down Anna's spine. Ever ready to see herself as having committed some tort, she followed him into his office, feeling unattached guilt.

"Do tell, Peter?" she said, pretending to sit back comfortably in her chair. She got out a cigarette and groped in her pocket for matches. O'Toole did not smoke himself—not tobacco anyway—but his office, unlike her own, was large and airy.

"I've got to be blunt. Some people have tender feelings about this sort of thing."

"Oh yes?"

"You don't mind?"

"How can I tell?" she replied, wishing desperately for a match.

"Okay. Here goes. It's about your employment. What are you doing to get a job?"

"Nothing at all. I'm putting off the evil day."

"Well, you shouldn't put off, you know. I can write you a good letter and you can get another one from . . . oh, Gore or James or someone."

"What's the situation here?"

"There is no situation here as far as I know. That's why I'm mentioning this."

"I sometimes think of quitting, you know, Peter. It seems

unreasonable to keep going from job to job like this. It makes me feel like a mendicant."

"Well, there are the success stories too, you know. Look at me. Eight years as a lecturer, then suddenly raised to this height."

"True." O'Toole really liked being chairman, Anna realized. Her esteem dropped a notch.

"The thing is, to be quite plain, if you don't apply all around, people think you're not serious."

"And if you do they think you're a fool. 'Haven't I seen this letter twice before already?' they say. 'Just drop it behind the radiator there, will you?' "

"You've got to be persistent, and being persistent means starting early. That's the secret of success."

"What do you mean by early?"

"Last month, if you really want to know. But now is a good enough time to start."

"All right." Anna looked despairingly at O'Toole. Would she have to raise the subject of matches?

"Another thing." He looked at her with a pretense of severity. "Are you going to publish something?"

"Probably not."

"I wouldn't put it like that to other people, Anna. Can't you say that you're working on anything? It would be good to mention in a letter."

"Okay. I'll think of something you can say."

"You don't have to be snotty about it."

"Sorry. Nice of you to help, really. It's just that I feel dread."

"It's okay to tell me that, but don't go saying things about dread to—well—James, for instance."

"Right."

"And do try to get up something that you can send off to a journal, won't you? 'Pending acceptance' is better than a great big hole on your resumé."

"Right. True."

"What about a cup of coffee?"

They walked in silence up the stairs to the coffee room. Anna calculated that with fifteen minutes on coffee she could still do an hour's work before her aesthetics class.

Jimson was not there, Anna was relieved to see. Two people from the English Department, Spong and Emily Dowell, were talking quietly together on the sofa. Emily Dowell was an older woman, a spinster, with the timid appearance of a rodent. Her specialty was Canadiana, which always brought out the best in

CAMROSE LUTHERAN COLLEGE
LIBRARY

O'Toole. He started in immediately on his Catharine Parr Traill imitations. Spreading a not-too-clean handkerchief over his hair, he began in a cracked voice to describe soap making in the backwoods.

MacGregor came in with Frau Bertelsmann. He caught Anna's eye after a minute and she began to blush violently; meanwhile, Bertelsmann was saying something to him in an undertone which made him nod and smile appreciatively, bending his head down towards her to hear.

"For this soap making you need two pounds of the best pig shit . . ." began O'Toole in falsetto, stirring a paddle round in an imaginary vat.

Bertelsmann looked on momentarily in disdain, holding her coffee mug with the tips of her fingers. Behind her, MacGregor continued to look over at Anna with a faint, special smile, his eyes very bright. Anna blushed even pinker and glanced down at her lap, then looked up anxiously as Bertelsmann towed him out of the room.

"I didn't say horse shit, I said pig shit . . ." went on O'Toole, looking around severely at an imaginary pupil.

Anna drank her coffee rapidly and got up to leave. Still watching O'Toole over her shoulder, she came up short against Jimson entering the doorway.

"Hello, Anna." He turned her back into the room again. "You've got to tell me what this is all about now."

"I must go and work on my lecture, Michael. No time to chat."

"I'll keep on phoning until you tell me everything, I warn you."

"Later, later," said Anna, wriggling to get around him as he blocked the doorway.

"I don't believe a word of it anyway."

"What?" Anna was halfway down the corridor. She turned around, walking backwards.

"These friends of yours. You've never mentioned them before. Why should I believe they even exist?"

"She had it this morning," called Anna. "A girl. Twelve pounds." She backed through the stairwell door.

Instantly, someone behind the door seized her arm. The door fell to with a soft whoosh and MacGregor, now holding both her arms, pressed her against it, apparently so as to prevent anyone trying to enter the stairwell.

He looked down at her with the same smile he had been

wearing in the coffee room. "What are you telling Jimson about a baby? Twelve pounds is very heavy."

"Oh, an involuted lie I was using on him last night to make him get off the phone." She answered the smile and felt a blush beginning all over again.

"I know about babies," he said seriously. "Get your details from me. Twelve pounds is too heavy."

She relaxed her weight against the door and put her hands up under his elbows.

"All right?" he asked softly. "About last night, I mean?"

"Better than all right."

"I've been looking around for you."

"I had to talk to O'Toole."

"So I gathered."

"We don't have much time," she said apprehensively into his lapel. "Someone might come up the stairs."

"I know. Come with me to my—"

"No, no. I have to prepare a lecture right away. What about tea?"

"After 3:00. Thank God, the housekeeper is looking after things this afternoon. Where shall I meet you?"

"In my office? Michael is on my heels, though."

"So I see. I could eliminate him without too much trouble, I think."

"Okay."

"Just a minute then." He gave her an elaborate kiss that started at her forehead and ended by her left ear. They began to descend the stairs together. Pausing on the seventh floor to open the door for Anna, he murmured into her hair as she went under his arm:

"I've been thinking about you all the time."

Closeted with Michie at 3:00, Anna subdued her impatience and continued doggedly to write up her curriculum vitae. Large gaps under Publication, Work in Progress, Papers Presented, forced her to alter the standard format she was using. With a pair of scissors and a glass bottle of glue she was pasting together bits of two older typed versions in such a way as to compress these headings out of existence.

There was a knock on the door. Michie leapt up from his chair and dashed around the desk like a tennis champion going for the handshake. All visitors were for him. Anna held consultation with students in empty classrooms.

MacGregor came in and sat down in the chair beside Anna's

filing cabinet, uninvited. Michie gaped at him, uncertain whether to take up his teapot or not.

"Professor MacGregor?"

"Professor Michie? I've just come to have a word with Professor Callaghan here."

Anna watched in admiration as with this cynical stroke MacGregor sent Michie flying for his teapot.

"What are you doing?" he asked, looking at the mass of scraps on her desk.

"Getting some kind of decent curriculum vitae together. Just let me get the glue off my hands." She took out a piece of tissue much worse for the wear.

"Have this." He gave his handkerchief.

"My talk with Peter this morning was about no job here," she said.

"Surely someone is going on sabbatical?"

"February, March, April and a bit of May," she said sadly. "Here today, gone tomorrow. You were in favour of that."

"Yes, but not for you. I was in favour of it for me," he said, smiling.

"Let's go," she said, standing up. "I hate even looking at this."

"Right. How many sweaters do you wear these days?" He picked up a tangled pile from the top of the file case and began straightening them out.

They went out to the elevator together. No one challenged this. The foyer was empty of faculty and students alike. Anna began to relax as they went around the corner of the Library. They glanced at each other sideways as they walked along, savouring their anticipation.

"I can't take your arm till we pass this row of lace curtains," he remarked.

"It was good Michael wasn't hanging around this afternoon," she said. "He often comes in to bait Michie."

"Oh, I was looking forward to seeing him. He would have been able to identify me as the twelve pound baby, I daresay."

"Wouldn't you mind his guessing?"

"I still have some remnants of competitiveness in my soul."

"What about the lace curtains, though? Michael's a terrific gossip."

He took her arm. "I doubt he'd enjoy telling the story," he said simply.

Later on, as they lay in bed, Anna was singing him part of her "emphatically not a . . ." song of the night before, while he stroked the long locks of her dark hair that fell across his chest. They had decided to put off having tea to the last possible moment.

He asked suddenly, "Shouldn't I be doing something about . . . ?"

"No, it's all right. I'm doing something."

"What?" he asked, leaning up on his elbow.

"Pills, you know."

"Yes," he said slowly. "I suppose you must."

"Do you mind?" Anna was surprised.

"No. It always seems—so unnatural."

"Like taking the train or flying?"

"No, like stopping something that ought to happen."

"Are you—were you a Catholic?"

"Vicious Protestant. Not any more. There aren't any churches on this continent."

"You should meet my classes."

"Not like Scotland." He pronounced this word in a treacly kind of voice that Anna much admired. She slid out of bed, saying it over several times under her breath in her best imitation.

The stillness from the bed attracted her attention, and she stopped brushing her hair to attend to it, glancing at him sideways.

"Are you looking at me?" she asked.

"Yes."

Anna began to think about her appendix scar and looked down at it apprehensively.

"You don't mind standing naked in front of a man?"

"Depends on the man. Is he naked also, for instance?" She sprang to the bed and twitched the covers off him.

"Don't," he said, pulling them back.

"Sorry." She knelt on top, looking at him seriously. "I liked it, you know. Looks are nothing."

"Looks are not nothing. I like looks. I love looks. Why do you think . . . ?"

"I am extremely vain, as you will soon recognize, if you haven't already. One definitely shouldn't pander to it."

"Anna," he said simply. Liking the way he said it, she realized he hadn't said it before.

"It's tea time," she remarked, catching a glimpse of the clock and feeling touched.

As she warmed the teapot, a concession to what she felt must
be his custom, she was trying out his pronunciation of the 'a' in
'Anna'. He appeared at her elbow, today in a blue shirt with the
sleeves turned back.

"Don't you ever wear anything?"

"Never."

"What about the windows?" he asked, reciprocating in a kiss
with considerable enthusiasm.

"For heaven's sake, Ian. You've been married." She surveyed
him, her hands on her hips.

"This is not like being married," he said briefly, giving her
his austere look.

"Oh well. I haven't been," she said defiantly, decanting the
boiling water into the teapot. This she carried with two mugs into
the living room.

"Milk? Sugar?" She went toward the kitchen.

"No, I'm habituated," he said, catching hold of her in the
doorway.

"The best thing is the strangeness—having you here like
this." Anna, now feeling slightly chilly, pulled her shawl off the
only chair and put it around her shoulders, sitting cross-legged on
the floor.

"Do you do this—sort of thing—often?" he inquired, blowing
on his tea.

"No. Never, really." She looked up, embarrassed.

"You're unusually straightforward." He gazed into his cup.

"But I liked you."

"Oh?"

"You're very unusual yourself."

"No."

"The Scotch-drinking episode in the Russian section, for
example."

"More usual than you might think." He lay down on one
elbow.

"Not for me. My acquaintances—since I started teaching—
have been more of the Michael model."

"Have you . . . ?"

"Don't be absurd."

"Not absurd."

"I really don't do it all the time. I thought I'd explained that
already. Michael's all right—in certain ways—" she qualified,
"but he belongs to a genre. It gets boring."

"Why do you say that?"

"Well, why do you dislike him yourself?"

"Because he's a bastard."

"What does that mean?"

"A prig. More specifically, he was taking up your time."

"My time." She reflected. She had had so much time. Now she had hardly any time at all. He was glancing at his watch.

"Your children."

"Yes. I have twelve minutes."

"Can you . . . come back tonight? Don't mind—if you can't."

"I mind." He drank his tea quickly. "I think I can. It may be late, though."

"Is it far to walk?"

"No. Luckily."

"Well . . ." she followed him into the kitchen. "It was nice."

"Goodbye, then." He put down his tea cup on the drain board.

"Goodbye." Anna faltered. "I . . ."

"I'll be back," he said, going out the door with his coat.

Chapter 10

Anna reflected on the afternoon in various positions all over the house. In the bath she thought about what it had been like in bed. Eating dinner, she thought about the conversation at tea. Straightening things up and making the bed, she thought about the walk home. At last, waiting beside the window with some sherry, she thought about his children. The evening wore on.

"This is worse than anything," she sighed, putting down the sherry and looking out the window yet once more. Someone was on the fire escape. Anna held her breath. It seemed to be the right kind of step. When he appeared on the landing, she already had the door open.

"Have you got anyone looking after the children?" She had given the housekeeper a good deal of thought.

"Yes." He flung off his coat and took her in his arms.

"Good."

"Why are you suddenly wearing all these clothes?" He plucked at the sleeve of her dress.

A number of possible funny replies occurred to Anna, but she said nothing. He went over to the light switch immediately and flicked it off, then came back to where she was standing.

"Give me your hand," he said abruptly.

Not yet accustomed to the dark, Anna stretched out her hand and brushed his chest. He took it in the warm, dry grip she remembered and stood there silently.

"Is everything all right?" she asked anxiously.

"Better than all right."

They stood in the dark holding hands for some time.

At last he said, "Would you think I was a fool if I said I loved you?"

"I was going to say that myself this afternoon, but you left."

"I was afraid you were going to say something else, so I left."

There was another long silence. Anna didn't breathe for a while, then gulped down a sudden mouthful of air.

He took her tightly in his arms at once. "It's not so easy," he murmured at last, reassured again by Anna's quiet breaths against his chest. "I have to sort everything out, it seems. It was rather like a summer holiday for a while—this afternoon. But then . . ."

"You put the children to bed . . ." Anna burrowed her head against him. "I care for you," she said, finding it easy to say this in the dark, and knowing that it was true.

Not replying, he gently released her and began to unbutton her dress. Running his fingertips lightly down to the solar plexus and back up to her collarbone again, with a sudden swift movement he turned her dress back over her shoulders and into a circular heap on the floor around her feet.

"What's all this?" he asked.

"You know perfectly well."

"You're not wearing anything on top; why do you wear these?"

"Let me help." She helped.

"I'll carry you."

"You can't."

"Certainly I can. You aren't heavy," he said, grunting slightly.

Much later Anna woke him. "Do you have to go home? It's past midnight."

"I needn't go yet."

She propped herself on her elbow. "Would you like anything? A drink of water, a piece of cheese?"

"No thanks."

"May I turn on the light?"

She reached for the bedside light on the orange crate she used as a table. The cat perched blinking on the pillows.

Sitting up, she said: "I have some Scotch. Would you like that?"

"I've given it up."

"Really?"

In response, he buried his face in her sheeted lap. She stroked his hair peacefully. Presently she asked, "Do you know the feeling as though your bones were liquefying? I get it just when I see you sometimes. Several times today."

"Yes, I know it." He rolled over on his back and smiled contentedly at the ceiling.

"Especially this morning when I saw you first," she went on.

"Yes."

She slid down beside him. "You too?"

"Couldn't you tell?"

Presently he began to quote, " 'Till a' the seas gang dry, my dear, And the rocks melt wi' the sun . . .' "

Anna tried to lift her head to watch him producing these mellifluous words, but he held it down on his shoulder.

"Say some more. I like the way you say it."

"It should be sung."

"No, no, say it," she pleaded.

He turned her over and lay on top of her, putting his elbows down on either side of her face.

" 'My love is like a red, red rose
   That's newly sprung in June
   Oh, my love is like the melodie
   That's sweetly played in tune.' "

He had tears in his eyes.

"It's beautiful," said Anna, her bones melting.

"It makes me cry." He was smiling softly.

They lay for some time gazing into each other's eyes, not saying a word.

Anna woke up at 6:00 with a start. A faint splash from the bathroom reassured her, and instantly she went back to sleep. When she awoke again, it was to the sound of a glass clinking in the kitchen. Not really awake, she leapt out of bed and rushed around the corner.

He was standing by the kitchen sink in the faint glimmer from the street light outside, completely dressed except for his overcoat and rubbers. He had been having a glass of water out of her cream cheese jar.

"Ian! Are you going? I was asleep." She rubbed her eyes. "It's morning."

The feeling of tweed against her naked skin was oddly familiar. Anna realized that it expressed the substance of certain daydreams.

"Was someone with the children all night?"

"Yes, she promised to stay over."

"Thank heavens! Will she do it often?"

"Once or twice a week. I'll have to see."

Anna put her nose against the familiar lapel and rubbed hard. "We'll manage," she said.

"I'll see you later." He freed himself gently. Anna watched obsessively as he put on his overcoat and rubbers.

The same day, eschewing the coffee room, Jimson, O'Toole,

and ignoring Michie as well as she might, Anna began to write a paper. An idea from her dissertation seemed exploitable, and abandoning the editing job, she began working it over, transferring paragraphs from the typescript into her inky, laboured handwriting. At 4:00 she flung the bundle of written pages into the wastebasket, crying "Pigs!" and left the office to Michie.

There was no one in the coffee room and MacGregor was not in his office, as she ascertained by attempting to call through the switchboard from a pay telephone in the lobby of the Arts Building. She went briefly to the Library and read the inscription on the door of the Henry W. Woods Memorial Collection. Then she went home.

The dishes were clean. She had a cooked tea involving a bag of decaying green beans, the last edible thing in the refrigerator. Glancing at the sherry on the shelf, she went back to the kitchen and made a sponge cake. It was getting on for 7:00.

The phone rang. Anna picked it up, fearing it was Jimson. MacGregor had not been wont to use the phone. It was a wrong number. She took the cake out of the oven and balanced the pan upside down on her coffee mugs. It was 7:45.

She put on her coat and went out for a walk. Halfway to the river, she went back and scribbled a note detailing the route she intended to take. She pinned this to the storm door with a hairpin stuck between the window and the glass, but the wind blew it down. Eventually she anchored it on the fire escape with a spare boot, kicking aside the snowdrift.

Feeling trapped, she walked the route she had outlined. No one waited on the landing when she returned. The telephone was ringing. Anna dropped her key down between the doors. Retrieving it, she jammed it upside down in the keyhole, then right side up, and burst through the door. The telephone gave one of those rings that indicates the caller has given up. Anna picked up the receiver, listened to the buzz for a moment, and put it down with a crash.

She lay on the rug in her coat and riffled through the telephone book. There were several I. or Ian MacGregors. All lived in the vicinity of the University. None listed a middle initial.

It was 9:00. She unmolded the sponge cake and washed the dishes from her meal. She made a fresh pot of tea. At 10:03, she finished the tea and began running a bath.

"What on earth am I doing?" she asked herself. A middle-aged lover with three children, not even particularly good looking. He did have a slight paunch, although not as many freckles as Anna had been expecting. His eyes were pale green. Anna looked at her own eyes in the mirror. They were dark brown, with clear, bluish whites. She brushed her hair, and her teeth. She got into the bath.

She had never had such a gentle lover. There was no question of the flashy technique that had marked some of her previous encounters with men in bed. Ian had a kind of intuitive genius. He would be shocked by a sex manual. Anna laughed uncomfortably, looking at the sponge in her hand. "Place your left hand on her right buttock, simultaneously drawing your off-side leg up under her . . ." Anna began to scrub her face energetically. The thing was that he really liked it, all of it. Anna closed her eyes and put down the sponge.

And then he had said poetry in bed. No one had ever done that before. It made him cry. She shivered, lying back with her eyes still closed.

The telephone rang.

Anna leapt out of the bathtub and rushed to the living room, gritting her teeth. It was very cold outside the bathroom.

"Hullo."

"Hullo." He seemed to be whispering. "I cannot come over."

"Oh."

"I'd like to see you, though."

"Shall I meet you somewhere?"

"Yes. All right. We could take a walk."

"Where shall I meet you?"

"Do you know where I live?"

"No."

"It's about five blocks from you." He gave the address. "I'll wait on the porch, then."

"Did you call earlier?"

"No. Why? Didn't you answer the phone?"

"I went out for a while and of course when I got back—it had stopped ringing when I got to it."

"Probably Jimson."

"Perhaps," she said cautiously.

"Goodbye."

Anna flung on her clothes and emptied the bathtub. The cat, who relished sitting on the edge of the tub during a long bath, gave her a disapproving glance. She ran out of the house and slipped painfully down the icy fire escape. Suddenly she began to cry. Why had she wanted this? Crying, she walked two blocks. She found a bit of paper in the depths of her pocket and blew her nose. Then she began to run again.

The house was a tall, gloomy, wooden structure, shaded on all the visible sides with spruce trees. The porch was actually an enormous ill-lit veranda. He was sitting patiently on the steps. Anna stopped at the end of the walk. He came down it and took her arm.

"Hush. Lucy is watching."

"Lucy?"

"Lucy is nine. She'll be wanting to inspect you."

"You haven't told her! Ian, she's only nine!"

"No, of course I haven't. But she's feminine, isn't she? Her bedroom window is on this side."

"Is anyone with them?"

"No."

"You ought to go back," she said fiercely, withdrawing her arm. "Is Lucy the oldest?"

"Yes. Have you been crying?"

"I fell down the fire escape. I ran part of the way. It's just the cold."

"I shan't be able to stay out long. I needed you."

"You couldn't—? No, probably not."

"We'll have to see what she says."

"Who?"

"Lucy. She has a head on her shoulders. She knows me very well, and she knows herself and the others."

"She's certain to mind. I would have."

"You'd be surprised."

"Wouldn't you have?"

"Lucy is quite different to me. She's more like her mother."

"How will she tell what I'm like just by looking at me?" asked Anna in melancholy.

"I don't know," said MacGregor gravely. "She's always right, though."

"What if she's wrong?"

"Wait and see. She won't be."

Anna bowed her head to fate. She saw that he regarded women as quite alien in an important way. Her present sadness was in the same class of mysteriously feminine things as the intuitions of his nine-year-old daughter. At the same time, she saw that he would not understand an account of her day. He had spent a full afternoon of administrative work and teaching, followed by an evening with his children. The idea that someone could have nothing to do but wait for a lover would strike him as impossibly wonderful.

Her tears were freezing in the frost, stinging her eyes.

"Don't worry," he said, putting his arms around her and drawing her behind a lilac hedge, now moribund in the winter weather. "She's really always right about people."

"People always say that about their children. But it's just because their children are like them—reflect their opinions."

"If that is truly the explanation then it has the same effect," he said reasonably.

"You're right. I'm being an idiot. Ignore this." She fished for the paper at the bottom of her pocket, but he produced his handkerchief immediately.

"What are their names and ages, please?"

"Lucy is nine, Jane is seven, and Gregor is four."

The reign of Bateson had terminated three years earlier. A few of Jimson's choice phrases floated into Anna's mind.

"You are really the most admirable person I've ever met," she said sincerely, walking along beside him.

"Oh?"

"Don't be offended. I've never known anyone at all like you."

"Mm."

"In fact, I love you," she said humbly. He took her arm again instantly.

"What is Jane like?"

"She plays with trucks. It's the influence of Gregor. He has a very powerful personality."

"Don't you like her doing that?"

"I prefer animal characters, myself."

"Like Winnie-the-Pooh?"

"Much more interesting. Lucy was always a one for that."

"Does Lucy still play with them?"

"Sometimes." They were walking very slowly. "She's much more of an adult now."

"We've come a long way. Should we turn back?"

"She doesn't like me to drink."

"She's afraid for you."

They walked along the riverbank in silence.

"Go on about imaginary animals," said Anna anxiously. It was very cold. The stars glittered above the streetlights like tiny particles of ice.

"There was a fox called Tod. A covenanting fox."

"He promised to defy the 39 Articles?" asked Anna, laughing.

"He covenanted," said Ian firmly. "That is in the blood. But he broke his solemn promises."

"And then what happened?"

"Once he was eaten by a whale."

"The Old Testament. I suppose that's in the blood too."

"Yes. Then his wife left him." He spoke into the frost impersonally.

"This Tod had a wife?" Anna asked, uncertain whether to go on.

"Named Lucy, of course. Perhaps we should turn around here. We must have come a mile."

"Oh God."

"Anna—do I make you cry?"

"Not at all. Not at all." She still had the handkerchief, a warm, moist ball in her cold fist.

"Anna."

They stood together, embracing in the cold, while she wept for his loneliness and her own. He made no protest, although she was sure he did not understand. After a time she began to feel very happy.

Chapter 11

It was Thursday and the department was meeting over the report of the external reviewer. It was couched in such guarded language, hedged in with provisos and qualifications, that Anna had been unable to make up her mind whether it was favourable or not. She waited upon the meeting to see. If the consensus was that it was unfavourable, she expected to have an entertaining time.

Anna liked her colleagues at this university, but the conditions of her employment made it impossible for her to feel more than detached sympathy for their concerns. She had already started to make one of her grocery and errand lists on the back page of the report, and she hurriedly tore this off and stuffed it into her skirt pocket as she walked down the hall to the seminar room where they met.

"Tearing it up? I agree with you," said James, joining her quietly.

"You think it's bad, do you?" asked Anna. James sat down, spreading out his notes and placing a sheaf of clean, white paper before him.

"I think it stinks," he said, unscrewing the top of his fountain pen.

"Getting on with it, are you, Jim?" said Eddy, coming in and drawing out a chair for himself sharply. "You must be pleased with this." He slapped the report against his thigh.

"No," said James, getting on with it. He did not raise his eyes.

"What do you mean—no?" cried Eddy, rising half out of his chair and riffling the pages of the report with his thumb. "He singles you out! Look at this! Page twelve, paragraph three: 'There is, however, one member of the department who should be commended for his activity in this area . . .' "

"I hereby call this meeting to order," said O'Toole, rapping the table. Gore, ffrench, and Peterson were busy getting their notes arranged. "Let's have a reasonably short discussion of this report first. There are some other agenda items we have to get to later."

Eddy sat back down and began to read the report over from the beginning, frowning.

"There seem to be two main complaints against us," said Gore. "Our research record is lousy and we can't teach. What more do you want?" He looked around, grinning sourly.

"It's not that bad . . ." said O'Toole, off to a slow start.

"No, it's worse!" cried ffrench. "The whole lot of us only sit on sixteen committees! Look at page twenty, here!"

"No thanks to you," said Peterson sibilantly, "You aren't on any of them."

"I haven't the time," said ffrench coldly. "Unlike some of the rest of you, I—"

"—play the guitar," finished Gore, winning a look of hatred from ffrench.

"David has said that Andersen accuses us of poor teaching," said O'Toole. "I don't read this that way at all. I think he's been very complimentary about that . . ."

"Check out page sixteen at the top, then," said Gore. " 'Caters to the clientele . . .' I don't know whether you read that as a compliment or not, but I certainly—"

"Even if it is complimentary, it surely doesn't apply to you," said Peterson. "A man who spends half the first term in Philosophy 1 teaching the students how to use quotation marks could hardly be so described."

"Ah, so you think drawing the cosmic egg and talking about wholeness is teaching philosophy," said Gore, with a triumphant glance around the room.

"Disagreement about the subject matter of Philosophy 1 is normal," said O'Toole. "The main thing is that Andersen thinks—"

"—that we give them what they want," went on Gore. "Yes, that's just what I object to. I want to dissociate myself from that entirely."

"What did you think of what he says about the teaching, Anna?" O'Toole was trying to create a diversion.

"I thought it was positive, really," she said. "He's very cautious, though, isn't he? Too many 'as it weres'."

"Not to mention 'buts' and 'howevers'!" cried ffrench. "Here's an important transition! Page seventeen, right after the teaching assessment, he goes on, 'However, the same cannot be said for the other, more important domain, as it were, of academic activity . . .' "

"That really gets my goat!" Eddy began to shout, pounding

the table. "He means research! Research *more* important than teaching! How dare this jackass come down from Toronto and try to pass this garbage off on us!"

"He admits that we do publish," murmured O'Toole, getting his word in by keeping his voice down so that everyone had to listen.

"You got a note into *Mental Activity* last year," said Gore, counting on his fingers. "Then there were my two modest little efforts . . ."

"And Jim here," said O'Toole.

"Yes, how many was it last year, Jim, a hundred and six?" cried Eddy.

"That makes thirty-three," said Gore, imperturbable. "If we divided that by six, it would be really quite respectable."

"Well, we can't expect him to do it that way," said ffrench shortly. "I had a note myself, David. You haven't counted that."

"Ah yes. On proportionality of tone to string length. In the *Proceedings of the New Guinea Philosophical Association.* I remember now," said Gore ironically, bending a finger back.

"I also published last year." Peterson had his eyes tightly shut.

"Sorry. Can't count reprints. You wrote that ten years ago."

"This counting is a mug's game," said Eddy. "Who knows whether any of this garbage is any good? Nelson's pretty proud of his thing on the guitar," he pointed at ffrench. "But there aren't any Pythagoreans around any more. They all drowned themselves or something when they noticed the square root of 2! And having an old article translated into Swahili doesn't mean it's any good either!" Peterson turned his head slowly in Eddy's direction, the eyes still closed.

"Why don't we ever hire anyone who publishes anything?" asked Gore suddenly. Anna looked at her lap, a flash of anger passing through her system.

"To bring our average up," said James, flatly. "Or what do you mean?"

"I mean new blood," said Gore. "What he says about stagnation here. Now, I agree with that."

"It has nothing to do with that," murmured James, taking the cap off his pen again.

"I don't know about that, Jim," said O'Toole. "He may be right here when he says we don't teach enough advanced courses. If we had some stimulation from older students . . ."

"Where are we going to get the older students to take these

advanced courses?" asked Gore. "If it weren't for Commerce and Nursing virtually forcing us down the students' throats, we wouldn't be able to fill a classroom."

"Most of you wouldn't," said Eddy, glaring around. He was a very popular teacher, Anna had heard.

"Well, I, for one, think this bears investigation," said O'Toole brightly. "I was having a talk with the Dean of Agriculture some time ago . . ."

" 'Cattle-feed and Existential Despair'!"

" 'Pig-swill and the Leap of Faith'!"

"No, 'Seed Grain and Some Recent Problems in Modal Logic'!"

"Okay, okay. It was just a thought. Some of those old Voc. Ags. have had an opportunity to ponder the metaphysical significance of things perhaps. You'd be surprised."

"What's a Voc. Ag.?" asked Anna. She was still feeling angry, but was trying not to let this show.

"Vocational Agriculture."

"Vocational Agriculturalist," corrected Gore. "American Gothic, The Man with the Hoe, you know?"

"Well, this has been a very interesting discussion," said O'Toole, promptly taking advantage of the agreement on this. "In summary, I'd say the review went very well and the Dean ought to be pleased with this." He patted the report. "Or not so displeased as with others." He looked around the table. "Agreed?"

"You mean French."

"Or History," said Peterson. "History is going to be in real trouble."

"As far as publication and research goes, I think we should join with Andersen in commending Jim here, and all make a special effort for next year. Right?"

"Oh, by the way, Peter," said ffrench. "Speaking of new blood and such things, why was my leave denied? I was only asking for half-pay."

"So you could play the bloody guitar," muttered Gore.

"I think I have a book in me."

"About guitar-playing."

"Well—and what if it is? I don't go for this moth-eaten view of academic —"

"The next item on the agenda is extension courses," said O'Toole firmly. "Several places have written in with their needs identification, as the man says: Cloverburg, St. Pierre . . ."

Anna looked bitterly around at the bookshelves. Why had she

expected to be entertained? She was of it and not of it. Of it enough to be attacked, but not of it enough to defend herself properly. They were all equipped with tenure, their salaries secure even if they were not all rewarded with yearly merit pay. I'm not even up for a temporary position here, she thought bitterly. I'm supposed to write articles in the intervals when I'm not packing my belongings to move. She caught herself up sharply. This self-pity was unworthy. What am I? Little Orphan Annie? She rolled up her eyes.

"And so," O'Toole was saying, "As usual, no one wants to do any of this, eh? Why are you looking like that, Anna?"

"Like what? Oh. Nothing. Sorry."

"Quite right, too, Anna," said Gore. "Teaching extension courses is the lowest form of academic existence."

"I've enjoyed it a time or two," said O'Toole.

"Like Voc. Ags.?" asked Anna.

"It's not vocational with extension students. It's hereditary," said Gore. "There's hayseed on the floor when you're picking up afterwards."

"Let's adjourn," said Eddy. "As usual, none of the real issues got discussed." He glanced at his watch. "I've got to go home. Pot-roast night tonight."

Anna drifted back towards her office. Jimson was coming down the hall behind her with Francoise. The History Department occupied the remaining offices on the corridor, although Jimson himself shared an office on the floor above with a junior classicist.

". . . and so, naturally, our review was a disaster," he was confiding to Francoise. "But that ought to make them sit up and take notice, or so I hope. Lift the lids of their coffins a bit, anyhow. Hi, Anna."

"Hello, Michael," said Anna, standing by her office.

"I haven't seen you about much lately," he said casually, reaching around her and pulling open the door. "Baby doing well? Or have you been sitting by the phone?"

"Very healthy," said Anna firmly.

"Fred Michie, as I do believe! What are you doing today, my dear man?" Jimson entered the office ahead of Anna. Francoise edged in behind her and stood in the doorway, blocking out the last rays of afternoon light. Michie had not yet turned on his reading lamp. Anna felt her way to her desk.

"This is good work you're doing here for History, Fred, my boy." Jimson picked up a page of typescript from Michie's desk and cast a critical eye over it.

"Someone in the division really must publish something by the turn of the century. The Dean is very worried about this," he said, shaking his head. "Have you heard anything about those five papers you sent off last term, now?"

Michie sat immobile at his desk. Anna turned her back on this scene. Jimson was being unusually vicious for the benefit of Francoise, she supposed.

"The journals are busy, of course. There's a long line-up ahead of you. I expect that things will improve by about 2021, and you'll get your crack at them."

Anna threw some things from her desk into the wastebasket. A balled-up page from the paper she had been writing the previous day had escaped her ruthlessness. Curious, she smoothed it out and read, "Of course, naturally, there are many imponderables in this area; however, as I hope to show . . ." She scrunched it back up again and threw it in the garbage. Resolutely keeping her ears closed to the thorough job Jimson was doing on Michie, she picked up her coat and sweaters and withdrew, receiving an equivocal wink from Francoise as she went out.

In the foyer, she passed ffrench and O'Toole having an argument. ffrench was bending forward on his toes, frowning, while O'Toole bobbed in front of him like a small dog barking up a tree. Anna supposed they were going on with their deferred discussion of the denial of ffrench's leave.

O'Toole, catching sight of her, began to make beckoning gestures, while ffrench's frown deepened to a scowl. Anna stopped uncertainly. The denial of ffrench's leave was certainly nothing to do with her.

"How did you like the meeting, Anna?" O'Toole came up to her, trailing ffrench. "Were you amused?"

"I always manage to have a good time."

"Everyone does his best for you, I must say. Don't you think Anna's presence helps us put on a good show, Nelson?"

"All very well for her. She finds it funny now, perhaps. She wouldn't find it so funny five years from now, I'll be bound."

"I'll be bound," repeated O'Toole thoughtfully, *"Carpe diem."*

"So you're sure there's no chance of even unpaid—?" ffrench took in Anna's continued presence angrily. O'Toole was holding her by the coat sleeve. "I'll share my thoughts on this with you later, Peter," he said, and stalked away.

"Very interesting man," said O'Toole, beginning to walk along with Anna, still clutching her sleeve. "A prey to his enthusiasms."

"There's no need for you to hold on to my arm now. He's gone."

"You are a reassuring presence for me. I cleave to you in times of stress."

"There's really no chance that Nelson will get leave?" asked Anna.

"Not a hope, my little friend. The Administration will never give him the dough, and we can't let him go on unpaid leave, can we? They might get some funny ideas about a five-man Philosophy Department. So much cheaper. Although I must say, Andersen has backed us up handsomely on the issue of teaching loads."

"What about Isaacson? He got a sabbatical. I'm replacing him. So there must be money."

"Yes, it was a sabbatical or the loony bin. Our Dean is a man of compassion."

"Just idle curiosity, of course."

O'Toole sighed. "How's the paper coming?"

"Not." Anna turned down the path beside the Library. "See you tomorrow."

She walked home slowly. The cat and the telephone awaited her. But possibly he would be able to come tonight.

Chapter 12

By the weekend Anna was exercising more self-discipline. As many women do when they have a lover, she felt extremely energetic and healthy: her appearance had taken a turn for the better as she noticed delightedly every time she looked in the mirror. She had finished her curriculum vitae and laboriously typed about twenty-five letters of application on the Dean's secretary's typewriter before the end of the week. She diagnosed all this as a case of having a lover.

On Saturday she tackled her thesis and spent the afternoon crawling around on the living room floor collating pages and inking in the charts. For this task, she had pulled on an out-at-the-elbow maroon sweater with a V-neck and a pair of faded blue jeans. At 7:30 she had almost finished the editing job, a task that, as she now saw, she had been avoiding not only because of its inherent unpleasantness, but because, once finished, she would have to write something else. She went out to the kitchen and made a cheese sandwich and poured herself a glass of milk. She ate standing at the counter, peering covertly at her own radiant reflection in the mirror over the sink. If she worked very hard, she would have the thing in a mailable package by 9:00.

There was a stamping noise on the landing outside the door, and Anna dimly made out the outline of MacGregor's head and shoulders through the curtain. This was a surprise, for she had not been expecting to see him at all on the weekend.

"Is it cold?" she asked mildly, leaning out the door. "I've scarcely been out."

"Freezing." He buried his icy fingers under her sweater at the waist as he pushed her inside. Anna twisted away, then took his hands in hers to try to warm them.

"I didn't expect you."

"A kind friend has taken everyone to her house for a staying-over party." He shed his coat quickly and hung it up in a now well-established pattern.

"How wonderful! What if someone gets homesick in the night, though?"

"I gave your number. You don't mind, do you?" he asked anxiously. "I didn't tell her much about you."

"She doesn't know me anyway."

"It's Helen Bertelsmann. She has two daughters. They're much older, but they like to play with my children."

"Oh."

"You look incredibly beautiful in that outlandish getup." He gestured at her old clothes. "Mysteriously shining eyes . . ."

"Mysteriously unbrushed hair, mysteriously messy house . . ." Retreating backwards through the living room door from his advance Anna fell over a cardboard box of dissertation materials onto the rug. Kneeling over her like one wrestler getting another down, he freed one of his hands and began deftly to unfasten her jeans. Laughing, Anna reciprocated, not so deftly.

Later he murmured, "On the hearth rug . . ." and reached for his shirt.

"Are you chilly?" Anna sat up.

"No."

She took the shirt out of his hands. "I want to look at you closely."

"In cold blood like this?" He lay down on his back and put his hand over his eyes.

"On the hearth rug, and the kitchen table, and one or two other places yet to be discovered," said Anna feeling his ribs with her fingertips.

"You once said it was better in bed."

"Better than the Library. I don't really like cars, either."

"Have you given it a lot of thought?"

"Not a lot of thought. I had several lovers, you know. Not for some time, however. I seem to have given up sex when I began to teach."

"When was that?"

"Four years ago."

"Good heavens."

"What's 'good heavens'?"

"Well, first of all—" he pondered, still with his hands over his eyes, "four years is not a particularly long time—from one point of view—but from the other—"

"There is a spinsterish side to my personality."

"No." He sat up. "Not at all. You don't know anything about that. The way you are, so soft and smooth and—"

"Dark, oblong, unlimited," said Anna promptly.

"Yes, and at the same time, with men like me lurking all about in every classroom, just—"

"Drooling and slavering."

"It makes one doubt the essential wholeness and goodness of the universe." He pulled her shawl around both their shoulders. "Would you like some tea?"

"No, I'd like to tell you something." He turned her head towards his face with the hand holding the shawl. They looked into each other's eyes. "Helen and I," he said, and stopped.

"Oh no," said Anna quickly, turning her head away again. "Now? Lately?"

"No. Some time ago. Last spring. She liked it more than I did."

"Did you just—stop?"

"More or less." He turned her head back. "She's a good friend. What are you thinking?"

"I'm jealous," said Anna slowly. "That's silly."

"Not necessarily. I told you because I thought it might matter."

"Was it like this?"

"Not a bit like this." He pulled a curling piece of her hair out from under the shawl and ran it through his fingers. "This is entirely different."

"How—different?" She wondered why her belief that she had been the only one had been so important to her. Was it just pity that had attracted her, or was she really in love?

"One cannot say. I like Helen. She's a very fine person. But with you . . ."

Anna waited, her heart beating. Why was this so momentous? He seemed unwilling to make further comparisons.

"When did you first notice—about me, I mean?"

"When I first saw you, of course."

"Of course? Right there in the President's house over the toothpicks and Swiss cheese?"

"Mm. You were with O'Toole."

"You thought—" she prompted, and wondered whether her vanity wasn't taking her to an extreme.

"I thought I wanted to have you." He smiled faintly, remembering this thought. "I also thought that it was extremely unlikely that it would happen."

"I spent the whole Christmas holiday trying to figure you out," she said.

"I was going to tell you—out there in the road. You didn't wait long enough to hear."

"I was furious."

"I wasn't sure whom you were furious at."

"Not at you."

"When did you first . . . ? I still can't believe it's come true like this." He was tugging slightly at the curl.

"I had a lot of daydreams all through Christmas. But it seemed so idiotic. I'm very susceptible. After all, being kissed at a drunken party—how much does it mean? So I didn't think you were serious."

"What sort of daydreams?" he asked happily.

"Oh well. The usual sort of daydreams. I had a combined night and daydream once, in which it seemed you really were making love to me."

"I wonder whether I could have felt any reverberations from that? Was it late at night?"

"Yes, I think so. I was in bed."

"I didn't have much time to think about you except late at night."

"In bed?"

"Yes." They both began to laugh.

Someone was knocking on the kitchen door. Anna leapt up and pulled on her jeans. MacGregor disappeared with an armful of clothing into the bathroom. "It's probably my landlord getting the rent," she called, pulling down her sweater. Smoothing her hair with her hand, she went through the kitchen.

"Surprise!" said Jimson, bursting in. He was holding a tall paper bag and had two wine glasses clenched in his knuckles.

"For heaven's sake, Michael. Can't you call up first or something?" Jimson was looking in amazement over at the doorway behind her, and she realized that she was in for it. She turned around. MacGregor, fully dressed but in his shirt sleeves and sock feet, was leaning against the door frame, lighting a cigarette.

"You only brought two wine glasses, Jimson," he remarked.

"Too bad." Anna was nervous. "I don't mind drinking out of the bottle, though. It was a nice thought, Michael."

"What are you doing here?" Jimson seemed surprised out of his suavity.

"Professor Callaghan and I have been having a pleasant tête-à-tête. Did you bring a corkscrew as well?"

"Never without one," said Jimson, seating himself and

withdrawing the bottle from the bag. "Anna doesn't recognize a need for these amenities."

"The rest of the house is an awful mess, Michael. We'd better drink here." Anna sat down slowly, pulling out another chair for MacGregor. If the other room was an awful mess, why had she been having a tête-à-tête there with Professor MacGregor? "I've got my thesis spread out all over everything." She tried to catch MacGregor's eye, but he ignored this lifeline, drawing his chair up with hers so that they faced Jimson side by side across the table.

Jimson went over to the cupboards and took out a mug. He put it down beside the glasses and poured. "Here you go, Anna."

"I'll take the mug," said MacGregor, putting his hand deliberately over hers as she stretched it out.

"Very good," said Jimson, savouring a sip. "Much better than the last one we had, I must tell you, Anna."

"That was a passable Moselle, as I recall." Anna was desperate to make it clear that there had only been one predecessor to the occasion.

"Yes, well—a German wine. German wine is good, some of it, but it is, nonetheless, German. This, as you observe, is a white Burgundy."

"Slight overtones of sharpness, against a firm, quite nutty base." Anna was holding her glass up judiciously.

"Not sharp, exactly," Jimson said with a frown. Glancing at Ian, she saw that he also was frowning down at his mug.

"What I came by to ask you, young Anna, was: would you like to go to the pictures?"

"Tonight? No, as you see . . ."

"We have other plans," said MacGregor, continuing to frown at no one.

"I didn't realize that you were in charge of Anna's social life."

"I am paying Professor Callaghan a visit. Your dropping by has been an unexpected pleasure."

"Ian and I were just . . ."

" 'Ian.' 'Professor Callaghan'!" Jimson spoke in falsetto. Anna was surprised to see that he was angry. "You don't seem to be in agreement about how well you know each other!"

"Michael, please . . ."

"What is it to you, Jimson?"

Anna put both hands over her face. Why was Jimson minding so much?

"Never mind what it is to me. As a onetime chum of Anna's here, I didn't expect to be pushed off to the side in quite so cavalier a fashion. Avoiding me, and lying, and so on . . ."

"Don't get excited, Jimson."

"Well, well, Anna." He stood up. "I'm glad I was the first to know."

"Are you going then, Jimson?"

"Sit down and finish your wine, Michael."

"In fact it's rather amusing." He took up his wine glass and drained it. Anna looked up at him, trying not to cringe at what she feared he might say next. "When you wanted to hear all the stories going the rounds about Professor MacGregor here, I thought—"

"Don't make a fool of yourself, Jimson."

"Go home, Michael," said Anna, getting up and wringing her hands.

". . . of course, father-fixation, probably . . ."

Anna left the room and lay down full face on her bed. Jimson's voice could scarcely be heard through the pillow. After a time, there was no sound from the kitchen. The murmur of voices terminated in the click of the back door.

MacGregor sat down on the bed. He stroked her back in silence for a time. She rolled over.

"Well—that's that," he said.

"Why was he so vicious? It's not as if he had any reason at all."

"From Jimson's point of view there are only two types of people in the world—people he can use, and enemies."

"Why did I get shifted into the enemy class so suddenly?"

"He doesn't like me."

"No, I know."

"Jimson has always been a public menace as far as I'm concerned. This is the first chance I've had to let him know directly. I rather enjoyed it."

"How did you get rid of him?"

"I gave him a few homilies about his manners, and he elected to leave."

"Ian, it's quite true what he said about my asking him about you. It was a long time ago. I didn't really ask, but I egged him on to tell."

"You can't be responsible for the snakes and toads a chap like that carries around in his gullet."

"I hated myself all the time he was telling."

"Shall I comb your hair? It was probably that most of all that got under his skin. Here, look." He picked her up, not without an effort, and carried her over to the mirror. Anna looked curiously in at a harlot, with long, love-tossed locks, pink cheeks, and dark, shining eyes. The fair curls of the man who was holding her were also in upheaval, and the skin of his face seemed smoother and tighter than usual. He was not looking at the woman in the mirror but at the one in his arms.

"I see what you mean. You too."

"It would be a waste, really."

"What?"

"Combing it. It will be mussed up again so soon."

"Where are you taking me?"

"Where would you like? The front hall? The arm chair? The hearth rug again?"

Chapter 13

There was a general faculty meeting the following week on Wednesday afternoon. Anna, who really had no part to play in these proceedings, decided to indulge herself by going. She knew that Eddy was going to speak on the teaching evaluation theme, and she looked forward to this with covert pleasure. Eddy's use of the word 'jackass' as a term of contempt was one of Anna's favourite things. She worked well and steadily on a little paper for one of her classes entitled "How are Transcendental Arguments Possible?" Somewhat late, she took a seat at the back of the enormous chemistry theatre. At her right hand was an isolated geologist, Frame, whom she knew slightly from the Christmas dance. Directly ahead and below, the engineers sat en bloc. The committee chairmen read at a podium off to the side of the theatre. The President and vice-presidents and their henchmen sat behind the demonstration table with its sinks and gas taps.

MacGregor got up and read the report of the Library Committee, a rather dreary document with overtones of doom and predestination in it. Closing her eyes and not listening to his words, Anna let his accent flow over her skin. He had not been with her for two days. Gregor was having the flu. MacGregor came in only to teach his classes. They had had two extremely short telephone conversations about this; he believed in getting straight to the point on the telephone, a quality that Anna appreciated. This morning there had been a note in her mail. It started in without salutation:

I shall probably not be able to come again as Gregor is presently running a temperature of 101° and the fever goes up at night. If I catch flu myself, this could go on for more than a week. My mother was of the opinion that I have a weak chest. Please take good care of yourself and don't pine. I see you sometimes from a distance. You have an unusually graceful walk. There are some other things about you that I think of constantly. You should burn this letter as it is covered with germs.

Anna opened her eyes again and watched him get down from the podium. He was, undeniably, a rather awkward figure. He was thinner than he had been before; his tweed coat fitted more loosely. In the past, her perceptions coloured by Jimson's stories, she had seen him as slightly pathetic—making headway against odds. It occurred to her now that this was not a true picture. Within this framework he had dignity and the respect of his colleagues. While he was not handsome, he was not ill looking by the standard set by those around him.

He was going straight home. He paused by his chair on the aisle to collect a file folder and his overcoat. He ran his fingers absently through his crisp, curly hair as he glanced around at his peers. Someone else was droning at the podium below. Anna stirred in her chair, wishing to go out with him but uncertain whether she could do this without attracting notice. This tiny movement caught his eye, and he fastened his whole attention on her face throughout the last seconds of the stair climbing. Anna felt as though she were caught in the beam of a searchlight.

He went swiftly out the door.

The regular committee reports went on, and it was some interval of time before they got to the Special Report of the Committee on Teaching Improvement and Evaluation. The substance of the report was familiar to everybody and Professor Vladimirov, who had been delegated to read it, struggled only slightly to articulate through his thick Slavic accent.

The proposal, as Anna had gleaned from elevator conversations with Eddy, was to give prizes once a month to the best teacher in every discipline. Eddy was deeply disturbed by this plan. His worry was about how the judging was going to be done. The proposal was that there should be a committee formed of students and staff to visit everyone's class once a month.

Eddy was now speaking to this point. He was reading from a filing card which he held before him at waist level.

"Ladies and gentlemen, as an expert in my field, which is concerned with values, I want to raise the voice of protest first and foremost about the composition of the committee which has brought this report before us today. Differing as I do from the result of their deliberations, I think it fair to point out that they lack the special expertise in the field of values"—here he looked up from his notes and briskly began to speak extempore—"which would distinguish their thoughts in this area from the thoughts of, say, a herd of jackasses. I, for one, am not going to tolerate having some jackass who is not even in my discipline, which I repeat, is concerned with values, coming into my classroom and making some asinine judgment about my teaching capabilities. And furthermore . . ."

Here the chairman of the committee rose on a point of order and began to "bring clarity to a few points." He begged to differ from his esteemed colleague, Professor Wiebe, about the character and composition of the committee. There was a representative from every faculty: one from Arts and Science, one from Agriculture, and one from Medicine, from Nursing, from Home Economics, from Engineering, from Commerce . . . Further, he feared that Professor Wiebe was muddled in his thinking when he supposed that this committee was to do the evaluative business of the proposal. The evaluative body was to be elected monthly by a mail ballot in every discipline or area. He sat down, his snake-like voice dying in the air against the renewed roar of Eddy's protest.

"However you look at it, Mr. President, however you look at it—" Eddy stabbed the air with his forefinger, "it's a mug's game! Everyone here knows just as well as I do the atmosphere of envy and jealousy—! And who is to judge the judges? Let me ask you that? Am I and my colleagues going to spend all our time judging each other?"

Here the chairman of the committee rose again and began laying out an extremely complicated timetable for the mail ballots, made out as an example for a universe of one hundred eighty-three faculty members.

Eddy rose to it again and again until Anna was glutted, her desire to hear him use the word 'jackass' outstripped by its repetition.

". . . and in the alternative," roared Eddy, "I would not be willing to allow anyone outside the field of values—just any old jackass, in effect—to adjudicate any aspect of my work—which is values, Mr. President!"

The faculty in uproar. Boos, hisses, cheering, and cries of "You tell 'em, Eddy!" and "Take it off!" came from all quarters of the room. Anna leaned her forehead on her knees, sick with the tension of suppressed laughter. Frame was looking at her anxiously.

"Are you all right?"

"Fine. Eddy is superb, isn't he?" Anna choked.

"He's dead right," said Frame seriously.

"I know."

"Cheer up," whispered Frame. "We're going to win on this one!" Did he think she had been crying?

The President was calling for order. O'Toole arose gravely in the lull and addressed the chairman of the committee. O'Toole, Anna felt sure, liked this sort of gaiety for the same reasons as herself. He was speaking, in a low voice as usual so as to make himself heard, on the issue of the prizes to be presented to the best teachers. Had the question of choice of prizes been considered by the committee? What prize could make it worthwhile for "some slug-a-bed in Economics—just as an example, of course" to up his performance to commendable levels in a given month? A gold brick? A trip to Hawaii? Where was the committee going to find the funds for this?

O'Toole proposed that the motion calling for approval of the committee's report be tabled until a sub-committee had been struck to come up with some answers to these serious questions. O'Toole went on to warn that deliberation in this area would not be easy—the type of reward would surely need to vary from discipline to discipline, the amount of expense involved being greater, as he delicately put it, "in certain backward areas."

After prolonged debate on this point, the report was tabled on O'Toole's motion, and the Committee on Teaching Improvement and Evaluation instructed to form a sub-committee.

The business of the faculty went on. Anna stayed until 5:00 and then went to the coffee room. Most of her colleagues were there already, flushed with triumph, drinking the last of the thick sludge at the bottom of the coffee urn. For once the Philosophy Department was all together on an issue.

In Anna's opinion, O'Toole had stolen the laurel wreath from Eddy by forcing the matter into a backwater committee. Eddy was acknowledging this gracefully as he knocked back a large bottle (Family Size) of Coca-cola:

"I saw old Pinch-penny sniffing the breeze when you mentioned expensive prizes."

"Yes, his nostril expanded and his eye rolled."

"It is always much the best policy to get another committee struck when you want to frustrate a motion," said Peterson to O'Toole.

Outside the Arts Building, Anna met Frame taking a large pile of books from the Library to his office.

"That was good, wasn't it?" he said, smiling shyly as she came up to him on the path.

"Where would we be without Eddy and Peter?" replied Anna.

"They're both in your department, aren't they? I wondered why you were so wrapped up in it."

"It's been a matter of general interest for weeks," said Anna, returning the smile. "Philosophy *is* concerned with values, you know."

"It must be nice." Frame was wistful. "In my department nobody talks much to anybody else."

"How odd that must be." Anna caught one of the books as it toppled off the pile. "Going back to work?"

"Yes, I have to. You know Fred Michie don't you? Doesn't he share his office with you?"

Anna nodded.

"We're pretty much in the same pickle. The Tenure Committee meets next month. We came here in the same year, Fred and I."

"You're not worried, I hope."

"Oh no. But one never knows, really. Good geologists in my area are a dime a dozen."

"It's the same in every field nowadays." Anna carefully balanced the book against the knot of Frame's tie. "All the best, anyhow."

Anna walked home slowly through the thick February dusk. The academic streets, lined with trees and large, comfortable houses, were silent and empty because it was the dinner hour. She looked through the warmly lit windows framed by plants and something better than lace curtains. This was what settled academic home life was like. A pleasant, bitter-sweet languor was upon her, and she lingered to appreciate it fully.

The next morning she went into the mailroom with a sense of anticipation. He had not telephoned; there would be a note.

Gregor was much better last night, and this morning his temperature is down to 99°. I am not showing any symptoms yet. I wonder if we could risk meeting this afternoon after my 1:30 class? My office would be best, I think. The course of the disease is very unpleasant, so you must decide whether you should come or not. I am not sure I shall be able to stand it if you do not. I merely mention this.

It struck Anna that the two letters he had so far sent were ideally neat. He had teacher's handwriting on the English model, but there were none of the usual blots and tailings off, and no words were crossed out. She wondered whether this was the effect of making several drafts.

"What are you reading, Callaghan? Love letters?" Eddy suspected Anna of being a feminist and sometimes addressed her by her last name without honorific.

"What is it women do in men require, Eddy?" asked Anna.

"What do you mean?" He looked up from a book circular, alarmed.

"The lineaments of gratified desire," Anna answered herself. "It's by William Blake," she added hastily, as terror threatened to replace alarm in his features.

"Oh, a poem."

"Don't tell Eddy things like that, Anna," whispered O'Toole, popping up suddenly by her elbow. "He's not a very big boy. Come and talk to your uncle if you want to recite dirty verses."

He had begun to read her letter over her shoulder and Anna folded it quickly.

"Come along then," said O'Toole. "Your uncle wants to talk to you seriously for a change." They went up to his office.

"I got that resumé of yours. It's a nice trick to leave out all mention of publication, but it won't work. No, no, Anna, these eagle eyes are just like adding machines. One, two, three papers, subtract a point for no conference presentations, half a point for a "pending acceptance," that makes one and one half points, which has to be offset, of course, against the fact that she's female and has the same middle name as my mother. So let's say she gets half a point. That's the way they do it."

"What can I do about that, then?"

"Look, think up something and write it down. I'll have a look at it, take a measure of its thickness with my calipers here, and write a nice letter saying how much I think of it."

"No."

"What do you mean, no? I'll even give you a title. I have a list of titles here somewhere." He took out his pocketbook.

"No, I said."

"How's the thesis editing coming along?"

"I sent it off. It's done."

"Oh." O'Toole looked at her slyly. "Any troubles? I haven't seen Jimson buzzing around your head for quite a time."

"No, he's fallen by the wayside."

"Good-oh! I assume from your serene looks that you don't mind if I say this."

"No, I don't mind. I'm quite all right. I've been working hard lately."

"I wonder—are you hanging around old Mr. MacGregor's garden, then?"

"It's disgusting of you to read other people's mail."

"Just a glance. From what I could glean, it was all about his health." O'Toole was not in the slightest embarrassment about this. "I should add that I like the man. He and Jimson are of quite a different stripe. He does like his wee drop o' whiskey—a taste I share." He looked at her sharply. "So do you, now that I think of it."

"Stop trying to take my pulse, Peter."

"Well—mind the gooseberry net and the flower pots," said O'Toole.

"Such a nice little blue jacket," he crooned, blowing her a kiss.

She went out crossly and closeted herself with Michie, putting her letter with its predecessor in the locked middle drawer of her desk.

Chapter 14

Anna went down to the English Department at 2:30 sharp. His class would have been over at 2:20, but she allowed him the spare ten minutes to shake pursuit from students and colleagues. The fourth floor was devoted to English, a larger department than Philosophy, although a less lively one. There were pictures in the intervals of wall between the offices. She went along the hall looking at these and reading the names on the doors. Bespectacled W.B. Yeats hung next to MacGregor. She had never been to his office before.

The door opened as she was raising her hand to knock. He stood aside rather formally to let her enter and closed it quietly. "I know your step," he said.

They looked at each other, a few feet apart.

"I shall not kiss you."

"No?" She looked at him teasingly.

"Only on the cheek."

"Both cheeks—and the forehead."

"Sit here." He put her in a chair and went around his desk to sit down.

"Now, what can I do for you, Miss Callaghan?" she mocked.

"No, not that. Just let me look. I never have enough time to look."

She glanced around the room, accustomed to his close scrutiny and comfortable with it. He did not have many books. A very large Shakespeare lay open on a chair that was apparently devoted to holding it. A much-thumbed copy of *Great Expectations*, an English I text, was the only worthy object on the desk. There was a dusty vase of pussy willows on the filing cabinet. No photographs or other homely forms of decoration were to be seen. Someone abour four feet tall had drawn a funny face in the lower left hand corner of the blackboard. She smiled at him.

"Damn!" he said.

"What?"

"Never mind. Tell me something."

"You look tired."

"I thought I was too tired to . . . Looking isn't good enough it seems. Or, to put it another way, it's too good."

"Have you been staying up with cold baths and things for Gregor?"

"Cold baths, and ice cubes, and 'May I have another drink of water, Daddy?' "

"Do you tell stories?"

"Sometimes," he said guardedly. "Please talk about yourself."

"O'Toole is hounding me to write a paper."

"I'm surprised at him."

"He's a cynic. 'Throw down some trash' is the rallying cry. He wants to be able to put something about it in his letter of recommendation."

He frowned. "There really isn't going to be anything here?"

"ffrench applied for leave, but he didn't get it. Peter thinks it's hopeless."

"Will you be here this summer?"

"Depends on money. Maybe they'll get up a summer school course, and maybe I'll be allowed to teach it."

"Where will you go, if not?"

"I don't know." Anna was desperately thinking of how to change the subject. He was silent.

"I sometimes have ideas, but they never turn out well on paper," she said. "The more I refine them, the less interesting they seem."

"Yes. I did not finish my dissertation for that reason."

"It's pride, really, don't you think?" said Anna tentatively.

"Yes, probably. Something else too. Not wanting anyone to know what you think at all."

"Some form of paranoia."

"Perhaps. . . . Tell me something else."

"Well . . . More about O'Toole. He is guessing about you and me. He caught me reading your note over for the fourth time this morning."

"You should have burned it. Did you?"

"The germ theory of disease was not a big thing in my upbringing."

"Did you really read it four times?"

"Six in all. I read the other one over twice this morning for good measure."

"I got yours too." Anna had laboured over a reply the previous evening and finally settled for writing "I love you" in the middle of a sheet of ring binder paper and putting it in a sealed envelope. "I have it by heart," he went on.

"If only I could write that well ordinarily."

"I have to go in about five minutes."

"Will you get some sleep tonight?"

"I expect so. I can't come, anyhow. Hold still. I'm going to imagine something." He was looking at her intently.

"Won't you tell me what it is?"

"Tomorrow." He swivelled around in his chair and went to the window with his back to her. Taking a crumpled package out of his pocket, he put two cigarettes in his mouth and lit them both. He turned around, offering her one of them, then suddenly snatched it away and put it out in the sardine tin.

"I forgot."

"Tomorrow," Anna pleaded.

"I hope so." He took down his overcoat and escorted her to the door, managing to do this without touching her at all. The elevator swallowed him a moment later. Vacantly Anna made for the stairs.

The next morning Anna woke up with a violent headache accompanied by a sore throat, swollen sinuses and the beginnings of a racking cough.

She staggered into the University to teach her class. The note in her mail box was very brief. It said:

"I've got it now too."

Anna wrote these same words on a piece of paper and dropped it folded in his box. She locked away this third letter with the other two and went home.

All day she stayed in bed, eating and drinking sparingly and trying to sleep. She had taught the earlier of her two classes and cancelled the other one. It would be a waste of everyone's time.

Being sick alone in her barren apartment Anna found frightening. She dozed and read away at a novel, but at frequent intervals she was subject to spasms of fear and self-pity. She imagined things that she had not thought about since she was a teenager: her own dead face in a coffin, dying in her sleep alone, not being able to drag herself to the telephone.

The book she was reading was not very good. She dreamed feverishly of her aesthetics class. "Aesthetics is about criticism," she was explaining to them. "I can't tell you what is good. I can only tell you what that means." She woke up quite suddenly, wondering whether this made any sense.

The telephone never rang. On the third day she was well enough to play limited games of soccer with the cat. She drank large quantities of Scotch and milk to keep herself dozing. Her body was stiff all over.

At 1:00 in the morning the telephone rang. Anna pulled herself together drunkenly. She had not eaten anything for twelve hours in the mistaken belief that the milk was enough.

"Are you all right?" he asked anxiously.

"Yes—no. I think I'm better."

"It's bad, isn't it?"

"Have you been staying in bed?"

"More or less."

"Sleeping a lot is the only remedy. Does anyone else there have it? Lucy or Jane, I mean?"

"Jane had a mild case at the same time as Gregor. Lucy's all right so far."

"Is Lucy nursing you?"

"Yes. She made blanc-mange today."

"What a sweet puss. I wish I had a Lucy."

"You're all alone, aren't you?"

Anna had the feeling that this had just occurred to him. Trying to be fair, she told herself that it was better to be alone than with two sick children.

"Can you teach?"

"Yes," he said. "I'm ambulatory now. Are you?"

"Not so far. I'm not sure about tomorrow either."

"I'll see you in the morning," he rang off abruptly.

When Anna woke up, she realized that the Scotch and milk had been a fatal error. After throwing up for the first time in twenty-five years, she crawled back to bed. She lay there miserably wondering whether she could keep an aspirin down long enough to do any good. At 11:30 she was able to drink a glass of water.

There was someone at the kitchen door. Anna pulled a sweater over her nightgown. She was already wearing tights on her legs for warmth. She went into the kitchen unsteadily. It was Ian.

"My God! You look like death!" He put a basket down on one of the kitchen chairs and picked her up. Anna held on desperately, hoping she wouldn't have to be sick again. He tucked her into bed, fluffing the pillows, and went back to the kitchen. Anna thought dismally about the glasses and bottles and plates in the sink. She put her head down over the edge of the bed, a remedy she had been using all morning.

"What are you doing that for?"

"I was sick this morning. I don't want it to happen again." At the end of this speech, she threw back the covers and ran for the bathroom. The glass of water had not been a good idea. He was holding her head down efficiently.

"All right, I think," said Anna, crying a little.

He put her back into bed, then took a thermometer out of his breast pocket and began to shake it down. Anna wiped away her tears and docilely opened her mouth.

"You don't have a very high temperature," he said at last. "It's less than 100°."

"It was probably what I drank last night."

"What was it?"

"Scotch and milk."

"Ugh."

"I was trying to stay asleep." She closed her eyes. He went into the kitchen with the thermometer. Returning, he tucked her up very securely, then lay down beside her with a book, pushing the blankets up against her so that he wasn't weighing them down. He rested his head against part of one of the pillows. She heard him turn a page.

A few hours later, she woke up. The book was lying face down on the coverlet. He was running water in the kitchen. She rolled over and looked at the book, holding it before her nose to see it clearly. It was in Gaelic. She felt shaky, but better. Was he doing the dishes? She remembered being sick the second time.

"Oh Christ," she said, and began to curl her toes alternating one foot with the other. After a time, the water stopped running, and he came into the room.

"You're awake." He put his hand on her forehead. "Better?"

"Much." He smelt of Scotch.

"Did you do the dishes?"

"Yes." He sat down. "I had a drink. I had two drinks. The bottle is almost empty."

"I don't mind. I never want to see it again."

He looked down at his knees.

"What about your classes?" she asked.

"Just reading courses. I postponed them."

"You shouldn't have come at all. It's a complete waste. I look awful. I was sick. You did the dishes. You've broken a promise like that fox of Lucy's, just because of me."

"Would you like me to comb your hair?"

"You mustn't stay."

"The housekeeper will be there all day and all night."
Delicately he untangled a snarl.

"I love you," she said miserably.

"Lucy made another blanc-mange this morning. Could you
eat some shortly?"

"Does she know you brought it?"

"She made it for you."

"Really?"

"Yes, I told you—she never makes a mistake." He was
working away at her hair, doing a thorough job.

Later in the afternoon he went out for bread and more milk.
Anna put on a lot of make-up and washed it off again before he
came back.

"Read me some of this," she demanded. She brought him the
book and put it down on the rug beside the pillows and the shawl.

"It's in a foreign tongue."

"Yes. I want to hear you read it."

"Shall I translate?"

"No." She propped her head against his trouser leg. He began
looking through the book. At last he started to read in a different
voice than the one he had been using on the Library Committee
report. Anna listened contentedly.

"Do you like it?" he asked, apparently surprised. He had read
for some time.

"Yes. It's the first time I've ever heard it spoken like that. How
did you learn it?"

"At my mother's knee."

Anna sat up and looked down at him. He was half-lying on
the floor with his back against the pillows and the wall.

"Where were you born in Scotland?"

"In Glasgow. You have no slums on this continent." He
frowned.

"Did you grow up in a slum?"

"No. We were better off than that. Proud poor."

"Why were you poor?" Anna was fascinated. Almost all her
university acquaintances were Europeans and Americans and
were backgroundless as far as she was concerned, sprung as adults
from the head of Zeus.

"My father died when I was an infant. I have two older sisters.
We were brought up by my mother."

"You went to university."

"I went to a very good school."

"Fichte and Proust," Anna teased.

"Latin and Greek," he said, pulling her down comfortably against his shoulder. "Tell me about yourself."

"My parents are teachers," she began. "I don't have any siblings. We lived in a small town."

"In this part of the world?"

"Eastward." She waved vaguely in the right direction. "On the real prairies."

"The real prairies," he said thoughtfully. "What are they?"

"No one at the university would know," she replied slowly. "Or if they knew, they've forgotten."

"Why do you say that?"

Anna thought of Gore's remarks about hayseed all over the floor. She pressed her lips into a friendly place between his neck and the open collar of his shirt.

"When I was a boy, I used to dream about the red Indians," he said. "But since I've been here . . ."

"You've been to Regina," said Anna, laughing. "That was what we used to say about people who had never gone anywhere."

"What is it like to be you, I wonder?"

"What is it like to be you?"

They looked at each other attentively.

Still later, Anna had a bath. It was getting dark outside. He prowled around the door. When she came out, the whole apartment was dark.

"Are you there?" Anna groped her way towards the bedroom.

"Just here."

"Where is that?"

"Here. Right here."

She found him standing by the bed.

"Oh Ian. I love you. Do you mind me saying that?"

"I love you too."

He was still wearing his clothes. Anna began to divest him of his shirt.

"What were you imagining the other day?"

"Which day?"

"In your office. You said you'd tell me tomorrow."

"Oh, then."

"Tell."

"I can't."

"You said you would."

"I'll show you."

Chapter 15

There were several more miserable days during which Ian nursed Lucy through her case of the flu. Anna began to teach again on Tuesday, and the notes resumed on Wednesday.

> Lucy's temperature went to 104° this morning. We have had the doctor in again. I don't know what I should do without Helen. She has the other two at night. The housekeeper is sick also. I shall go mad if I don't see you soon.

On Thursday he continued:

> Lucy is improving. Children recover from this more quickly than adults. You did not say how you are in your letter. Helen has generously offered to take them all to the mountains this weekend if Lucy is better. That would almost make up for everything.

Anna mournfully pondered the recurrence of Helen Bertelsmann's name in these letters. In the first note she appeared as a sick nurse; in the second she was taking an active role in Anna's love affair. Anna like her doing neither of these things. She wondered obsessively whether Bertelsmann had spent the night, or several nights, at Ian's house. She wondered whether they had had long, late-night coversations about herself, Anna. She had a vivid picture of Ian standing up against the sort of dark wooden mantelpiece she was sure his house contained, saying casually, "You mustn't think I am taking this seriously at all, Helen," while the Bertelsmann, compressing her lips, poured him a cup of tea. She also began to wonder whether the Bertelsmann affair was perhaps only one of several, the one he had felt obliged to mention, because . . . She shook herself free of these meditations and locked the two letters away carefully.

She had not once seen Jimson since the fatal Saturday, now two weeks past, when he had come to her apartment. It amazed her to realize this since formerly scarcely a day had gone by in which she did not come across him entirely by accident. Anna was making no special effort not to see him other than avoidance of the coffee room, so she presumed that he must be taking steps to stay out of her way. Her virtuous attendance to her lecture notes in the office was putting the screws on Michie, she noticed. However happy he might be to be waited upon by Jimson no longer, he was not getting much done while she was there.

No ripple of scandal was reaching Anna's feelers. O'Toole made some sly allusions to nice brass buttons occasionally, but she felt he was not a gossip in the Jimsonian sense.

Late on Friday afternoon Anna went into the coffee room, feeling safe. Jimson believed in the two and-a-half day weekend. The younger members of the French Department were having a post-departmental meeting colloquy. Anna poured herself a stagnant cup of coffee. It was 5:00.

She sat down beside Francoise Hibert on the sofa. Francoise was looking sleekly attractive, as usual wearing extremely pale stockings, her legs appearing winter bare under her black skirt. Anna wondered, not for the first time, whether this was Parisian or eccentric. They smiled at each other in greeting.

Gauthier took up where he had left off on the subject of the department head. "What animal does he most remind you of?" he asked dreamily, addressing the assemblage. "Pig with overtones of elephant, or elephant with overtones of pig?"

"Depends which end you see first, the snout, or the ample ass of his," said LeMarchand, an epigram artist whom Anna had once seen crossing swords with O'Toole, to the greater glory of Ireland.

To Anna's convalescent eye, they all seemed to stretch their necks and scream at this. Anna put down her cup untasted. Francoise was giving another of her ambiguous winks. Anna got to her feet and tiptoed from the room. In the hall she met Helen Bertelsmann efficiently carrying a tea kettle to the tap.

"Hullo—er—Helen," said Anna.

"Professor Callaghan."

Anna stopped uncertainly, wondering whether the Bertelsmann would want to divulge something. She was a handsome woman, very well made-up and wearing good, tailored clothes. Anna examined her critically.

Helen was smiling thinly. "Have you recovered from the flu? I have not been in much lately myself, but I have not seen you going to your class." They shared a classroom interval between 1:20 and 1:30 and sometimes passed with formal salutations in the hall outside.

"Oh yes, I'm all better. Did you have it yourself?"

"Last week. It is very contagious, no? Luckily I share some of my housekeeping arrangements with Professor MacGregor. Last week he looked after my affairs and I have been able to help him this week." Her articulation in English was remarkable, Anna thought. She spoke without the use of the letter 'r'.

"Oh—good. His daughter is sick." Anna resisted the impulse to make this into a question.

"The little girl is very attached to him."

"It is kind of you—" began Anna, but stopped herself from going on to say why.

"Do you mind if I tell you something personal, my dear?" Bertelsmann looked at her intensely.

"Not at all. Shall we—?" Anna made a vague gesture towards shelter in the stairwell. They were just outside the coffee room door.

"No, no. It is just that your skirt is . . ." Anna looked down. Her skirt was twisted around her waist with the zipper in front.

"Oh, thanks."

Anna walked home, achingly lonely. She did not look into the windows of the cosy houses as usual. The unexpected mildness of the mid-February season was giving her no pleasure. She was going over and over the Bertelsmann conversation in her mind. Shared housekeeping arrangements. Did they usually . . . ? How close together were their houses? (She felt sure that Frau Bertelsmann owned a house.) Furthermore—here she put her jealous thoughts away—if Lucy was very attached, how could Ian be so cruel as to send her off to the mountains just after an illness? Oughtn't he to go? Wasn't she being extremely selfish in preventing him from looking after his children properly? She divorced Ian from his wife and married him to Helen several times.

"Although," she put her key in the lock of the kitchen door, "her daughters are much older."

Exactly how had he looked after Helen's affairs last week? Gregor had been sick. No mention had been made of Helen in last week's notes. Anna took off her coat slowly. The dishes had not been washed since Ian had done them on Monday afternoon. Had he also done Helen's dishes? He had been such a tender nurse. She remembered with love and shame how he hadn't minded her being sick. Horribly ashamed of her thoughts, Anna sat down at the kitchen table and presently began to cry.

The long Friday evening and the longer Saturday morning Anna devoted entirely to jealousy-evasion techniques. She washed her hair but did not look in the mirror to comb it as a punishment for her vanity at being better looking than Helen. Later, catching a glimpse of herself in the kitchen mirror she saw that her parting had gone irreparably crooked so that she looked Iroquois when she tried to straighten it. She re-washed her hair.

"Is Lucy better?" she asked breathlessly in the doorway.

"Yes, much. Your hair is wet."

"I washed it twice today. It came out looking very peculiar the first time."

He was tired. He sat down heavily at the kitchen table and looked at her wordlessly as she stood, arms akimbo, in front of him. He had lost more weight, and his face was lined with fatigue.

"Ought she to have gone?" burst out Anna. "Wouldn't it have been better if she had stayed home in bed?"

"Who?"

"Lucy—your daughter, Lucy. She went to the mountains with Helen, didn't she?"

"Oh yes, they all went. What is the matter?"

"I just thought perhaps you should have let her stay."

"But she wanted to go," he said, wonderingly.

"Oh, Ian, I have been taking up so much of your time lately . . ."

"You haven't been taking up nearly enough of my time lately."

"I thought . . ."

"Come here," he said softly. Anna sat down on his knee and put her head on his shoulder. "What is it, Anna? Tell me."

"I missed you horribly."

"Was it really *horrible?*" he asked, teasing. "Would you say it was *terrible*, now?"

"It was *awful.*"

"I enjoyed your letters, though," he remarked, kissing her gently on an important spot behind her ear. Anna's letters had all been repetitions of the first one.

"I wish I could have done something—like Lucy's blanc-mange, or—Helen," she said dropping her voice on the name and wishing she were dead.

"There was nothing you could do."

"Helen had it well in hand." Anna tried to get up to mask the bitter energy in this remark.

"She helped, as I think I told you." He held her down.

"She mentioned that it was lucky you shared housekeeping arrangements. You looked after each other's affairs."

"I got her mail. She took the children at night. When were you discussing this? She can't have been in much lately."

"As she herself said. I met her in the hall yesterday afternoon." Anna succeeded in getting off his lap and walked across the room wringing her hands. The roar of her self-hatred was getting too loud for her.

"Anna!" He pursued her through the living room door. "How long have you been brooding like this?"

"Hours and hours. I tried not to, but I started in right away whenever I wasn't—well—counting or singing or something."

"Would you like to know everything? I'll tell you everything." He backed her against the wall behind the armchair.

Anna kept her eyes cast down and bit her tongue viciously between her front teeth. She was not going to say no to this because she did want to know, but she was certainly not going to say yes.

"Starting from the beginning: I have known Helen for twelve years, since she first came here and before her husband died. She was a friend of my wife's, and I was a friend of Friedrich. After . . . I did not know how to look after Gregor properly at that time, so Helen and I got a housekeeper to share between us. University salaries . . ." he began to dry up.

"Oh Ian," said Anna helplessly. "What a pig I am."

"No, it's all right." He let go of her arms and got out his cigarettes, lighting two at once. "I don't want you to go on thinking about it and making things up." He gave her one of them and sat on the arm of the chair. Anna remained standing against the wall with the vague idea of punishing herself. She kept her eyes cast down.

"About a year ago," he began, clearing his throat, "we were at a party together. For some reason I was not drunk as usual, and I thought, why not? We were both very lonely, what with . . . one thing and another . . . Helen is still very attractive even though she's my age, so I . . . we went to her house and got into bed."

Anna said nothing. There was no question that she wanted to hear about this.

"It didn't turn out very well the first time, but we tried it again about a week later. I had given up drinking altogether at that point, and—well, it went better. After a while I stopped, though—after about a month—" he said precisely, "primarily because I wanted to drink again, and the two do not go well hand in hand, but also . . ."

There was a long pause, while he smoked his cigarette, holding it cupped in his hand in a way that Anna particularly liked.

"It seemed rather pointless," he said at last. "I thought that Helen would like to re-marry, and I was taking up too much of her time for her to have any social existence. As for me, it was just some sort of . . . physical exercise—momentarily pleasant, but not very interesting. Do you know what I mean?"

"Yes," said Anna in a low voice. Her vanity was at rock bottom, and she was surprised at his gentle intuition when he went on.

"It is not like that with you at all. I said that before, didn't I?"

"Yes," she said again, her heart swelling.

"Not even in the beginning, when I was just thinking you were too beautiful to be wasted on that son of a bitch Jimson and wondering what you would be like with your clothes off and so on. I used to turn into a jellyfish when I saw you at forty feet. Helen does not have that effect." He took her cigarette away and put it out in an ashtray.

"I am sorry," said Anna. "I am sorry. Have I spoiled everything?"

"Let's have some tea. Do you want to know what you make me feel like from two feet off?"

Anna looked up. "Yes," she said humbly.

"I've forgotten already," he said, pulling her tightly against him.

She had, of course, spoiled something, she reflected, later on in the gathering dusk of the afternoon, as he slept with his head in the crook of her arm. He was unaffected as yet, but her own consciousness no longer had the sparkling, pellucid clarity of the first days. They were beginning now to 'have an affair', she thought, with all the inevitable squalor which is attached to the phrase and to the reality behind it. She reflected that someday, not soon perhaps, he might start to drink in preference to making love with her, and after what he had said today about the pointlessness of sex with Helen, she realized fiercely that she could never forgive him if that happened. It occurred to her almost as a comfort that they did not have much time before she would be leaving the university and the town.

Chapter 16

February wore on and was replaced by March. The battle in the French Department reached a new pitch of acrimoniousness. Michie had the flu. After Anna had sent him some books and papers on receipt of a note meticulously detailing his needs, she was rewarded by a few words of thanks on his return. After this he often said some greeting when she entered the office.

A few letters of refusal began to drift back to her in response to her applications. "Dear Ms. Callaghan: After an initial sorting out of candidates we have arrived at a short list of names. We regret to have to tell you . . ." "Dear Ms. Callaghan: Budgetary restraints have forced us to withdraw the position for which you have applied. We regret to inform you . . ." Anna was quite prepared for this and she was sure that her colleagues, aside from those receiving similar letters, were innocently unaware that anything was happening with regard to her future prospects.

She had a conversation with Ian about this. He, like the rest, hired in the years of university prosperity, was happily blind to the situation.

"What are you reading?" He was sitting by her filing cabinet in his overcoat, waiting to take her home. Anna was putting things away.

"A letter from my publisher." She passed it to him slowly. She did not want to blight his happiness with thoughts of the future.

"Why did they advertise a position they don't have?" he said, throwing it in the wastebasket.

"Because they're pigs. They *might* have a job, and they want everybody in North America to apply, just in case."

"What on earth for? The administrative work is a complete waste."

"Yes, but it lets them know they're still alive. *Cogito ergo sum*, you see."

"Good heavens," he said briefly. "Do you get many like this?" He retrieved the letter and spread it out, frowning, on his knee.

"Lots."

"Have you heard anything favorable?"

"Princeton has made me an offer but I'm still waiting before I answer them to hear from Harv-. . . ." Anna stopped, embarrassed.

"What does O'Toole think of all this?"

" 'You'll only get cash if you throw down some trash.' That was what he said the other day at least."

"Isn't there going to be anything *here?*"

The course of their love affair was running smoothly. MacGregor had worked out a totally new arrangement with his housekeeper and had rescheduled his reading courses. He saw Anna every day, either in the late afternoon or evening, and they both were thriving on this regimen.

One day she met Jimson while she was waiting in a queue for the Library check-out desk. She caught his eye accidentally and he looked away at once, then evidently changed his mind and came over to say something.

"Hello, Anna. You're looking radiant, darling."

"Thank you, Michael."

"Very polite, too."

"I'm just taking out some books, as you see," she said uncomfortably.

"It's a bit late in the year to be doing your homework. Have you heard anything good on the employment front lately?"

"No—have you?" This type of conversation was constant among her peers. She began to relax.

"Yes, I have something in my pocket. But I'm waiting on other things."

"You'd rather take them?"

"Yes, indeed."

"Why? What's the offer you have?"

"Sierra Leone."

"Oh."

Anna moved up into position before the library assistant.

"Well, ta-ta! - Give my love to Ian!" he added dropping his voice.

Several days after this Anna received an invitation to a party from a couple in the Music Department named Bloom; Leopold and Mary Bloom, pleasant, middle-aged people with European roots, Mary a pianist and Leopold a violinist. She knew them slightly. She had once gone to hear Mary read a paper on the theory of musical keys. Anna was still trying to learn something about aesthetics.

She told Ian about this that night. Unexpectedly, he turned out to have been invited too, and she felt easier about wanting to go.

"You won't mind about me drinking?" she asked. He was very frank on this sort of point.

"Not at all. I like to watch you drink. Your eyes dilate in an interesting way."

"And you won't be tempted yourself?"

"Lucy will insist I take a bottle of ginger ale to present to the hostess, I expect."

"Lucy is so well organized and thoughtful." Anna was beginning to worry badly about not having met Lucy.

Anna arrived early. She gave Mary a chrysanthemum, the last crop from her Christmas plant, and a frosty bottle of German white wine. Mary, in return, gave her a scented European kiss on both cheeks.

The room filled up slowly with people and smoke, and Mary turned her sophisticated attention to the other guests. Ian had come in, caught her eye, and settled in the sofa corner with Spong, seeing her happy with the Blooms.

Parties had a curious effect on Anna. Before a party and in the early stages, she felt excitement and anticipation. At best, she began to feel melancholy loneliness by the middle. Sometimes this deepened to fury, as at Christmas.

She was entering the lonely phase when she found herself in the kitchen with two male linguists and Helen Bertelsmann. The linguists were arguing with Helen at first about some Indo-European phonetic item, but later turned to a violent, intra-disciplinary discussion which involved higher mathematics and diagrams on paper napkins.

"I had a friend once who wrote the entire first draft of his dissertation on paper napkins," Anna remarked to Helen, who was making only a pretence of interest in the conversation.

Helen looked at her severely. "In Europe this would be unremarkable," she began. "Students work in cafes, in bars, and they talk, talk, talk to each other. Here we find the students in isolation in their library carrels reading light literature."

Anna started guiltily but dismissed the thought that Ian would have mentioned this.

"Do you think they really are more serious in Europe? One gets the impression from French films that it's all in the way they dress."

"What do you mean by this?" asked Helen rather aggressively.

She was wearing a strictly tailored suit, which made the best of her trim middle-aged figure. Anna, who was wearing the dark red dress which made the most of her breasts, put down her beer bottle and began to go into her French student routine.

"The duffle coat, and then, a woolen scarf, thrown carelessly over the shoulder, like this! (Knotted before the mirror, ahead of time, naturally.) Then they sit on the backs of chairs, and read sentences out of books to each other!" Anna perched on the back of a kitchen chair and pretended to read. " 'All happy families are alike . . .' " She realized with a familiar joyous shock that Ian was present. He was smiling at her joke, his eyes crinkling pleasantly at the outer corners.

Helen, unsmiling, appealed to him instantly. "The air of intellectual excitement at European universities, they have nothing like this here, no? It is so sterile, such isolation . . . lack of seriosity."

Anna like this word so much that she almost lost the thread of his reply. He seemed to be agreeing whole-heartedly.

". . . and no decent beer to be found."

"When I was in England, I noticed that there was a lot of talk about beer," she remarked, picking this up as the foundation of another joke. " 'Do you like tea? Yes? Do you like beer? Yes? Well then, you must be all right.' "

"The beer of Germany is splendid, much better than British beer, especially around Heidelberg, near where I come from. It is very good for the health to drink this beer. Doctors offer it as a prescription for disorders of the gall bladder, the spleen . . ."

"But beer is not really good for you," said Anna, her Puritan forebears suddenly uppermost.

"The beer of Heidelberg is said to clarify the blood, assist in circulatory movement, relax the bowel . . ."

"Beer is good for you, Anna," said Ian, getting a bit of quiet pleasure out of an emphasis on the 'you' part. She remembered what he had said about her eyes and, judging the party to have gone on long enough to make this acceptable, went over and stood close beside him. He put his arm around her waist stealthily. She realized that Helen was making her angry but that he continued to be unaware of this. He looked peacefully from her face to Helen's.

Helen was also annoyed. She made a ppphht! noise with her lips. Suddenly Anna recognized that it was a shock to Helen that Ian had his hand on her hip. This was the *ad hominem* to top all *ad hominems*, and Anna's anger departed. Helen was looking on at the linguists again with pretended interest. One of them was stabbing at the other's paper napkin with a cheese knife.

"*This* is entirely wrong. It's *this* part! I cannot agree . . . !"

"I must—I have no wine in my glass," said Helen, and left abruptly.

"Ian," said Anna urgently, "doesn't she know—about us?" She looked up at him with eyes which, as she was now conscious, were dilated.

"Well, possibly." He spoke cautiously. "I have my arm around your waist."

"I noticed. Is that all she knows about it, that you have your arm around my waist?"

"Well—certain inferences . . ."

"Ian, I think she just made them," said Anna wildly. She began to feel terribly upset for Helen. "Please go and talk to her!"

"Do you think . . . ?"

"Yes."

He freed his arm and went towards the dining room door with a perturbed expression. He came back to stand in front of Anna. "You don't mind if I . . . ?"

"No, just come back some time."

"All right." He went through the doorway.

Anna listened to the linguists for a few more moments, then sauntered through the rooms. Ian and Helen were nowhere to be seen, but she felt a certain optimism about this. She was identifying herself with Helen.

On the other hand, she thought, dallying on the outskirts of a conversation about Mozart, why should I think she cares about it that much? I am in love with him, but is she in love with him?

But even if she isn't, Anna argued, eating a piece of cheese, it is a blow to one's pride to see a former lover loving someone else.

If he does love me, she thought dubiously, somewhat later, listening to Mary's interpretation of the Mozart piece under discussion.

Much later, she wondered what she was doing at the party at all. The conversation had reached the point where Anna, drunk herself, could no longer take pleasure in its drunkenness. It was after 1:00, as she saw, catching a glimpse of someone's watch.

She went back into the kitchen, but he wasn't there. One of the linguists emerged with a beer apparently from behind the refrigerator.

"That's just the dress for you, Anne."

"Anna."

"It suits you. Fits you very well. I like it."

"Thank you."

"I'm going home now. Like a lift?"

"No thanks."

"Aw, come on; let's swing, baby!"

"No!" cried Anna, suddenly in a rage. She hunted for Mary, who turned out to be at the piano and missed her wave. Then she went out into the hall and put on her sweaters and her coat and boots, and started off the porch for home by way of the thawing streets.

He met her at the bottom of the walk, just turning in through the hedge. "Anna! What are you doing here?"

"I'm leaving in a fury. I mean in a hurry." She spoke freezingly.

"I'm always talking to you in the road at the end of parties." He seemed amused.

"True," said Anna, dodging to escape between him and the gatepost.

"I took Helen home." He caught her cleverly.

"Oh? You left quite a long time ago for that."

"You were right about her. She was very annoyed."

"There is something about you which annoys women."

"Yes," he said sadly, pushing her through the melting snow on the lawn to the dark side of the house. "It was lucky I got here just at this moment."

"Oh? Why?"

"Because it is just the right moment, that is why."

"Where are you taking me?" Anna began to struggle, laughing in spite of herself.

"This is a wooden lawn chair. Nearly as good as the kitchen table. Not as good as the hearth rug. We'll hear your comparison with cars in a short while."

In the end they went back to the party. First, they went out by the alley and inspected each other's clothes under the street lamp. His shirt needed tucking in. Anna did this inexpertly.

"We can't do it the *right* way, after all."

Turning her around, he said, "The hairpin situation is dire."

There was amost no one still at the party. The remaining guests were sitting in a contented circle in the living room.

"I thought you'd both gone home," cried Mary, giving them each an energetic kiss. Leopold pressed coffee with brandy in it on Anna. Ian found his ginger ale bottle in the kitchen.

Anna had a new glimpse of what her walks home in the evening sometimes revealed: this was what a settled academic life could be like. They sat back against the soft cushions of the sofa and let the even tenor of life flow in their quiet conversation. At last she was inside one of those warmly lit windows, framed with plants and curtains.

Ian turned out to know the Blooms very well, and Anna again had the insight that her earlier picture of him had been entirely false. He talked of what was real to people who thought constantly of abstract matters, and they understood him very well and respected his judgment.

After a time, when they were alone with the Blooms, Ian slid his arm down from the back of the sofa to her shoulders and she found herself in a warmly lit annex inside a warmly lit cavern, a place where she had always yearned to be. The Blooms smiled affectionately at Ian, and Anna felt that their love and approval extended to her.

When, at last, it was time reluctantly to leave, Mary gave Anna a tender kiss and said in her ear, "You are just right for him, my sweetheart."

The end of this party shed its luminescent glow over Anna for the whole of the next week. She walked to her 8:30 class with her heart melting, even at that barbaric hour, for Mary and Leopold and Ian, and all that they stood for.

Anna had very severe ideas before this about the academic ideal. As the child of high school teachers who looked upon education as the standard of excellence in mankind, Anna had been bred a bluestocking. Education should have its acolytes and its initiates, and she had always felt herself to be very much a spear carrier in this procession. Now she began thinking about it as part of a whole way of life. It was a way of living that she saw around her every day in her settled, middled-aged colleagues, one which she could not fully participate in because of the impermanent conditions of her employment. They were submerged in it: the educational process dictated the order of their working lives and filled their leisure hours with enjoyment. Anna longed to have this.

Chapter 17

Her birthday was at the end of the week. She was about to be thirty. She was uncertain whether this would be worth mentioning to anyone beforehand. Finally she told Eddy. He was enchanted.

"Callaghan—Anna here is thirty today," he told MacGregor in the mail room.

"Really?"

"And she isn't married yet. You'd better get cracking on that, Callaghan! The best time to have a baby was nine years ago!"

"Oh come," said Anna.

"Yes indeed. Those little fellers need so much attention, and before you know it—bingo!—you're an old crochet wandering around on a cane, and you haven't even the patience to read them a story!"

"I'm not an old crochet yet, surely?"

"You ask him," said Eddy, jerking his thumb at MacGregor. "She should have a baby, right?"

"Yes, she should," said Ian, thinking about this.

"What am I? A brood mare or something? One can be thirty in peace, surely?"

"It's a nice age," said Ian. "I remember it well."

"Yes!" cried Eddy. They were almost the same age, Anna recognized, shocked. "Do you remember what dancing was like when we were young?"

"I do."

"And the movie theatre was still the movie theatre!" cried Eddy. "Women wore stockings! Do you remember that, MacGregor?"

"I'm sure Professor Callaghan doesn't know the meaning of your words. You must explain to her about movies and stockings."

Eddy looked puzzled.

"Begin with stockings, please," said Anna.

"Well . . ."

"I'll do it, Wiebe," said Ian calmly. "I'll explain the two of them at once. When Wiebe and I were young, you see, Professor Callaghan, there was an archaic custom called 'going to the movies.' Rather like watching T.V. in a large hall, it was. One took a companion of the opposite sex, and that's how these 'stockings' come into it. Women in those days wore a curious garment called 'stockings' which covered the leg up to but not above the thigh. The custom was that you took the woman's hand, but after a time, if things were going well, you gave her the bag of nuts and put your other hand on her knee. Now as you slid your hand up the leg, you see, there was a wonderful place—this gap between the . . ."

"You're embarrassing Eddy," said Anna.

"He knows what I'm talking about, that's all."

"Many happy returns of the day," he said that night, as they were having a late cup of tea on the rug.

"It's strange that I should be so old. It seems only yesterday that I was twelve."

"Does it?"

"Actually, I don't feel much more than that most of the time. I'm always wondering what I'll be when I grow up."

"I'd like to think you were over the age of consent."

"What was this exchange you were having with Eddy this morning all about, anyhow? You seemed to be in agreement."

"I thought I'd explained it at the time quite thoroughly. Stockings and movies, and so on."

"You really shocked him, telling in front of a woman like that," said Anna, laughing. "But what I meant was you seemed to agree that I ought to have a baby."

"Yes, I think he's right about that."

"Why?"

"It's a natural thing for a woman," he said slowly.

"Oh—like your views on contraception."

"The bodily changes aren't ugly and unpleasant as some people appear to think. A woman is never so beautiful as when she's pregnant."

"Being sick for three months."

"Smooth skin, glossy hair, shining eyes." He smiled. "Like you are now only even better."

"You exaggerate," she said, feeling secretly pleased. "Nineteen hours in labour, and all the other things, too: swollen ankles, horrible doctor's examinations, having your pubic hair shaved, stretch marks . . . ," she went on.

"Strange cravings."

"That's a cliché."

"Not entirely. A woman doesn't become lovely like that just for nothing. You'd see for yourself. And I'd like to be the one responsible," he added.

"I've never really seen what the man had to do with it. Sex and getting pregnant are quite distinct."

"No, they're not. What are you, an ignorant savage?"

"I admit there's a causal relationship."

"It's more involved than that. I wish I could show you." He got to his feet and carried his teacup to the window where he stood with his back to her.

"And then," went on Anna stubbornly, gazing at his back but continuing to lie on the rug, "What about a woman's career?"

"Motherhood . . ."

"Motherhood is not a career. You spend all your time thinking about—oh, teething and diapers and cooking dinner. If you're married, that is. And if you're not, you race back and forth from the typewriter to the formula on the stove . . ."

"It's a richer form of existence." He sat down on the radiator and lit a cigarette. "Why should a woman want a career when she has that special bond—with a little thing that was once a part of her own body."

"My God, Ian, *you* want to have a career, don't you? Do you think the other half of the human race is so different from you males?" She sat up on her heels, beginning to feel annoyed. "I suppose it would be different if we were bright green, or communicated only in whistles, or something! But you can see very well that I'm a human being, not a Martian!"

"*Do* I want to have a career?" he asked slowly. "Why should anyone want a career?"

"Independence. Security, Self-sufficiency. Besides I like to think about something other than cooking every once in a while."

"I'd rather not have a job—or do any work for money at all—if there were any alternative."

"If everything were different then everything would be different, of course. But you can't found an argument against the equality of women on that premise." Anna was arguing vehemently.

"I didn't say anything about equality."

"It's implicit in what you've said so far that you don't think women ought to be on the same footing in society as men."

"Society." He sighed, and came over and sat down beside her.

With part of her mind, Anna was aware that he was trying to stop her from quarrelling by decreasing the physical distance between them.

"Like D. H. Lawrence. Women are mystic forces. They think with the other half of their brains. If you can call it thinking!"

"I hate thinking." He put his hands on her shoulders, exerting a little backward pressure.

"Then you'd much better have been born a woman," said Anna triumphantly, struggling for balance.

"Sometimes I fail to see why women are attracted to men at all."

"I should have thought it would be much more problematic the other way around from what you've said."

"No. Men are gross, ugly things," he said. "They have beards. They have rough voices. They snore." He rocked her shoulders back and forth gently.

"But that's all right, though. Whereas, if a woman is the wrong shape or size or something, it's not all right, it's not all right at all."

"I suppose there's something inherently unfair in that," he said, looking anxiously into her face.

"They are all around us, every day. Look at Emily Dowell, for example. She must have been a bright young girl. But she was never a bit pretty, and so . . . And Irene Engelbert, and that woman in Economics, and . . . and so on." Anna suddenly started to feel sad. "And me, too."

"You!" He toppled her over backwards, and lay down on his stomach with his arm across her chest. "You haven't been listening to me closely enough," he said, smiling again.

"I have too. You like looks. You love looks. It's the same thing, only the other way around."

"Your nose," he said, frowning. "It's . . ."

"What's wrong with my nose?" cried Anna, putting her hand up to cover it immediately. She met his eyes. After a while she began to laugh.

"Oh hell!" she remarked. "Too bad there aren't any good convents around any more."

"You would not do well in a convent, Anna. You should be somebody's wife."

Anna thought of taking issue with this, but remained silent, watching his face.

"Mine for instance," he said, tentatively.

"I know why—you'd like some more children!" said Anna, trying to make a joke of it now.

"I'd like you to have them."

Anna thought about this conversation often over the next few days. Anna had a sexless mind. Her enlightened parents were responsible. The question of sex never arose for her in her day-to-day dealings with students and her colleagues. It explained in large part her sexual abstinence since she had begun her teaching career. She tended to see her relationships with her peers, mostly men, in purely professional and social terms.

Ian, as she now knew, was entirely different. He had always seen her in a completely sexual way, as a pretty, desirable woman. Anna was very taken with this thought. Even in their early encounters, while she had been wondering what to say next, he had been thinking about what it would be like to be her lover. Anna chuckled happily as she thought about several intervals of silence, interpreted by her at the time as gloomy or awkward.

A new idea struck her. Since he saw everything in sexual terms, he probably believed that she did too. Anna had been aware for some years that she was not like other people in this, but it was now sharply brought home to her. She secretly tried out looking at some of her colleagues with Ian's perspective.

Returning a book to ffrench, she mentally removed his clothes. He was eating a sandwich at his desk.

"Thanks for the book, Nelson." His long, pallid form emerged from the shirt and trousers, the cavernous chest, the shrivelled belly. Anna hastily covered him with a sheet.

"Not at all. You see, the proper analysis of music is quite different from other art forms. The score is so much less important than a text." He flicked a crumb off his pant leg with his thumbnail, a particularly long one, cultivated for the guitar.

"I think I didn't really appreciate that before," she said, beginning to back out of his office. Was there some connection between the size and shape of the phallus and the thumb? She recalled hearing this somewhere.

"Most people don't. You ought to learn to play a musical instrument," he called, as she backed around the corner.

She also tried this out on Gore and James but balked at Michie. With Eddy she was embarrassed to attempt it.

"Anna, it rests my poor old eyes to look at you." It was O'Toole. "Come with me to some secluded spot—or grot—and let us dally in the shade." He cast her a languishing glance as he hurried past. "Something, something about the hair of some nymph or other." He disappeared into his office with a handful of freshly sharpened pencils.

No, thought Anna, this approach is wrong for me. It occurred to her that one of her first thoughts of Ian had been a sexual one. I am not really a dessicated old maid. I simply have the right thoughts about the right people.

Examining the argument they had been having, she saw that he had been much too clever for her. By reducing everything to personal terms, Ian had obscured all the reasons for her position. On the other hand, she felt sure that this was not just a successful debating technique. These personal things mattered more to him than they did to her in the end, even though his subtle appeal to her vanity had betrayed her. She realized that he was quite serious about what she began to refer to privately as 'this mystic nonsense' about women.

Anna's mind reeled when she thought about the discussion of pregnancy and motherhood. The idea that a pregnant woman is more sexual she dismissed as poetic. Ian knew much more about details of child-raising than she did, and the fact that he could think that it would be a perfectly satisfactory thing for a woman to devote her whole life to stunned Anna. Not only that: it was natural, it was right that it should be this way. Anna expanded her nostrils and rolled her eyes up into her head.

The end of the conversation she suppressed entirely. She did not want to take him seriously. The subject of Ian's wife was taboo for Anna—she imposed silence strictly on this matter—and the idea that he might divorce and want to marry her was one that she uprooted vigorously and at once.

Chapter 18

They had a department colloquium one Tuesday afternoon in mid-March. The department was permitted no money to fund visiting speakers, so they relied on the distant chance that someone accidentally passing through would desire to convey some of his philosophical thoughts to them. There was a small honorarium raised out of pocket when this occurred, as it rarely did.

This time the speaker was to be a man of some reputation from one of the other western colleges in town to visit a sick aunt. His name was Evelyn Joyce, and Anna knew him slightly.

They were taking him out to dinner afterwards on a share-and-share-alike basis, and for this reason, Anna was wearing a silk blouse with a good deal of lace on the collar. In her office she put on powder and lipstick to further enhance herself. She was becoming quite unselfconscious about Michie. In the fall term she would not have done it, knowing full well the hatred primping evoked in the masculine academic's breast.

Michie was behaving oddly of late. He often sat at his desk doing nothing or typing very slowly and then ripping up the paper without reading it. Anna was paying very little attention to this, however, and she supposed that he had some sort of spring fever.

So did they all. Their long winter enclosure together induced claustrophobia and worse. At the last meeting of the French Department a fairy-tale specialist named Rimsky had challenged Gauthier to a duel, and it might have taken place right in the seminar room had not some bodyguards of the Dean rushed the door. The milder weather of March was no relief, for it was a time when no one had a moment to spare; final exams were to be prepared and term papers were due.

MacGregor was hanging about in the hall outside her office pretending to talk to O'Toole. Since they were not to be together that night because of the dinner party for Evelyn Joyce, Anna guessed that he had come by to catch a lonely glimpse of her going off in her finery.

"And so, short of a suicide—not entirely to be discounted, that—or a murder, of course—" O'Toole broke off and leered at Anna, halfway in and halfway out of her office.

"Anna, where have you been all my life? Why have you come to me like this in my toothless old age?" He looked slyly at MacGregor out of the corner of his eye. " 'In me thou seest the glowing of such fire,/That on the ashes of his youth doth lie...' "

" 'This thou perceivst, which makes thy love more strong,/To love that well which thou must leave ere long.' " Ian capped the verse with a touch of melancholy.

Somewhat disconcerted, Anna looked from the one to the other. What had they been talking about?

"Strangely apt," said O'Toole, thoughtfully. "MacGregor here was just asking whether this department would have a teaching position open for next year."

"Oh?" said Anna.

"He seems to be taking a commendable interest in the problems of other Arts Departments," went on O'Toole. "Oh, by the way, have you met? I never can remember these things. Professor Callaghan? Professor MacGregor. Professor MacGregor? Professor Callaghan."

"They know each other already," said Eddy, coming down the hall and straightening his tie.

"Really? Very good then. Are we all set? Has Gore escorted Joyce to the classroom I wonder?"

"Ready to go," said Eddy.

"Come along then, Anna," said O'Toole, propelling her briskly forward. "Don't lallygag like that."

Professor Joyce was a dissolute-looking man, rather jowly, with hair growing out of his ears. He shook hands all around, then went to the top of the table and spread out his notes.

"This is a chapter out of a book I'm writing," he began, "and I may have to skip over a few bits—time constraints and so on."

Anna sighed quietly. In her experience this meant a number of awkward pauses while the speaker shuffled backwards and forwards through his notes, trying not to leave any ends dangling. She looked around. O'Toole, an eager beaver, had a fresh sheet of clean, white paper and a pencil. James had brought a folder which contained the paper he was writing this week. He now placidly took up his pen and began to write, the nib travelling smoothly across the page. Eddy was sitting tensely forward. Peterson, his hands folded on his chest like a bird's feet, was already dozing.

Anna suddenly brought her attention back to the lecture. It was well underway.

Her degree of attention varied. Like someone on a swing, she would pump all her force into a massive burst of intellectual effort, then sink back down into a private low, where she didn't seem to have any conscious process at all. This would be succeeded by the backswing, or negative side of the parabola she was describing, in which she was subject to a fertile field of visions, imaginings, and daydreams.

Thus, by fits and starts she began to take in the subject of the lecture, which seemed to be an attempt to resolve Zeno's stadium paradox by mathematical means. There were a lot of mimeographed sheets which Joyce passed out as he got to the more technical part of his talk, detailing the solution he proposed. Anna was staring stupidly at one of these, getting somewhat behind in her comprehension of the lecture, when Joyce was interrupted by Gore.

"Surely you mean 'and' here, not 'or'."

Evelyn Joyce started. "Where do you mean?"

"Here on page 2, B12, little a, Roman numeral ii." Gore held up a sheet and pointed. "Just here, you see?"

Anna looked at B12, little a, Roman numeral ii. He certainly should have put 'and' and not 'or'.

The whole room was abuzz. ffrench and Eddy were conferring in an undertone.

"David's dead right." said Peterson, back from the land of Nod. "You mean 'and'."

"Let's see. How much does this matter now? Let me just . . . Perhaps you're right." Evelyn Joyce began to shuffle backwards through his lecture.

"Who cares?" said Eddy, suddenly. "We all know what he means. Let him get on with it."

They all looked at him in horror.

"You see," said Gore, "it matters a lot, Eddy. You'd be surprised how much logic touches everyday life. Did you ever take Philosophy 1? Or did they—"

O'Toole interrupted, tapping his pencil against his teeth. "Perhaps Professor Joyce would—"

". . . or did they teach that back at Slippery Rock State Teachers' College?" continued Gore, unperturbed.

"Yes, I would like—"

". . . always taking people up on semantic points!"

"Let me draw you the elementary truth table for—"

"Eddy, for heaven's—!"

". . . just get my hands on—!"

O'Toole stood up. "Now then, Professor Joyce has decided . . ."

Eventually, Evelyn Joyce read the rest of his chapter, breaking off now and then to describe how it would go when he corrected the small logical error on page 2, B12, little a, Roman numeral ii.

They went out to dinner. The restaurant had been chosen in preference to the Faculty Club for the known cheapness of its liquor. Anna, as the only woman present, was placed in a chair next to the visitor. Only O'Toole's wife ever came to these affairs. The other wives complained of the dullness. On this occasion Melissa was at an Oxfam meeting, as O'Toole confided to Anna, taking the chair on her other side.

"Now what you need is bread and milk, and a pot of camomile tea," he said, pointing it out in an imaginary spot on the menu. "You've been stealing carrots from Mr. MacGregor, again. Don't deny it, my little friend. I saw your whiskers quivering there in the hall this afternoon."

He was already on his second rye and water. O'Toole loved to talk and could go on in this vein for hours. Anna munched on an appetizer, turning her head and shoulders towards Evelyn Joyce.

"How do you find it here, Anna?" Joyce leaned toward her confidentially. Simultaneously, O'Toole leaned toward her confidentially as well, so as to hear more clearly. "Rather backward, or . . . ?" went on Joyce, slurping down a double Scotch.

"No, I like it," said Anna. "I'd like to stay but alas . . ."

"Too bad."

O'Toole leaned forward to do one of his Anna Callaghan imitations for Joyce's benefit.

"And so I am looking for a job, dear Professor Joyce. I can't tell you how interested I was in your lecture today," he said, dewily.

"Nothing in my bailiwick either," said Joyce crisply. "We advertised, but it came to nothing. The Dean put his foot down. Budgetary problems, of course."

"I know," said Anna, giving O'Toole a kick with the sharp heel of her shoe.

"Ah, you applied, did you? I'd forgotten. Really, this administrative work is a tremendous bore. How do you find it, O'Toole?"

"I see your glass is empty, Joyce. Do let me . . ."

Later on, with dessert and cognac, they came to the scurrilous gossip in their trade.

". . . and so," said Joyce, draining his balloon glass with a gusty sigh of satisfaction, "when he returned from his sabbatical, he found no fewer than two of his colleagues encamped in the front hall, while his wife, unlike patient Penelope . . ."

Anna looked around at her colleagues curiously. They were all following this narrative with varying degrees of fervour. Eddy had gone straight home after the lecture to have dinner with his family, as was his custom.

"We had something like that here once—" began Gore, leaning forward. O'Toole was summoning a waiter with one hand, meanwhile privily consulting the contents of his wallet.

"Poor old Maxwell." Joyce was unwilling to be interrupted with the tale of some backwater scandal. "This was *Bib* Maxwell, you know. Maxwell at Harvard. Poor old Bib."

Anna took note of Joyce's present unbuttoned condition of drink with secret pleasure. The hair seemed to sprout forth from his nose and ears like newly watered vegetation.

"I knew Maxwell and his wife very well at one time," said Peterson.

"Yes, but this was his *second* wife." Joyce accepted a fresh glass of Remy Martin from the waiter's hand. "Not poor old Maisie."

O'Toole had apparently made a budget cut, as the rest of them were drinking beer.

His eyes clenched shut, Peterson opened his mouth to speak. A new competitiveness was in the air. Anna hoped he would have something to say for poor old Maisie.

"Mind you, I have a very young wife myself," said Joyce, his gaze wandering from Peterson's face. "She's had a pretty rough time of it, poor kid. The custody of the children . . ."

He went on at some length about the divorce. His present wife had been the wife of someone quite eminent at Joyce's university, and there were a variety of complications. Anna guessed that he was giving them all a treat, like a minstrel bringing the news of Arthur's court to some kingdom in a remote part of the world.

"Consequently, Barth lost the editorship and I trundled off to become a simple Dean," concluded Joyce. "Divorce is never easy."

His audience was becoming more restive.

"Have you heard about what happened to Geoffrey Bateson?" asked Gore quickly.

"Bateson? Let's see. I knew a fellow named Bateman when I was chairman at—"

"No, no. Bateson at Harvard. The Religious Studies man."

"This Bateman had a rather trying time with his women, too, as I—"

"This Bateson was our blue-eyed boy here," said Gore. "When Harvard snapped him up, a lot of people thought—"

"Not I," said Peterson, leaning forward around Joyce. "There was something fishy about the man from the beginning. I always thought so."

"You were certainly right about that," conceded Gore generously. "This stuff about plagiarism is nothing. He may not even have a Ph.D. Where was it supposed to be from anyway, Peter? Oxbridge?"

"Sorbonne, I think," replied O'Toole.

"Quite a scandal, is it?" inquired Joyce genially.

"There was more to it than met the eye," remarked Peterson, ignoring him. "I always said that MacGregor—"

"Judith MacGregor was sleeping with him right under her husband's nose," Gore explained, getting ahead of Peterson's story.

"Ah." Joyce nodded, tilting his glass over his nose.

"The youngest child was only about six months old at the time. MacGregor, of course, can't count. They didn't teach arithmetic when he was in school. Hadn't been invented."

"Keep your hair on, dear," said a small voice in Anna's ear.

Anna pressed her hands together in her lap. So many sessions of gossip had she been present at, added her own witty contributions to. This, she felt, was a worthy punishment. But it was not yet complete.

"This woman—what did you say the name was? I seem to remember something about that. I read a paper here that year. I expect you all recall it." Joyce looked around, smiling.

"Judith MacGregor," said Gore in his thick voice. "Lovely woman. Big tits. Big eyes. What more can you ask? Wasted on MacGregor."

"Chairman of our English Department," explained Peterson.

"Deadwood," said Gore.

"Now that's a problem we all have," said Joyce sympathetically.

"I wonder," said the small voice of O'Toole, "if you have the time, of course—could you just tell me the square root of five to the fourth decimal. I most awfully want to know."

"To tell you the truth about this fellow Bateman . . ." Joyce was now sure they had exhausted the MacGregor-Bateson theme.

"I correspond with someone at Harvard," interrupted ffrench. "That's how we first got word about the Bateson mess this year. Interesting man, Prask, this friend of mine. Plays the recorder. He's a linguist. They prefer wind instruments usually. Anyhow . . ." he looked around dramatically. Anna was searching in her purse for a pen.

". . . anyhow, he says that the MacGregor woman has ditched old Geoffrey now."

Joyce sat back in his chair discontentedly. The home team was winning the pennant.

On a page torn from O'Toole's pocket book, Anna was laboriously trying to work out the square root of five. Peering over her shoulder O'Toole offered her some assistance.

She got a ride home from the restaurant somewhat later with Peterson, who was delivering Joyce to the home of his aunt. Peterson was tireless in his determination that Joyce should come to appreciate how cold it became in the wintertime on this part of the prairies. They dropped Anna off and she crept up the fire escape to her kitchen door, exhausted, drunk, and sad.

The telephone was ringing when she put her key in the lock. She ran into the living room, not bothering to close the kitchen door. It was Ian.

"Is everything all right?" he asked.

"Yes. Yes. I'm all right."

"Have you been running?"

"I just came in. I heard the telephone outside."

"I thought you might come in about now."

"But why . . . ? Nothing's happened has it? Nothing bad?" Anna heard her own voice, shrill with anxiety.

"No. I don't know why I called, really. Do you . . . ?"

"Yes."

"I'm coming over," he said decisively, and rang off.

Chapter 19

Anna was being taken on a MacGregor family expedition to the local zoo on the last Sunday in March. Lucy had proposed this trip and specifically requested that Anna be brought along. Anna was to meet them at the MacGregor house since Ian said that it would never do for them to come to her apartment.

"We don't want visiting here," he said firmly.

"Why not?"

"You don't know about visiting. Visiting is—well, banana peels, and sticky fingers, and Gregor chasing the cat under the bed."

"I wouldn't mind."

"You don't know the meaning of your words."

Anna reflected that this was an odd position for Ian to take, as he held that women were naturally maternal, but she held her tongue. He obviously loved his children, but his descriptions of child-raising were always without illusion.

It was a very warm day and the sun was shining on the pools of water in the streets. Anna had put off her sweaters entirely in favour of a heavy woollen dress and her shawl. When she came up to the spruce trees shading the MacGregor lawn, a straggling procession was coming off the porch. A pretty, delicate-boned, blond little girl waited patiently by the gate, holding a basket that Anna recognized. Gregor and Jane were having a tug of war on the porch steps. Ian, standing halfway down the walk, was watching this over his shoulder, his arm suspended horizontally in the air in front of him. Evidently he had been just about to look at his watch.

The instant Anna's presence became known, the tableau dissolved. Lucy opened the gate and Anna looked down at her, smiling. She had imagined Lucy as older and larger, somehow.

Ian appeared behind her. "Lucy MacGregor. Miss Callaghan," he said formally.

"Anna," said Anna firmly. She put out her hand. Lucy took it, not as an adult would, to shake, but as a child does, to hold. Anna was touched.

There was a roar from the porch.

"Come on then, you two!" cried Ian impatiently, "We're going now!" Gregor came instantly off the porch and ran past them through the gate. Jane followed more slowly, whimpering slightly. Gregor had won the battle.

Gregor was a stocky, self-possessed child who came to slightly above Anna's knee. He paid no attention to her or any other adult. Anna recognized admiringly the impermeable sphere of childhood that surrounded him. Only his sister Jane, a larger, shyer version of himself, was fully real to him.

They drove to the zoo. Anna sat in back, placing herself strategically between Gregor and Jane, and they all three played rock, scissors, paper, with Lucy kneeling on the front seat to watch. Anna had never been in a car with Ian before, and his driving gave her a secret sense of amusement. He drove with extreme, almost obsessive care, and in certain mannerisms reminded her of her grandfather, who had once got a ticket from the police for driving too slowly. Anna supposed that it was 'because of the drink'; she had believed before this that he did not have a car at all.

Ian bought five tickets at the gate, refused to buy any popcorn or candy, and took the lunch basket out of Lucy's hands.

"Where shall we go first?"

Anna had been to the zoo many times before. In the early fall term it had been a Saturday haunt. As a consequence she had very well-defined opinions about what to see and what to avoid.

"The rattlesnakes!" cried Gregor, pulling Jane along with him in the wrong direction.

"What do you like best, Lucy?" asked Anna. She refused to believe that Gregor really preferred the rattlesnakes.

"The elephant," said Lucy. They went to see the elephant.

There was a new sign on the elephant's compound that described the difference between the Asian and the African elephant. The number of toenails was different, it seemed. Anna began to memorize this, wishing she had a pocket book to write it down in.

"It's your turn, Anna," said Ian, watching her do this with a smile. "Where shall we go?"

"The tigers," said Anna, and they went to see the tigers. "There are seven different kinds of tiger," she remarked as they strolled through the park.

"How do you know these things?"

"As you see," pointing to the sign on the tigers' cage as they came up to it.

After about an hour of this the chidren became footsore. They found a sunny knoll of grass and sat down on it, Ian spreading his coat underneath to protect them from the damp but still frozen ground. There was not much room on the coat so Gregor sat on Ian's lap and Jane sat on Anna's, while Lucy unpacked the basket.

Everyone had made his own lunch. Peanut butter and jam for the small fry; Ian was eating a bologna sandwich absently. Anna had brought cream cheese on rye in her pocket, but accepted butter and jelly on white from Lucy, who anxiously watched her eat it.

"Don't do that, Gregor; it's disgusting," said Ian, trying to prevent his son from licking the jam off one half of his sandwich.

"I hate bread," said Gregor, defiantly continuing.

"I want something to drink!" Jane began to imitate Gregor.

"Milk," said Ian, taking the sandwich away from Gregor and simultaneously getting to his feet.

"Lemonade! or Coca-Cola!" cried Gregor.

"Milk."

"I'll get it," said Anna hastily, as Ian began to go through his pockets for change.

"No, no." He walked off toward the concession stand, leaving her alone with them.

"Did you know that elephants prefer pink lemonade?" Anna asked Lucy.

"Do they like it better than peanuts?"

"No, just better than plain lemonade."

"How do you know?"

"Oh, chatting with them. One picks these things up."

Anna felt that this had been an immense success. They were all three staring at her.

"What were their names? Was it the elephant here? Can we go back and give him some?"

"Who's this?" said Ian coming back with the milk and looking around at them, pleased at their good manners.

"The elephant," said Lucy. "She talks to the elephant."

"What's his name?" repeated Jane, impatiently.

"I never can understand what they're saying," said Ian, happily. "They talk through their noses."

The afternoon went on. When they went to the reptile house, Anna refused to go in and went off to play with a parrot instead.

Ian came up behind her as the parrot was nibbling at a sunflower seed on her outstretched finger.

"Ian! What are you doing! This is a public place!"

"There's nobody about," he replied, not letting go of her.

"What have you done with the children? You didn't leave them alone with the boa constrictor?"

"They're in a treehouse. We're going to the caribou next."

"Oh good. Animals with fur, you know."

They had tea in the conservatory, a huge banana tree bearing fruit over their heads. The children were getting tired. Anna began to carry Jane, who was small-boned like Lucy.

"You don't have to do that. She can walk."

"No, I can't."

"You carry me, Daddy," demanded Gregor.

"You see?"

"We need a little horse," said Lucy. "I could ride the horse."

"A very little horse," said Ian, wrestling with Gregor.

"About the size of a chair," said Anna.

"Smaller than that."

"I could keep it in a little box," said Lucy, leading the way.

"They're nice children," said Anna later, in bed.

"Mm. That's the nicest they've been in a while."

"You're very patient with them."

"No."

"Well—no shouting, and slapping, and things like that."

"That's different from being patient."

"Anyone can see you pay a lot of attention to them. Gregor has a very big vocabulary."

"Did you really like them?" he asked, rolling over and putting his elbows down characteristically on either side of her ears.

"Yes. Children in particular—particular children, that is— are different from children in general," said Anna. "Did Lucy have a good time?"

"Oh yes. We have an elephant named Lmumba, now." He had stayed home with the children after the zoo expedition and had come over very late.

"It was fun," said Anna drowsily.

"I wish . . ."

Anna kept her eyes closed. She was not sure she wanted to hear this wish. He sat up on the side of the bed.

"Could you live with them?" he asked.

"Are you thinking of taking a holiday?" Anna's wits were alert. She had known for some time that this moment was coming.

"No. I'm thinking about being married."

Anna pulled one of the pillows over her face.

"You're not divorced."

"But I could be." He began to take the pillow away.

"You said this was different from being married."

"It is." He gave up on the pillow.

"Well, then . . ." Anna sat up. "Why should we alter that?" She gave his arm a shake. "You're not bored with it or anything?"

"No. But . . ."

"Ian," said Anna urgently. "What is, is. I don't have a job here for next year. There isn't going to be any summer school."

"O'Toole said they think highly of you. Nobody ever wants to teach extension courses. You could . . ."

"No, I couldn't," she said, more positively than she felt. "I need a real job. Extension courses don't pay enough."

"That wouldn't matter."

Anna set herself to look into his eyes. He looked away at last.

"You cannot go away from here."

"I don't *want* to go away. I *want* to stay."

Walking to the university the next morning she resolutely kept her mind off this conversation. Present happiness in the face of an uncertain future was all anyone could demand of life. Her thoughts in suspension, as usual at this time of day, she enjoyed the sunrise glittering against the melting ice in the puddles.

Her 8:30 class was coming to the end of a section of the textbook, and Anna was pleased to have timed the curriculum so perfectly. Next week they would begin to review for exams. She left the classroom amidst the press of students and found herself unexpectedly confronted by Francoise Hibert.

"Come and drink a cup of coffee with me," said Francoise in a very friendly voice.

"All right," said Anna, surprised. "I've given up the coffee room, though."

"Good. Then we'll go to the cafeteria."

They stood in line for the coffee machines with a large crowd of students ahead and behind them. Francoise chatted away neutrally about the difficulties her own 8:30 class was having in mastering the subjunctive. She proved an expert at seizing a table in the packed, smoky room, simply moving in on a lingering pair of students and beginning to clear off their used cups from in front of them. She then disposed her textbook and her lecture notes over the whole surface of the table in such a way as to discourage a similar manoeuver by anyone else.

Anna began to drink her coffee, smiling in admiration. Francoise was clearly a very forceful match for Michael Jimson.

"I chose to talk to you because you are a woman of my own age," said Francoise, beginning to come straight to the point, whatever it was.

Anna, taken aback, remarked, "We're not the only ones, although I admit there aren't very many. There's that woman in Economics . . ."

"No, no," said Francoise positively. "We are, in certain ways, alike."

"Undoubtedly we are, in some ways," began Anna cautiously.

"Also, you know Michael." She pronounced this name in the French way. Anna thought how very much Jimson must like this.

"I don't really know him so well." Anna was sure that whatever Jimson had told Francoise about herself, it had not been the truth. Her lips twitched.

"I do not care about that," said Francoise, catching this. "It does not matter."

"There was nothing between us."

"No. There was nothing between you. Good. Michael and I have been having an affair."

Anna began to get the idea. They were having an old-fashioned talk. "You know that he's married," she said solicitously. "You shouldn't allow yourself to become too involved."

"His wife is a bitch. She does not care for him. He talks of getting a divorce."

"Oh no," said Anna. She shook her head. "No, definitely not."

"I know what you are thinking. Men never marry their mistresses. With us it is different, however." Francoise looked down at the table, no longer sounding so positive.

"Do you want to marry Michael?" Anna asked, picking up her cue, but also curious to know the answer.

"Yes, yes," replied Francoise impatiently. "I want—but should I take this step?"

Anna felt like saying no to this immediately, but she asked instead, "Are you very much in love?"

"He is so charming, so sophisticated, don't you think?" said Francoise looking up with a wistful smile. "We go to a restaurant and he orders . . . Things must be perfect. He learns French from me. It is so sweet." She laughed tenderly.

"But you shouldn't let that sort of thing influence you, surely. I mean—restaurants and so on," Anna said, feeling slightly sick. "Marriage is a very bread-and-butter sort of thing. Solid virtues are what you want."

"I think I am naive," said Francoise good humouredly. "I come from the Gaspé. I have eight brothers and two sisters. My parents have these solid virtues. But for me . . ."

Anna gaped at her. Her entire picture of Francoise collapsed into a thousand fluttering fragments. The pale, sophisticated stockings, the winks. Francoise was a Canadian like herself, from an even more backward environment. She began to identify at once.

"Are you a Catholic?" she asked. She decided to use every means at her disposal to try to dissuade Francoise.

"Yes—or no," said Francoise. "I would not let his divorce hinder me in this. Many of my friends are married to divorced people."

"Would you like to stay married, though?"

"Of course. Who would marry who does not wish to stay married?"

"Possibly someone who has divorced once would not mind so much to do it a second time."

"The cases are not the same. I am not like Michael's wife. She is—pouf!" Francoise made her waving gesture in front of her face.

"Well, another thing. What about your job? Do you have a permanent position here?"

"Permanent, impermanent. French lecturers are always needed," said Francoise laughing. Anna started to like her suddenly. She had a really charming smile, her teeth flashing suddenly in a triangular mouth.

"But Michael doesn't," Anna remarked.

"Ah, that is . . ." Francoise fell silent.

"It's very important, after all. He'll probably get one, all right, but it'll be somewhere else. You shouldn't dream of marrying when there's no chance of living together."

"Yes," said Francoise. Anna had the impression she was not taking this point very seriously. Perhaps she thought she would be settling down shortly and producing ten little Jimsons, as she would if she married one of her own people.

It was after 9:30. Anna began to want to see what was in her mail. She started to gather up her things.

"I think you should think about this very seriously before you do anything," she said.

"Yes," said Francoise. "Michael must talk to his lawyer again this week."

Stunned by the thought of Jimson actually doing anything of the sort, Anna rose.

"The mail should be in."

"Does your lover send you letters?" said Francoise, teasing. Anna blushed.

"I have had older lovers myself," said Francoise proudly. "They send so many letters, always in these used envelopes with somebody else's name crossed off at the bottom of a long list."

They walked out of the cafeteria. Ian used that kind of envelope just as everyone did in interdepartmental mail. Anna wondered whether Francoise regarded the use of a new envelope as the quintessential test of a romance.

"Is he nice in bed?" They were passing a group of students in line for the check-out. Anna looked around nervously. "Those men with pale blue or green eyes—I think they are often cold."

"I am in love with him," muttered Anna, getting as close as possible to Francoise's ear. She thought about how interested Jimson would be to hear this news. On the other hand, it was true.

Chapter 20

The mail was still being sorted, so Anna waited patiently a few minutes, perched on a radiator under the window in the mail room.

Francoise was not being completely open with her, she felt sure. It was possible that Jimson would have mentioned divorcing his wife, or even, in a fit of enthusiasm, marriage, but Anna refused to believe that any real initiative in this area could come from him. So it must be that Francoise herself was the real mover, despite her pretence of asking Anna's advice. What she really must have wanted from me, Anna reflected, was some opinion about whether Michael would go through with it. Anna felt comforted by this. She was quite sure Jimson would never do so, even if he got as far as seeing a lawyer.

She reflected for some time on her new picture of Francoise. Francoise had that type of French prettiness which consists not in regularity and beauty of feature, but in the animation of the face and an assured style of dress. Anna had always felt rather like a cow in Francoise's presence. Now that Francoise's naivety had been revealed, Anna began to feel a motherly kind of admiration for the girl's charm. She must be quite a lot younger than I am, Anna decided. Francoise was so pleased with herself that she had had middle-aged lovers. Had she really been sleeping with Spong?

Anna suddenly thought of the conversation with Ian of the previous night. A renewed feeling of superiority to Francoise's predicament overcame her. She, herself, Anna, was not allowing Ian to trifle with the idea of divorce or marriage. Even if Ian became serious, she, Anna, would be quite firm.

But he was serious already, Anna realized suddenly, horrified that she could even make a comparison between Ian and Michael. She projected herself down off the radiator with a shudder. A secretary had just finished stuffing mail into her box.

There was a small slatch of the usual junk. Anna threw some book circulars into the wastebasket and tore open a rejection letter: "Dear Dr. Callaghan, It is with regret that we . . ."

Unexpectedly, there was a note from Ian as well. They had seen each other less than ten hours ago. Smiling at the brown manila interoffice envelope with the names crossed off the front, Anna slit the Scotch taped flap with her fingernail. Looking behind her hastily for O'Toole, she opened out the page. The wish Ian had made last night was now at the forefront of her mind.

As usual it began without salutation. The handwriting was peculiar. There was a blot on the empty lower half of the sheet.

Something very bad happened last night after I went home. I must see you. Come to my office when you can.

Anna's hands were shaking as she folded this up and put it in her pocket. One of the children is ill, has died, she thought. Lucy decided she didn't like me after all. He's hurt himself—no, he can't have, he wouldn't be here. Perhaps after last night's conversation, he had a bottle of Scotch and . . . She opened the note again as she walked down the hall. Was the handwriting unsteady, drunken?

O'Toole met her in the corridor. "Keep your chin up, kid!" he said cheerily. " 'Dear Ms. Callaghan: We are pleased to be able to tell you . . . because of the exceedingly strong letters of recommendation accompanying your application . . .' " He looked over her elbow at the note. "Ah, I see," he said with a meaning smile.

Anna was too agitated to follow this by-play. He raised his eyebrows. "Come and talk to your uncle now." He tried to take her arm.

"No, Peter. I don't have time. I . . ."

"Ah." His eyebrows went up again. "Well, then. Anytime you want a bit of kindly counsel from a wise old friend . . ."

"Thanks." Anna started into the stairwell.

"Going down?"

"Yes."

"Well, well."

In the English Department she passed Emily Dowell coming from the bathroom. Emily's mouse-like aspect was accentuated by her habitual choice of grey clothing. Anna tried to smile at her, feeling sick.

"Have you many more classes, Professor Callaghan?"

"Twelve or thirteen," replied Anna. "It's an awful time of year, isn't it? We're all so sluggish."

"I hate to see it come to an end," said Emily, sighing. "So little has been accomplished."

"I'm just going—to see Professor MacGregor—about something," said Anna, faltering. They had reached his door.

Emily remained standing beside her. Anna knocked timidly. "Come in," he called, his voice muffled by the door. Anna went in and shut it behind her. Something was badly wrong. She stood there helplessly, smelling the Scotch and looking wonderingly at his face. He did not move from behind his desk.

"Sit down, Anna," he said quietly.

Anna sat down, feeling the first stirrings of anger. He was just drinking again, perhaps, was that it? There was a momentary silence.

"Why?" said Anna. She looked at her hands.

"Last night after I—went home—I received a telephone call from Cambridge—from Harvard. From Judith, in fact."

"Oh." She shivered and looked up.

"She is coming back here tomorrow."

He lit a cigarette and pushed the package over the desk towards her.

"To see the children?"

"To try again," he said grimly.

"Try again," echoed Anna. She stared hard at her hands.

"Yes."

"I see. Do you want this?" There was a long silence. Anna stared stubbornly down. "I haven't any right to ask," she said at last and got up, feeling the onset of tears.

"Anna . . ."

"I'm all right," she said, putting her hand on the doorknob and bursting simultaneously into a sob.

She heard him muttering, "I cannot stand it," and tightened her grip on the doorknob. But it was impossible to leave. The tension in her chest was giving her hiccups. She put her hand over her nose and mouth to make herself stop breathing.

"But it has been three years," cried her mind. "She left her children. He's drinking already. It is impossible . . ."

He said quietly, "She said that she had been thinking about it a great deal lately."

Because Bateson didn't turn out to be quite what she had expected. Anna did not say this, but it was so well articulated in her mind that she felt that she had.

"She believes she has changed," his voice went on.

Why doesn't he hate her? Anna asked herself.

"She is their mother," he said expressionlessly.

So that was it. Anna no longer felt like crying although the hiccups continued to hold her in their grip. She felt like screaming. Taking her shaking hand away from her mouth, she began to grope for a piece of tissue. The only paper in her pocket was the note. She could not blow her nose on that. Turning around, she wiped it with the back of her hand. He was still behind the desk.

"I see," said Anna, steadying herself for a hiccup. "I'll have a cigarette, now."

"I cannot say no."

She lit the cigarette and blew out the smoke through her lips, still trying to deprive herself of oxygen to drive away the hiccups. "What shall I do?" she asked.

She felt a pang. He had been real to her. Had she ever been real to him? The only possessions he had of hers were six pieces of ring binder paper.

"I don't know."

"No." Anna felt a surge of anger at the stupid question and its emotionless response. It was time to go. She could walk. She had a cigarette to hold to her lips. She was not weeping.

"It was nice, Ian," she said trying to end gracefully. "We didn't have much more time, anyway."

He did not reply. She wondered what he thought now about last night.

"I hope it—works out," she said, managing to look at him again. She could not read his face. There was no sign of love or pain or any of the things that tore at her heart, not even anger.

"Goodbye, then."

He still did not reply, so Anna went out the door with an additional bitter grievance. He had left it all to her.

She saw nothing in the hall and nothing as she went mechanically up the stairs. There was no one, nothing to attract her attention away from the tension in her muscles, the aching pressure of her diaphragm. She went into her office without looking at Michie and put her head down on her arms. Pretending it was fatigue, she began to breathe steadily and sparingly out of her nostrils, wishing he would leave as usual. Instead, he remained where he was, and after a time, Anna realized that she heard someone sobbing. It was not herself. She looked around. Michie was standing at the window with his back to her.

"Fred?" she said hesitatingly. This was supposed to be his name. "Is anything wrong?"

All noises ceased. Anna listened to the silence for a while, then got up and left the office, taking her textbook with her. She had a class in fifteen minutes.

O'Toole, lurking in his office with the door half open, like a hermit crab, summoned her inside as she passed by.

"What's the latest?" he asked, motioning her to shut the door. Anna forced herself to smile and remained at the doorway, one hand against the jamb.

"I've got something to tell you," he whispered. "On the level. Don't just stand there."

Anna shut the door but did not sit down. She gestured with her textbook.

"Next year." He said telegraphically. "Extension courses. Cloverberg, St. Pierre, and possibly French Creek."

Anna's repressed anger rose to her lips. "What is this? Charity? I'm going to get a job—a job, Peter; I'm going to be a real person, just like you!"

"Don't get huffy. I had the idea perhaps . . ."

"Where do you get your ideas from, Peter? —Oh my God!" She realized the source of this idea suddenly.

"What's the matter?"

"Nothing," she said dully.

"I diagnose a case of too many letters of rejection. Rejection rejection, as we professionals call this syndrome."

"You're probably right," said Anna bitterly. "I've got to go."

Anna taught her classes thoroughly, meticulously, and, as a matter of fact, very well during the next days. When she was in class she had the illusion of control. At all other times she rode the stormy seas of despair. She was aware of nothing but a tearing pain, on which the company of other people or any sort of ordinary daily activity had only a narcotic, not an anaesthetic effect.

She tried reasoning with herself: she had not been thinking of it as anything but a love affair; it had been going to end soon anyway; his strange ideas about women and marriage were so wrong-headed it was well she was out of it; he was too old for her; she had been attracted by pity and had mistaken it for love; he had only wanted sex; he had only wanted comfort; he would probably be better off if he could patch it up with his wife.

While these undisciplined premises for different arguments were tossing in her mind, she had no time for anything else. She spent most of her time at the university with her head down on her desk and most of her time at home with her head down on the table.

On Tuesday evening and Wednesday morning she tried to force herself to feel jealousy. Any identifiable emotion would be preferable to the tearing sense of loss. She pictured Judith MacGregor as Gore had described her at the dinner party. She was probably blond, like the children. Large blue eyes, a curving figure. She repeated Ian's words again and again, "I like looks—I love looks," until they had no significance at all. Those words had been for her; she tried to feel angry that they could apply to anyone else.

Standing before the mirror in the bathroom, staring at her pale, wizened face without seeing it, she said aloud to herself: "His bones liquefied when he caught sight of her in the airport. The children were in bed when they went home. They made love on the hearth rug. 'Oh no, it is an ever-fixed mark,/That looks on tempests and is never shaken . . .' She was just as beautiful as he remembered her." She watched with curiosity as the artificially induced tears ran down her cheeks.

She did not cry very often. There was no room for anything but the pain. It was as though he had died or, worse, was missing and could not be found. He had said so little to her at their last meeting that she had no insight into his condition. Whether he was happy, whether he was sad, bitter, angry, drunk or sober, she could not even speculate. The interview between them, now examined and re-examined so many times, made no sense to her at all any longer.

She paid no attention to her colleagues or Michie. There was no one she could talk to. Since they had been very discreet, there was no sympathy or even ordinary curiosity directed towards her, even by Thursday when she was sure everyone must know of the remarkable return of Judith to the MacGregor fold.

On Wednesday in the early afternoon, she was proofreading one of her final examinations in the Dean's secretary's office, a glassed-in room on the second floor. O'Toole came out of the Dean's office and stood by her elbow. He was making a curious sequence of faces, his back to the Dean's door, now closing behind him. Anna went on reading slowly, her lips moving.

O'Toole cast her one of his languishing glances. Anna did not notice. He changed his approach.

"I hardly see you these days, little one," he said in a low, sympathetic voice.

"No," said Anna, putting down the examination paper on the edge of the secretary's desk and making a note in pencil on the margin.

"I have an idea you'd benefit from a talk with your kindly old uncle," said O'Toole, winking lasciviously at the secretary, a middle-aged woman with a stiff grey permanent.

"Oh yes? What about?" Anna gave the secretary the typed

sheet. The woman smiled reprovingly at O'Toole, who was pocketing a couple of pencils from the jar on the edge of her desk.

"This and that. Time and tides, mice and men," said O'Toole, trying to take Anna's arm and hurry her out of the office. "Just replenishing supplies," he said to the secretary, who was gazing at his pocketful of pencils.

"There are only a few changes," said Anna to the secretary. "My mistakes, mostly."

"Come on, come on!" said O'Toole, jogging her elbow.

"This word—" Anna pointed to the word 'ontology' in one of the questions, "I expect it's my handwriting."

"Not with an 'a', then?" said the secretary alertly, altering it in her own clear writing. The Dean came out of his office.

"Oh, O'Toole? Glad you're still here. There is . . ."

"That's all, I think," said Anna to the secretary, going to look over her shoulder.

". . . just another small matter I forgot to mention. Come in here again, please."

O'Toole followed him back through the office door, again making a series of faces over his shoulder. Anna was watching the secretary carefully paint over the letter 'a' with erasing fluid.

Mechanically, she left the office and went down the hall to the stairwell. Stair climbing absorbed quite a bit of time. She had forgotten about O'Toole entirely already. Nothing he could say would help.

Chapter 21

On Thursday morning Anna went over to the bookstore in the Students' Union Building. She had made up a list as usual. At the top it said: RING BINDER PAPER. Like most people who write a great deal, Anna had obsessive preferences for certain types of writing materials. She could not get binder paper from Supplies. She put her books in one of the pigeonholes beyond the cash register where students were supposed to leave their belongings to prevent casual shoplifting and went down the aisle to the paper section. On the way back to the cash register, she paused to gaze dully at the new philosophy titles.

Francoise Hibert caught up with her on the way out.

"It is nice, is it not—this weather?" she said, stopping Anna under a tree beside the path to the Arts Building. "On a day like this, one should try to get a tan."

"Too bad we have exams to make up," said Anna, trying to take in what Francoise had just said. She had the feeling that it did not matter what reply she made. The whole conversation could be crossed out and replaced by another one just as well.

"Are you very busy?"

"Not very." Anna looked around. What had she been going to do next?

"I must talk to you again about what we were talking about before," said Francoise.

"I don't think you should marry him," said Anna. It made no difference whether she said this or not.

"But why not? He has seen his lawyer. There is no big problem. She will agree, of course."

"Why should Michael's wife agree?" Anna didn't care.

"He can make her agree," said Francoise. "Michael is quite ruthless about this."

"Michael will probably get a job in the States or something," said Anna vaguely. "You couldn't go with him."

"Yes I could."

"You couldn't get a job yourself, though. American universities won't hire Canadians."

"Canadian universities won't hire Americans either. Not for permanent positions, at least."

"All the more reason why you shouldn't marry Michael," said Anna, trying to be reasonable. It was like talking to a child. Francoise was not thinking this through.

"We are speaking of doing it this summer," said Francoise tentatively.

"Will Michael be here? Surely his work permit expires by May?"

"He can come back as a visitor." They began to walk slowly towards the Arts Building. "Then he could become a landed immigrant, you see."

"True," said Anna, wondering whether Francoise expected Jimson to stay in Canada and live with her here on her salary. Explaining to Francoise the absurdity of this expectation struck her as too difficult, so she merely glanced abstractedly down at the three-foot circuit of ground around her feet.

"Do you think a white wedding is correct when the man has been divorced?" asked Francoise.

"I don't know." Anna changed this. "I don't really have an opinion."

"In the Gaspé, we would have a real big ceremony in the church. We would eat a pig. People dance, sometimes for three days." Francoise flashed her enchanting smile.

"Are you going home for it, then?" They were still some way away from the Arts Building. The remaining time of their walk, Anna felt vaguely, should be filled constructively with conversation.

"No, Michael would like it to be quiet—and tasteful," added Francoise with a slight interrogative emphasis on the last word. "We will do it here with just a few guests—my friends and people from his department."

"Oh."

Francoise was now taking an interest in Anna's abstraction.

"You are sad," she said, suddenly sympathetic. "Did you really love him, as you said?"

Anna's heart jumped in her breast. For a moment she couldn't see anything because of the searing flash of light in her eyes.

"These affairs can become so serious," sighed Francoise. "especially with an older one. You see, they are so much in need of security. Not like a young man."

Anna stopped and went off the path to the shelter of a honeysuckle bush. It would never do to enter the Arts Building like this. She was shaking all over.

"I am sorry it hurts you," said Francoise, putting a comforting hand on her arm. "His wife must be a bitch. Michael says . . ."

"Don't tell me what Michael says," muttered Anna, taking her arm away from Francoise and drawing the back of her hand across her trembling lips.

"It is better to be realistic, is it not? Michael says that you were a substitute for his wife. It is not good to stand in another woman's shoes. I know this myself from . . ." She did not finish the sentence. Anna forced her mouth into a smile.

"I expect you're right," she said. Francoise was giving her back one of her own arguments.

"Would you like to have some company? You must be lonely. You should come to my apartment tonight. It is bad at night, is it not?"

"I am really all right," said Anna. "Nice of you to offer."

"You should not refuse," said Francoise solicitously. "Michael would understand. He is so clear-headed. He could probably help you more than . . ."

"No, no," said Anna. "I'm better off alone. I'll get over this sooner or later."

They began to walk again.

"Do you drink?" asked Francoise in a low voice. "That is very bad, when you do that. I, myself . . ."

Anna shook her head. They were on the cement patio beside the shrubbery and the bicycle racks, still piled with melting snow.

They parted in the elevator. "See you later, Francoise," said Anna.

"It is nice to have someone with whom one can discuss these problems with such frankness," said Francoise.

Anna went to her darkened office and put her head down on her desk. Michie seemed to have a slight cold. She kept her eyes closed, concentrating on synchronizing her breathing with his. Only later did she remember that she had left her book in a pigeonhole at the bookstore.

The nights were bad. She was not getting any sleep. The only position in which she could still the uproar in her mind was with her head pressed against something hard. Sometimes she fell asleep at the kitchen table.

On Thursday night she took out the Scotch bottle she had

bought in November and stood it on the sink board. There was hardly anything in it. During her bout with the flu she had drunk well over half of it. Ian had had two drinks, she recalled. She put it back in the cupboard. If it were just a matter of filling up a certain space of time with oblivion, this would make sense. But she had no expectation that she was ever going to recover.

There was nothing to eat in the refrigerator. Anna put on her coat and sat down at the kitchen table. An unpaid bill presented itself. She took up a pen with the intention of making a list: MILK, APPLES . . . She was going to go out and get food. She put her forehead down on the table.

Some time later she went into the bathroom, still wearing her coat. She began running a bath. She dumped her clothes in the corner of the room and got into the tub. The cat was scratching at the door, trying to get into the bathroom. Anna got out of the bath and opened the door. She put a towel around herself and put her overcoat on top. She went back out to the kitchen and sat down at the table. The cat remained sitting on the edge of the tub, looking down with ever-renewed interest at the steaming soapless water. Anna had her head on the table.

It was Friday morning. Anna had slept with her overcoat on. She walked stiffly in to the university. Her 8:30 class went very well indeed. They had finished the material to be covered in the course exactly on time. Anna went straight to her office and synchronized her breathing with Michie's.

O'Toole knocked on the door.

"Anna?" he said, poking his head around the corner. Anna looked back vaguely over her shoulder. He took in her face for a moment.

"Sorry to disturb you," he said gently and disappeared, closing the door.

Anna taught her other class. Walking back up to her office, she began to feel panic-stricken about the weekend. She turned back to the ground floor and munched a sandwich without tasting it. She sat alone by one of the windows, trying to keep from putting her head down on the table. Back in her office she firmly made a grocery list. For some reason, Michie was not there. She put her head down.

I am going to go mad. I am already mad. Why am I taking it this way? . . . older one . . . other woman's shoes . . . sex and comfort . . . patch things up . . . what more can you ask . . . ?

It seemed to be getting later. The afternoon sun came low through the parting of the drapes and fell on one of Anna's hands, the one under her temple.

Someone was knocking on the door. Anna made a sound in her throat and tried to get out of her chair. Michie was not there to protect her. She hoped it was not O'Toole. She opened the door. It was Ian.

He shut the door behind him and took her in his arms. Anna's wild feeling of hope began to subside. He was just holding her tightly. He did not kiss her. He was reeking of whisky. Anna pressed her face into his shoulder, wishing that this moment would not end. Slowly she began to absorb some of the tension from his body. They were conveying pain to each other now.

He released her gently and sat down on the edge of her desk, now scrupulously tidy and cleared of books. Anna looked aside, standing in front of him. In no way had things changed.

Anna found her cigarettes on the floor under her chair. She got two out of the package and put them both in her mouth to light.

"I am all right," she said, giving him one. She was trying to comfort him for having made things worse. It could not really be worse while he was there; it would be worse later.

He was looking at her but not in the old way. She felt as though she were being hit repeatedly in the face with the flat side of a book. He seemed to notice her reaction to this for he turned his gaze down at the cigarette burning cupped in his hand.

"I cannot stand it," he said.

Anna knew that as long as he was still there she was going to be completely in control of herself. She felt the words she was going to say starting from the pit of her stomach.

"Yes, you can," she said, distinctly. "You've got to."

"Why should you say this to me?" He seemed to be gaining equilibrium from the effort of listening to her speak. The cigarette was still burning in his hand.

"You want to be married." Anna knew with deadly certainty what she was going to say. "You want to be married to the mother of your children. She admitted she was wrong. She came back. You have what you really want, Ian."

"No."

"Yes. If you went off with me now, what would you have? You wouldn't be allowed to keep the children. Something you believed in would be lost."

Anna took a puff on her cigarette.

"I want you," he said, tonelessly.

"You don't want me that much. Why are you drinking?"

"Why do you think?"

Anna put her cigarette out in the wastebasket with an affectation of competence. Imitating what he had done long ago, she took away his untasted cigarette and put it out as well.

"Have you told her about us? You should." She did not wait for a reply to the question. "You know you should."

"I cannot."

"You must." Anna was now so involved with the chain of argument that she was feeling absolutely nothing, as in her classes. "Have you been drinking all this time?"

"No."

"It is just because you have not told her. If you told her, all this would be gone—over." Anna made a small, sweeping gesture with the flat of her hand. She was really not feeling a thing. The reaction later was going to be absolutely awful, she knew, but did not care.

"No!" he cried.

Anna looked at his watch on the wrist lying across his knee. It was nearly 4:00.

"You have to go home soon," she said.

"Anna . . ."

"You cannot have me anymore."

"Ah," he said putting his hand over his eyes. Anna knew what he was feeling. If she stopped talking now, she would not be able to prevent herself feeling it too. But he was crying.

Holding him in her arms awkwardly, as he still half sat on her desk, and sobbing wretchedly into his jacketed shoulder, Anna began to feel wonderful.

He slid down off the desk and began to kiss her. Anna took great gulping bites of air between the kisses, her shaking beginning to subside and to be replaced by another, quite different sensation. With one hand, he reached out and grasped the doorknob, fumbling with the lock.

"No!" cried Anna, retreating to Michie's desk. "No! not here!"

They stared at each other wildly.

"Go out now! Go and I'll follow you!"

He was still staring at her, his hand on the doorknob. "Do you still have the key? Go to my apartment!" He nodded and began to open the door. He closed it again suddenly.

"You'll come!"

"Yes! Go! Now! At once!"

When he had left her office Anna blindly took up her shawl and coat, knocking everything off the top of the filing cabinet. She crouched on the chair inside the door, counting to sixty over and over again. The door began to open, and Michie insinuated himself between it and the doorjamb, apprehensively taking in her posture. Anna leapt off the chair, pushing his slight frame aside as she threw the door wide open and dashed for the stairwell.

Once outside the building, she began to run in earnest, splashing herself in the puddles, panting to a walk, and splashing again as she ran.

"What am I going to do?" her mind shrieked, "What are you doing, Anna?" but she ignored it. Up the fire escape to the kitchen door she ran, fingering the key in her pocket. She opened the storm door and put her whole weight against the one inside. Ian opened it from the inside, and she slipped against him.

Chapter 22

At 5:30 Anna got up from the bed, throwing on her skirt and blouse, and went alone into the kitchen. She took the Scotch bottle out of the cupboard, unscrewed the top, and poured the last three ounces down her throat in quick swallows, looking at herself in the mirror over the sink. She looked like a consumptive. There were dark shadows under her eyes. Her cheeks were scarlet. Her mouth still twisted by the raw whisky, she began to make coffee.

Ian came out of the bedroom in the golden afternoon light, pulling on his jacket over his rumpled shirt. Anna was putting the dripping filter container in the sink. She kept her back turned as long as this was possible, then took up one of the brimming mugs of coffee and passed it to him.

"You," he said quietly, taking both the mug and her hand. "You, you, you." It was no longer like being hit in the face with a book.

"Yes," she said. She gently disengaged her hand and sat down at the table. He stood over her, and she looked up at his face. The skin around his eyes was puffy, and the small freckles there stood out against the shiny skin. There were two sharp creases down his cheeks beside his mouth.

"It was not 'nice'," he said, still standing over her and holding her eyes. "Why did you say that on that day?"

Anna looked down at her hand on the table. There ought to be an imprint from my forehead here, she thought, a hollow place like the imprint of feet in the middle of cathedral steps.

"That is what one says, when—" she began.

"When one doesn't care about something."

"When one is pretending not to care," she admitted. "I thought it would be easier for you—for both of us—if I pretended."

"Easier!" he cried. "I thought I was going to go mad when you said that!"

"Well," she said, glancing up at him again. "There's pride, too. I don't even have that any more."

"No, neither do I. What does it matter?"

"You have to go home tonight."

"No. Yes. Do I?"

Anna stood up, her coffee untasted. He put his arms around her loosely, locking her into the circle.

"But you do. You know you do." She resisted the impulse to lean against his arms. He was silent.

"Tell me about it," said Anna suddenly. "Tell me everything."

"Everything?" he asked slowly.

"You see, you can't have it both ways, Ian. You are deceiving—Judith," she tried the name aloud for the first time. "But if . . . well, you see, you would be deceiving me too."

"Yes." He slackened his grip, and she pushed him into a chair.

"I didn't care so much about you and Judith being in bed, or—or anything," she said, noticing that she now really did care about it. "The awful part was having completely lost you. I didn't know where you were. You were just gone."

After a while he began to speak, still not drinking the coffee but without any apparent tension.

"I met her at the airport on Tuesday night. She is still very beautiful. She said again that she has changed. We had a drink together in the bar. She was nervous about seeing the children again, particularly Gregor, who doesn't remember her. When we went home Lucy was very upset, and Judith stayed with her for hours. Then we went to bed, and—" he glanced up.

Anna looked at him steadily.

"To use your words, it was nice," he said bitterly. "She said she loves me, and I said I love her—which is true in a way too. Then, the next morning she called up Helen, and they had a long conversation. I came in to teach. In the afternoon I saw you in the Dean's office with O'Toole."

Anna remembered being in the Dean's office.

"I—" he put his head on his hand, the elbow propped on the table. "It was like looking at a person I had never seen before. You never smiled. Your face— Don't you know all those lovely—?" He gave his faint smile. "Of course you don't. I was standing right by the glass, but you didn't see. So then I went away."

"At night we—well, it was the same. She wants me to keep the housekeeper. She says she needs to have a job. Judith was an historian. I got up early the next morning because of Lucy. She's dreadfully confused. Judith wants to put her in therapy, but I—

"I saw you teaching your class in the morning," he went on.

"You left the door open. I listened outside for a while, but I couldn't make out what you were saying. You seemed so controlled."

"Not weeping and screaming, you mean?"

"Almost—enjoying yourself."

"Well—yes."

"I would have waited for you but for that. However, I thought that you were . . ."

"Having a wonderful time."

"Better off, anyhow." He frowned and took a sip of coffee.

"And then—" she prompted.

"Well, things went from bad to worse. You were walking across from the bookstore with that Frenchwoman. I saw you out of my office window. Were you crying by the bush there?" he asked gently.

"Sort of. She's trying to make a confidante of me. I was resisting doing the reverse."

"And then I didn't see you at all after that. I went home early on Thursday because of Lucy. We had a bad time of it with her last night. Judith slept with her. Lucy wanted to stay with me—she does sometimes, you see—but Judith has Viennese ideas about that. Psychoanalysis is a terrible scourge," he added.

"So I thought about you all night, but I couldn't come to any conclusion and this morning, when I didn't see you again, it became obvious I was going to have to," he concluded abruptly.

"What about Judith then?" asked Anna. "Is she happy?"

"It is much as it was before, although with the children— Judith says it will get better. She says that she is like a stepmother to them at the moment. Helen is being helpful, as usual."

Anna thought remorsefully of her feelings about Helen. "And so you are going to go on with it?" she asked.

"I cannot do without you," he said with finality.

"Yes, but what will you do *with* me?"

He got up and poured his nearly full cup of coffee down the sink absently.

"I don't know," he said. Anna recalled that this was exactly what he had said before.

"What time is it, Ian?"

"Half past six."

"You must go home."

"Yes. Will you let me see you? May I come here sometimes?"

"Let's think about it. Go home in the meantime."

He came over to her and she stood up, putting her forehead against his shoulder.

"We won't have much time to be together," he said, stroking her hair.

"No," she said, meaning something different.

After he had left, she looked at the calendar in the living room. Classes would be over in five days. There was a three-week examination period. She calculated. Marking the last examination would take three days. She would have to have time to pack and settle her affairs. She would be gone by the fifth of May.

Everything was completely different for Anna. Over the weekend she began to become accustomed to feeling ordinary emotions again. On Saturday morning she woke up to a flood of jealousy, which she welcomed with bitter happiness. She wrestled with this all day, feeling each new pang like someone with a limb coming back to life after a tourniquet has been taken off. Throughout Saturday night and all of Sunday, she drank a very large quantity of liquor. The impossible part was over. He was no longer a positionless hole in space; he was on the same planet, functioning in a parallel form of life, eating breakfast in the morning, walking through the streets, playing with his children. She drank in the expectation of seeing him again.

She taught her 8:30 class on Monday and went back to her office. Michie was staring at his typewriter. There was no sheet of paper in it. She remembered the sobbing suddenly, and instead of sitting down at her desk, she went over and stood in front of his.

"What's up, Fred?" she asked, unaware of the change in her own features from the previous Friday. "How's your paper coming?"

He looked up vacantly.

"I destroyed it."

"Too bad." Anna was sympathetic. "I admire you for trying. I can't seem to come to grips with that at all, myself."

"It doesn't matter, anyway." This was a long and revealing speech from Michie. "I assume you have had a job offer."

Anna was stunned. Then she remembered her behaviour over the past week. The weekend had so far separated her from it that she had not once thought of the events of Friday afternoon since she entered the office.

"No—no," she stammered. "One never knows, of course. I haven't seen the mail yet today, and there are one or two places that still haven't rejected me."

He did not reply to this pleasantry, and Anna tried to divert attention away from herself.

"How's the tenure situation? You're up for it this year, aren't you?"

"I was," he said.

"The committee's met, hasn't it? Haven't you heard? Are the pigs holding out on you?" As Anna finished this sentence, her heart began to sink. "It isn't worse than that, is it?" she asked hesitantly.

"Yes," he said, looking steadily into air.

"I'm terribly sorry, Fred." She forebore to ask what he would do. People were asking her this question almost daily now. An older student in her advanced class had even offered her a job in his office, "as a sort of receptionist—if things don't work out."

"I'll clear out," she said after a moment's silence and picked up her textbook from her desk. Lecture notes were now completely unnecessary as they were having review days. Students who had not come to class all year were now attending faithfully, hoping to scrape something together from the hints Anna was offering about the final examination.

The mail was in, and Anna knew suddenly that there would be a note from Ian in her box. The only person in the mail room was Helen Bertelsmann, who was efficiently sorting book circulars, ordering them alphabetically by publisher for her files.

"Professor Callaghan," she said formally, as usual.

"Professor Bertelsmann—er—Helen." Anna withdrew her note slowly. Helen was not watching her, so she went over to the radiator under the window to read it.

I was not able to see you on the weekend because of Lucy. Judith wants to take her to the doctor today. I still have all your letters. It would be reassuring to receive one, although perhaps I should not ask. I love you, Anna.

When Anna turned back into the room, stuffing the note into her skirt pocket, Helen was still there. She seemed to be lingering.

"Would you like a cup of coffee, Professor—er . . ." Helen asked abruptly.

"In the coffee room?" said Anna dubiously.

"No, no. I have strictly given this up. I have a filter machine in my office."

"Yes thanks, then," said Anna, adding, "Just a sec. I'll follow you." Helen paused in the doorway and watched with comprehending eyes as Anna snatched up a pencil from the ledge under the mail boxes and wrote a line in the centre of a sheet of ring binder paper from the front of her textbook. She then tore off the top third of this sheet, on which the words CATFOOD and BUTTER appeared in bold print, and pushed the twice folded note in the used envelope through the slot in Ian's box. Anna had decided to come clean with Helen.

"Please call me Anna," said Anna, as they waited by the elevator. "I'm never really comfortable with 'Professor Callaghan'."

"I have become accustomed to the informality on this continent," said Helen. "In certain ways, this is to be preferred, although . . ."

They entered her office. It was pleasantly decorated with plants and had several comfortable chairs. Anna sat down in one of these, looking around her with lively interest. She had not expected Helen to have an office like this.

"What is your situation?" asked Helen, plugging in the kettle after giving it a preliminary shake. "You have no position here next year?"

"No," said Anna. "I haven't had any positive response from anywhere yet."

"Professor MacGregor has said something about your difficulties," said Helen.

"It seems to surprise him," said Anna mildly. "The academic world used to be different. How nice that must have been."

"What do you intend to do?" asked Helen, pouring water meticulously into the filter.

"If I get a job, of course, I'll go wherever it is. If not, I'll have to find something to support life. Either way, I expect I'll be leaving in May." Anna said this firmly, glad to be able to answer the question.

She had not expected more, but Helen seemed reluctant to let it go at that.

"You will be missed," she said, matter-of-factly. Anna wondered as she took her coffee whether this level of innuendo could be maintained.

"The MacGregors have difficulties," said Helen. "The eldest child is highly strung. She rejects the mother."

"I know." Anna's fingers shook, but she spoke placidly over her coffee.

"I believe it was a mistake for the mother to return." Helen's sharp grey eyes were fixed on Anna.

"Ian wants a family life," said Anna, trying to say what she felt was true. "I don't think he was happy going it alone."

"This way will not succeed," said Helen decisively. "The mother is very egotistical. Ian will begin to drink again very soon."

The strain was beginning to tell on Anna. It was like an oral examination in which the candidate, bound and gagged, was supposed to assent by gesture to only those assertions of the examiners she believed to express facts.

"I hope not," she said, turning her head away from Helen's scrutiny.

"Perhaps you will not be here to see it," said Helen shortly.

"What shall I say, Helen?" said Anna after a long pause. She had waited until she again had control over her voice. "I *should* go away, shouldn't I? As it happens, I can't stay anyway. In the meantime, though, you see . . ."

"In the meantime, I would like to help you," said Helen in a softer tone of voice than before. "I have seen that you have a strong character. But this is not always enough."

Anna took a long draught of coffee and then tried to meet Helen's eyes.

"It is first of all necessary to spend time with other people," said Helen.

Ian could not have asked her to do this. Of that Anna was positive. Helen had returned to her old post as Judith's friend in his mind. She thought of the grudging generosity of her own behaviour at the Bloom's party. This was reciprocation.

"You would like to come tonight to my house for dinner?" suggested Helen. "I have two daughters, one of whom you will find sympathetic. She is very intelligent, high-spirited, but serious. With the other, it is too early to tell."

"Yes, thank you," said Anna, dazzled by the promptitude and magnificence of this gesture. She put down her empty cup. The buzzer had gone for her next class.

Chapter 23

Anna drifted around the campus for a while after the class. Ian had made no arrangements to meet her, but she did not want to go back to her office. She made herself as visible as possible. After his recital of the events of last week, she had no doubt that if he was at the university at all, he would be able to find her.

Crocuses were coming out on the lawn. The spring was early and warm. He would only need to take a stroll outside. It would be the most natural thing in the world for them to meet here.

"Well, well," said Jimson, coming up to her as she bent over a crocus. "Anna Callaghan, I do believe."

"Hello, Michael." Anna wondered what Francoise had told Jimson about her.

"I hear there have been some little changes in your friend Ian's affairs."

"Oh?"

"You know what it is with me. People tell me these things."

Anna gave him a radiant smile of dislike. Better this than a false affectation of sympathy, she reflected.

"So what are you doing with yourself now, my child. Time to move on, right?"

"Right."

"I'm glad to be able to tell you that Sierra Leone is no longer for me."

"Really?"

"There is going to be an opening in my department. The historian, Michie, he who shares your office, will be scraped off the floor by the janitors this summer and carted away."

"And you . . . ?"

"It is not quite in the bag yet. However, I have a luncheon date with one of the assistant deans—" he glanced at his watch. "I hope to be able to present my point of view."

"Well, hurry off, then."

"Yes. Ta-ta, dear."

The crocuses temporarily spoiled for her, Anna went over to a lilac hedge and examined the unformed bud ends of the branches with careful fingers. So it was because of this that Francoise had not been concerned with the likelihood of having to live apart from Michael. Michael would get Michie's job and they would live happily ever after, teaching at the same university. Anna frowned, thoughtfully. She could see perfectly well now why this vision of the future would appeal to Francoise. But why was Michael eager to marry her? It did not fit in well with Anna's view of his personality.

Ian did not appear and Anna was finally forced to go back to her office. Michie had apparently not moved since she left. The typewriter was still empty. She went over to his desk again.

"You might have a look outside," she suggested. "The spring is wonderful."

"Would you like me to leave?"

"No, no. I just thought it might help if you—"

"Is Professor MacGregor expected this afternoon?" said Michie with sudden venom. Anna looked at him wonderingly. They had not met here often. Michie got up and went out with his coat over his shoulder. Anna sat down.

There was nothing to be done. The last term papers were not yet in. She had submitted all her exams to the printer the week before. They would not be written for nearly three weeks yet. The last day of lectures would be yet another perfunctory review, thinly veiling direct revelation of the material covered by the final examination. Idly, Anna took out a sheet of paper and wrote the word 'The' in the top left-hand corner. In her absent, uncaring mood, she had begun to write an article on aesthetics. She even had a title: "An Aesthetic without a Metaphysic." By 6:00 that evening she had covered five sides of three sheets of ring binder paper. Ian had not come.

She went down to the fourth floor and knocked on his door. It was too late to expect he would still be in. Anna put on some lipstick and powder in the women's bathroom and went outside to walk slowly to the address Helen had given her. The hour appointed was 7:00; she estimated that by walking very slowly, she could manage to arrive only fifteen minutes early.

She had begun to feel lonely, a mood which her relief at finding Ian again had held off over the whole weekend. The streets were drying, but Anna did not think she would take out her bicycle soon. Bicycling, she reflected, got you to and from where you wanted to go too quickly. It was better to walk. It gave one the impression of filling up the time usefully.

Helen lived in a house that was almost the identical twin of Ian's, separated from it by about ten blocks. The spruce trees in the yard were trimmed, and the bleached grass and mould underneath them had been raked clear of cones and needles. The house was in much better repair.

A girl of about sixteen opened the door.

"Mama!" she called over her shoulder. Anna was seventeen minutes early. It occurred to her that she was also empty-handed and that this was not polite by European standards. Helen did not seem surprised, and to Anna's amazement she received a kiss on the cheek.

The two girls, Cybele, eighteen, and Celeste, sixteen, were entirely North American. They were wearing the usual jeans and sneakers and plaid shirts, contrasting oddly with another of Helen's suits. After a few guarded exchanges with Anna, they left her entirely to their mother, ignoring Helen's instructions to them in German about homework and the use of the telephone.

Helen took Anna into the kitchen and poured her a glass of vermouth.

"Your house is so pleasant," said Anna, admiring an herb garden on the windowsill. "Helen, this is very kind."

Helen, pleased by her admiration, allowed Anna to peel but not to chop several kinds of vegetables. They were having a Chinese dish of some sort. Anna, who liked to cook very much but rarely had the opportunity, listened with secret amusement as, with great culinary erudition, Helen explained the origin and uses of the ingredients.

After dinner they sat for a while on the back porch in the spring twilight while the girls did their homework. Helen had a vegetable garden in the backyard in summer.

"How I envy you all this, Helen," said Anna, embracing the whole scene with her shawl-wrapped arms. "Every day I pass by houses like this and think how pleasant it must be to have a settled life."

"Sometimes it is too settled," said Helen neutrally. "With my husband I went to Germany every summer. But now, with only one salary, . . . I will be paying tuition for Cybele next summer. She goes to France to study. I have only the gardening and a few good friends."

"What more can one ask, though, really?" said Anna.

"Opera," said Helen, promptly. "Theatre. Music, not diploma recitals, but real concerts. Intellectual excitement."

"There is something deceptive about summer holidays in Europe, though, don't you think? I mean, could it be that wonderful all the time? I expect there's a good deal of dullness everywhere." Anna tried not to put this contentiously, thinking of the Blooms' party.

"Not in the cities," cried Helen energetically. "In the cities there is not a moment's dullness. Everywhere is music, plays . . . it is so lively, so stimulating."

"Did you grow up in a city?"

"Oh, no. In a little town. It would only be called a city on this continent."

"I grew up in a little town," said Anna. "A this-continent little town."

"But in this country," said Helen suddenly, "there is wilderness. Now that is something we in Europe do not have. In Canada that is something."

When they went inside at last, Anna was badgered by Helen into a game of chess with Cybele. "With Celeste one can play the physical games like field hockey or baseball. But Cybele is an intellectual."

Cybele, ignoring her mother's praise, set out the chess pieces on a small table by the fireplace. She was a much better player than Anna, but Anna speculated that Cybele did not wish to win too quickly. The ignominy of being called an intellectual oppressed her. Anna tried to take advantage of this and lost more slowly. Helen had taken up her embroidery some distance away, remarking that she would not interfere by helping Anna.

It was 9:30 and Anna realized regretfully that she would soon have to leave. Helen gave her another glass of vermouth, and she postponed the departure hour until 10:00, leaning back in the sofa cushions with her legs curled up.

The doorbell rang and Celeste again answered it, calling "Mama!" Helen went out into the hall, carefully shutting the glass door to eliminate the draught. There was quite a bit of talk outside the door to which Anna, staring into the gas flame in melancholy, attended not at all.

The glass door opened, and Helen came halfway in, looking distressed.

"Have you got the fire on, Helen?" asked Ian's voice, and Helen came forward into the room, propelled by Ian behind her.

He was carrying Lucy, who was wearing a nightdress and a blanket and had her head burrowed face downward into his shoulder.

Anna jumped to her feet, her eyes darkening in alarm. She was sure she should not be here. Helen looked around and motioned her to sit down again. When she had finished doing this, her heart beating wildly, she found Ian looking at her over Lucy's head with a surprised, happy smile from a chair by the fire.

Celeste had come in with them and was now making herself useful by sitting between Ian and the fire, stroking the bottom of Lucy's bare foot, which dangled from the blanket. Ian shifted Lucy carefully until she was lying across his lap in equilibrium, then looked up again at Anna and extended the smile equally to Helen.

Anna began to relax. It was clearly up to Helen to tell her what to do, and Helen had knelt down on the other side of Lucy and was paying no further attention to the Anna question. She was talking to Lucy tenderly in baby-German. Anna did not speak or move but kept her eyes fixed on the ruffled, blond head against the jacket.

After a time, Lucy held out her arms to Helen who picked her up and carried her out of the room, still talking to her tenderly.

"What's wrong with Lucy?" asked Celeste. "She's not sick again, is she?"

"Not really," said Ian. "Not yet anyhow. Lucy doesn't want her mother right now."

"Electra complex," said Celeste. "The child wants to murder the mother. Cybele has a case of that too."

Ian calmly took off his jacket and sat down again in his shirt sleeves, looking across the room at Anna. Tidy Celeste picked it up off the arm of his chair and took it into the hall to hang up. Anna stared back, her mouth dry. His being so much at home here filled her not with jealousy, but with longing.

They heard Celeste go upstairs after Helen. Cybele was in the basement with her recorder, playing "Du bist wie eine Blume" with fervour.

"Come here," he whispered. Anna got up hesitantly and went halfway across the room. He lay back in the chair, watching her walk towards him. She took another step. He looked so tired. "Closer."

"Please, Ian, I think . . ."

He leapt to his feet and took her in his arms. "Don't think," he said anxiously.

"I'll sit on the floor," she said, pushing him gently backwards. They sat down. Anna rested her head on his knees, kneeling in front of him.

"What are you doing here?" he whispered.

"Helen invited me to dinner." Anna sat back on her heels. "She said that a strong character is not enough at times like this, and one needs the company of other people."

Ian's lips twitched. "What would I do without Helen?" he said contentedly.

"What did the doctor say about Lucy?"

"A euphemistic version of Celeste's opinion."

"And so you brought her here."

"Yes, although—there was a long discussion about it beforehand."

"Will you leave her here?" Anna felt her questions were impertinent, but it was part of her longing that she had to know.

"As long as I can." He rubbed his hand over his forehead. "I'll probably stay the night. The others are all right with Lucy not about."

Helen came back down into the hall talking over her shoulder to Celeste, who was still upstairs. Anna could hear the uninterrupted murmur of Celeste's voice from above. She was telling a story to Lucy, from what Anna could make of Helen's German.

"Helen," said Anna, on her feet. "I'll go home."

"Since you're here, you're here. What can I do about it?" Helen shrugged, looking at Ian who remained lying in the chair. "Now please come with me, Anna, and we'll make some tea."

"May I come too?" he asked.

She shrugged again, then smiled slightly. "Oh, why not?"

Anna sat meekly on a kitchen stool buttering slices of bread while Helen interrogated Ian from the sink. He leaned in the doorway, looking tired and peaceful.

Lucy had disliked the psychiatrist and so had Ian. Helen did not ask for Judith's opinion but wiped her hands on the dishtowel very thoroughly, compressing her lips. Lucy had not spoken or opened her mouth all afternoon and evening.

"She spoke to me," said Helen briskly.

"What did she say?" Ian asked anxiously.

"She wanted a drink of water."

Ian pulled out a stool and sat down beside Anna, blowing on his tea. Helen put her hands on her hips and looked down at him.

"It is very simple," she said. "The child rejects her mother. That is what we say, pretending it is irrational. If she were an adult, we would say she dislikes her or hates her."

"Hatred, love—they're all irrational, aren't they?"

"No," said Anna cautiously, "One feels them, so they're not rational in that sense, but one can have reasons for feeling them." She drank some tea, feeling uncomfortable. To her surprise Helen elaborated the point.

"She has reasons for hating her mother."

There was a prolonged silence.

At last, Helen said, "Leave her here, Ian. Perhaps she will change her mind. You can't force her."

"No, I will not try to force her," he said, looking at the uneaten piece of bread and butter in his hand.

Cybele came up from the basement and sat with them, her practising done, and Anna's longing began to become unbearable. She got up to go.

"Goodbye Helen. Thank you for dinner," she said, fearing to thank her for too much. "Goodbye," she said more generally to Ian and Cybele.

"I'll see you to the door," he said firmly, taking her lightly by the elbow. Helen did not move from the sink but began to address some remarks to Cybele about homework.

Ian picked up Anna's coat and shawl in the hall and went out the door with her, trying to help her into them. They stood outside in the chilly, spring night under Helen's neat spruce trees.

"Good night, sweet Anna," he said gently. "I cannot come with you."

"No," said Anna, feeling the tears pricking at the corners of her eyes.

"There will be time."

"Yes," she said.

"There will be."

Chapter 24

There was nothing in Anna's mailbox the next morning, and she walked away from the mailroom without even a bill or a circular. O'Toole was standing before her office door. The moment he saw her he raised his arm to the horizontal crying, "You shall not pass!"

He whispered in her ear, "That was what the man said at my dissertation oral."

Anna laughed and O'Toole looked at her curiously. She reached for the door handle.

"No, no. Don't go in there. Don't you understand international hand signals? We were fated to meet in my office this morning." He hurried her down the corridor.

"Just a carefree chat with your chairman, that's all." He shut the door with elaborate care, as usual. "First of all, any word?"

"Nothing in the mail in any case," said Anna, holding up her hands palm outward to exhibit this.

"Nothing in the mail?"

"No."

"Nothing at all?"

Anna began to laugh at this elaborate probe. He raised his eyebrows and gave her an innocent, wide-eyed stare.

"Well, no news is good news. Or," he added cautiously, "sometimes it is."

Anna sat down in a chair and lit a cigarette, using her hand as the ashtray.

"Anything else you want to know?" she asked calmly.

"I had hoped that someday you would ask me this question." He paused.

"Yes?"

"How's Michie bearing up?" he asked, changing the subject. He sat down behind his desk.

"Not very well. He just sits there staring at his typewriter."

"Too bad. The Political Science faction is trying to eliminate History at this university altogether."

"Is that what did him in, then?"

"A factor in it, at least. I have overheard our mutual friend, Jimson, in the coffee room telling a colleague that History is not an academic discipline."

"Good heavens! Politics is not an academic discipline, of course, but I should have thought that History . . ."

"I have a weakness for it myself." He pushed the wastebasket towards her with his foot. "For heaven's sake, don't put that thing out in your hand."

"You're squeamish, Peter. How can you be on the Tenure Committee when you can't stand the sight of blood?"

"You'll find out someday for yourself. You, too, will . . ." He stopped, evidently remembering something.

"That's beginning to seem pretty unlikely, isn't it? There's always Sierra Leone, I suppose."

"Have you applied there?" he asked quickly.

"Don't be absurd."

"Some story is going the rounds about Jimson accepting a job there."

"He told me it was in his pocket."

"Oh? Well, he's taken it out again. He's going after this one in a most unseemly way, if I may say so." O'Toole pursed his mouth.

"Did he really accept it beforehand, do you think? The job at Sierra Leone, I mean?" Anna asked.

"On the most cursory assessment of his character, I'd say, yes, he did. Undoubtedly he's going to ditch them now."

"What a pig."

"You're so hasty. You've been chatting with him again lately, I gather."

"Not really. He seems to dislike me."

"That's one way of putting it." O'Toole sounded thoughtful.

"Does he . . . ?" Anna wondered whether she knew O'Toole well enough to ask about Jimson's malice.

"Oddly enough, he's been remarkably reserved about your affairs. I mean by that expression, of course, 'matters pertaining to you,' nothing more."

Anna laughed again, and once more O'Toole gave her a curious look.

"Peter, just in case I don't get a chance to say it before I leave . . ."

"No! No!" he cried, leaping up from his chair. "Don't you be the one to propose! I'm old-fashioned in this way!"

Later that afternoon, O'Toole made Anna come to the coffee room with him. She had been walking up and down the corridor, thinking about the paper she seemed to be writing but unable to get down to it because of the unhappy presence of Michie. There was no other task to be done. Anna had only two more classes to teach before it was all over.

Jimson was in the coffee room talking to the historian Speer in an undertone, when they came in.

"Ah, O'Toole. You're just the person I wanted to see," said Jimson, giving Anna a flick of his eyes by way of greeting. "Speer and I have been thinking of getting up a really good speakers program for next year."

"The problem is cash," said Speer earnestly. He was a grey-haired man with horn-rimmed glasses, previously in Jimson's 'deadwood' classification.

"If Political Science and History—or History and Political Science, rather," Jimson said, glancing deferentially at Speer, "could pool their resources with Philosophy . . ."

"What an excellent idea!" cried O'Toole. "You have some funds, I take it? Philosophy would be glad to share them with you."

"Surely you have something put aside for speakers," said Jimson, quick to catch implications.

Anna, much entertained, poured some coffee for herself and O'Toole.

"Let me think," said O'Toole, lounging in a chair. "Do you remember what we did about Joyce when he was here, Anna?"

"I believe you used the stamp allotment for his taxi fare," Anna replied reflectively.

"No, no. That didn't quite pay for it. I think I had to hawk a couple of chairs from the seminar room—to Engineering, if I remember correctly."

"It is madness, this penury!" cried Jimson, looking around him at the shabby room. "We should—our departments should petition the Legislature."

"We've been quite lax about getting speakers in the past, I agree," said Speer.

"I know of a number of men we could get—of interest to both our departments, too. Do you know Paddy Dillon?" Jimson asked Speer. "He's a pal of mine. He's doing some very interesting work."

"Dillon at Princeton?"

"That's the one. Then there's . . ." Jimson listed some other well-known people. He always remembered the nicknames.

Anna examined her feelings. Was she envious of Jimson? His getting Michie's job was almost a *fait accompli* since the presence of the man on the spot was a tremendous presumption in his favour. She wondered with contempt why he was lobbying so hard. She was not envious, she decided. She was only sad that she was going to be hired by no one.

Academic life had never seemed so desirable to Anna as it did at this terrible time of year. There was a scent of fear in the air. The students hurried back and forth from the Library with armloads of books. The Faculty was restless. But having longed for the end of classes throughout the long, dull days of March, Anna was now savouring every breath of the stale air of the Arts Building.

She walked slowly home that night, thinking about her problems. She was going to have to pack up soon. She had given notice on her apartment, but it would be worthwhile trying to arrange something with the landlord so that she could stay there during the first five days of May.

A car overtook her on the road. Cybele was driving it with Helen in the back seat. There was no one else in the car, so Anna speculated that Helen was trying not to give directions, as in the chess game. The car slowed to a stop, then began to back up carefully, "Hop in! Mama wants you to come for supper again."

Helen was making insistent pointing gestures from the back.

"Thanks!" said Anna, getting in awkwardly. "Are you sure . . . ?"

"You were not in your office today," said Helen.

"No. I share with Michie, you see." Anna turned around as Cybele began to drive off, after a preliminary nervous jerk of the clutch. "He's not in good shape right now. I'm avoiding . . . I mean, I'm trying not to bother him."

"Professor Michie in History? What is the matter?" Helen relaxed her severe expression.

"Denial of tenure," said Anna. "It must have happened quite a while ago." She recalled her conversation in February with the geologist, Frame. "But it seems to be hitting him badly just now. I don't believe he has any prospects."

"There is a position open in that department?"

"Yes. Jimson will be getting it, I expect. Do you know him?"

"Professor Jimson? I know him slightly." Helen indicated by her tone that this was as much as she wanted to know Jimson.

Cybele parked the car in front of the house after a discussion, in German on her mother's side and rudimentary English on her own, about the hazards of the garage. They went into the house. Anna took off her coat and followed Helen into the kitchen.

"I hope you didn't mind about last night, Helen. About my being here, I mean."

Helen poured out two glasses of vermouth and pointed to a stool.

"It was an accident," she said. "I invited you to dinner. Tonight I invite you again, you see?"

Anna sat down gratefully.

"I am not a neutral ground in this war," said Helen. "I have told you already in my office."

"Yes. Is Lucy still here?"

"Upstairs with Celeste. They play together, those two. Celeste goes to university in two years," she added. "She will major in field hockey."

They were having a vegetable soufflé for dinner. Anna was allowed to chop some things this time.

"Do you like children?" asked Helen bluntly, as they listened to the running feet up above.

"Well—some children," said Anna, thinking that she had said this to someone before.

"I disliked them very much before I married Friedrich. We were not going to have any." She put the plates in the oven to warm. "However . . ."

"As it turned out. . . ," said Anna, laughing.

"Yes, as it turned out. Friedrich was better with them than I. I became a parent after he died." She spoke matter-of-factly.

"You were wonderful last night with Lucy," said Anna, pleased that she did not mind praising Helen.

"Ian believes that the mother must love the child, and the child must love the mother," said Helen, washing parsley. "This is not so."

"He has strange ideas about motherhood, I think," said Anna thoughtfully. "Mystic bonds."

"It is enough if the children and the adult can respect one another. There is no mystic bondage."

Anna tried not to laugh.

"Bond," said Helen firmly, correcting herself.

"Sorry," said Anna. "Your English is really impeccable, you know."

"Bondage," went on Helen. "There is bondage. Homework, laundry, dancing lessons, swimming, cooking supper . . ."

"Not a bit mystic, all that."

"Judith could not endure this." Helen began to chop the parsley into miniscule fragments with an enormous steel kitchen knife. "She is also an intellectual. She was teaching here in the early years with us all."

"When did she marry Ian?" asked Anna.

"At the end of his first year here. It was the first year for all of us." Anna had the impression that Helen looked back on those years as golden; her husband had been alive then. "She is not a Scot like Ian. She is an American."

Anna's jealousy began to boil up again. It had been bad when she had only had the mental picture of Judith so generously sketched by Gore; it was worse to know that she was a woman much like Anna herself.

"In the beginning she and Ian were an inseparable couple. When Lucy came, she was determined to be perfect. Then," Helen scraped parsley off the blade, "she began to become desperate. Jane was barely out of diapers when she had Gregor. It was too much. She did not want Gregor."

"I don't suppose Ian could believe that," said Anna, finding Helen's description of Judith MacGregor's predicament appalling.

"No. He tried very hard to make himself useful. He was always the better parent anyway. But for Judith, nothing could make up for the loss of a few more years of her real life—her intellectual life."

"Oh God," said Anna, wishing she had something to do with her hands.

"And so," said Helen, mounding the parsley on the chopping board, "she made her decision. These stories—I do not know what you have heard—they are untrue. It was a decision."

"But—," said Anna, "it was reflected glory, wasn't it? I mean, a vicarious intellectual life through Bateson."

"She has finished her dissertation at Harvard," said Helen. She took the plates out of the oven. "It was a mistake to return. Why did she do it, this is what I ask myself."

"Panic, possibly," said Anna. "I couldn't bear to send my thesis to the printer for nearly two years. They had to force me to take soft foods for the first two weeks after I finished the oral exam. Perhaps it terrified her to be finished her Ph.D."

Helen passed Anna the hot plates silently as Celeste pursued Lucy through the kitchen into the dining room.

Later, the dishes washed and the homework done, they all five played the non-intellectual game of Hearts.

"Lucy beat Celeste at chess this afternoon," remarked Cybele, passing the Queen of Spades to Anna.

"Cybele told me what to do," said Lucy. Celeste put her tongue out at her sister.

"This game differs from Skat," said Helen, "in the following respects . . . Listen to me, Cybele, for you will play Skat with your colleagues next year . . ."

At 10:00 Anna went home. There was no one there. No message awaited her. She took off her coat and poured herself a drink. She had replenished her stock of Scotch on the weekend. She drank quietly until it seemed to be time to go to bed, then fell into a drunken sleep.

Chapter 25

After her 8:30 class the next morning, Anna went to the coffee room. There seemed no reason not to. The mail would not be in for half an hour. Michie was filling the whole office with a bone-chilling fog of despair.

Jimson was in the coffee room with Speer and another historian named Crystal, younger than Speer, a good looking, happily married man of about forty. He too had been on Jimson's hate list in the fall.

". . . and so we have been corresponding regularly since that time."

"So I've heard," said Crystal. "A Princeton postmark doesn't go unnoticed around here."

"I suppose not," said Jimson carelessly. "Of course, Paddy was in Oxford all winter. You must have heard about the letters from Nick Slater."

Anna inferred from this that Jimson was still marshalling his forces. She took her usual place on the sofa and placidly lit a cigarette. Spong came into the room and sat down beside her, nervously spilling his coffee.

"How many more?" he asked her hollowly.

"More?"

"More classes do you have?"

"Oh. One."

"What about Thursday and Friday?"

"But—" Anna panicked momentarily. "This is the last day of classes."

"It is?" He looked at her in alarm.

"Good God, Albert," said Crystal, who had been listening to this. "That's something you ought to be up on."

"Then—" Spong was coping. "I'll just have to do all of Milton in one hour." He sprang up and left the room.

"Now there's someone who needs a holiday," remarked Crystal to Anna. He had never spoken to her before. She had the impression that he wished to get away from the conversation with Jimson. He was a reserved person who ordinarily never came to the coffee room.

"We have three weeks of marking ahead of us," she replied.

"Incredible tedium," said Crystal with a sigh.

"No tedium in the teaching," said Jimson, who had been looking for an opening in this. "Not for me, anyhow. It's a question of style, of course."

"Did they give you another standing ovation this morning, Michael?" inquired Anna. She had been unable to believe Jimson's report that this had happened last year.

"Spontaneous clapping," said Jimson promptly. Evidently no jam could be too thick.

"They clapped for me once too," said Anna sadly. "I was taking off a pullover at the time."

"You have certain natural advantages," said Crystal. "Sometimes even for me their attention wanders to the front of the room, of course."

"I must go," said Anna. "Mail time."

"I'll go with you," said Crystal, rising to his feet. Anna was happy to see she was helping him to escape.

"Any good news?" asked Jimson. "They always telephone when it's good, though. I don't know why you're so obsessed with mail." He gave her a significant smile. Anna wondered whether Francoise had told him about the kind of envelopes her middle-aged lovers used. It was a detail that would appeal to Jimson.

"I still have a few places to cross off my list," said Anna. "I like to finish a job once I've started it."

She made for the door, Crystal on her heels.

"Jimson is making a lot of new friends," he remarked as they got on the elevator.

"I can't imagine why," said Anna briefly.

"It may not do him as much good as he hopes."

They got off the elevator.   ·

The note was short. "I love you," it said.

Anna walked back to her office and went inside, firmly shutting the door behind her. The thick cloud of Michie's misery swirled around her. She pulled the three sheets of ring binder paper towards her and read what she had already written. Then she wrote steadily until her next class.

After lunch there was a telephone call for her. Anna felt only a faint stirring of hope as Michie passed her the phone. A potential employer would not bother to find out her extension number. A job offer would come direct to O'Toole's phone.

"Hello," said a voice she vaguely recognized.

"Hello," said Anna inquiringly.

"Seth Frame, here." It was the geologist, Frame. "I wonder if I could . . . ? There's a beer fest this afternoon at the Students' Union Building, you see. Would you like to go?"

Anna allowed a certain pause to suggest that she was considering this offer very seriously but was having trouble fitting it into a busy schedule.

"Hmm. I'm not sure I have time," she replied. "Nice of you to offer, though."

"The beer is very cheap," he said encouragingly.

"No, really, I . . ."

"Please come. I . . . It's about Francoise Hibert." He was keeping his voice low. "I want to talk to you."

"Oh—well, in that case . . ."

"Good. Is Fred there?"

Michie had gone out without his teapot. "No. It was he who answered the telephone, though. He rarely sticks around to listen in on my intimate exchanges on the phone."

"I didn't recognize his voice. He is taking it hard, I hear."

"Yes. Very. Did you make it through yourself?"

"By a hair."

"I'm very glad."

"Well—see you later. About 3:00 I think. Do you know where the beer fest is?"

"I expect I can find it."

There was no difficulty in finding it. Loud music pouring forth from the open front doors of the Students' Union Building engulfed the whole campus in an echoing wave of sound. Wincing, Anna pressed her way through the crowds of rejoicing students to the desk where the beer tickets were being sold. Frame was waiting. She was five minutes early, but she had the impression that he had been there for some time.

Anna bought one ticket. Frame pressed two more on her.

"I always buy too many," he confided, shouting in her ear. "I usually think I'm going to stay a long time, but then I get bored."

Anna made a gesture of assent. She recognized a fellow sufferer from the party punctuality syndrome.

Walking ahead of Frame to the bar, Anna looked around the big room. It would be necessary to get the table farthest from any speaker and well protected by plants, partitions, coat racks and other sound breaks if they were to have any kind of conversation. She spied one and hastily went to take it, giving her tickets into

Frame's keeping. She made some gestures in what she hoped was the common parlance of the deaf and dumb to indicate her intentions. He nodded.

"Do you like this sort of music?" asked Anna in a medium pitch shriek, as he came back to the table. He had providently purchased four bottles of beer.

"Not much," he shouted. "I thought this affair would be the best place to have a private conversation."

Anna lit a cigarette. She was hoarse already. Frame indicated with some head nodding and music direction movements of his hands that the song was coming to an end.

"Francoise . . ." he said, as the last note began to die away. There was an immense amount of booing and cheering which drowned out the rest of this speech. Anna sat back patiently in her chair.

There was something wrong with the tape recorder. Two students wearing striped engine driver's caps with the peaks to the back began to work over the machine. The cheers subsided into sporadic hand-clapping.

"I'm worried about Francoise," said Frame in a normal tone of voice, leaning forward over the beer bottles. "I wouldn't be taking this up with you, but I saw you talking together the other day between the bookstore and the Arts Building. So I thought . . ."

"She was telling me she and Jimson are going to get married this summer," said Anna bluntly. She felt sorry for the timid Frame, but there was no point in beating about the bush. He probably knew this anyway.

"Why?" he said softly, beating his hand against his knee.

"Well, she's a pretty girl. Jimson is a pig, but there's no point trying to tell people things like that." Anna was feeling sorry, but wanted to get this over as quickly as possible.

"I know he wants to marry her," said Frame impatiently. "But what does she see in him? Why is she taken in like this?"

"He's a subtle pig," said Anna warily. "He shaves his bristles carefully. Actually, I don't see at all why he wants to marry her. It's much more plausible the other way around. He has a wife already."

Frame gave her the look of a mathematics professor discovering that his students didn't know how to divide fractions, an academic combination of pity and horror. "I see you haven't thought about this," he said.

The music started again and Anna devoted herself to her beer, thinking about it. Frame continued to give her the mathematics professor look, evidently hoping to spur her on to new depths of concentration. Anna was trying not to let her attention wander, but her ear was caught by the voices of some boys, probably Voc. Ag.'s, she decided, who were shouting at a nearby table.

"He hates God!"

"That's impossible. There is no God!"

"He hates him all the same!"

The song ended, and Frame took advantage of this to prompt her. "You're a Canadian, I suppose?"

"Yes," she replied. "So are you, aren't you?"

"Thank goodness," he said, adding simply: "That got me my tenure."

As the first pealing notes of the next piece started, Anna saw revealed before her all of Jimson's plans. Their devilish simplicity struck her full in the face. He was going to get Michie's job. He wanted Michie's tenure. The preferential hiring policy of the university for Canadians would set him back unless he became a landed immigrant and gave good earnest of taking out citizenship. Francoise had even mentioned this. This was why he would need to marry Francoise, to become an immigrant.

Anna began to make now-I-understand gestures to Frame, tapping her forehead to indicate the depth of her obtuseness. He smiled sadly, and addressed himself to his second beer.

The tape snapped again and a magnificent whirring noise terminated in a click.

"Who does he hate, then?"

"God! I said God! He hates God!"

"I don't know who you're talking about. Describe this person he hates!"

Anna now recognized an atheist from her 8:30 class in one of the shouters.

"Isn't there something you can do about it?" Frame asked quietly.

"What about you?" asked Anna. "Did you discuss this with her at all?"

"When she invited me to the wedding. She's not speaking to me now." Frame's gentle face showed signs of tears. "I'll get some more beer." He stood up.

Anna thought over her two conversations with Francoise. "Should I take this step?" she had asked. She had been on the level. Jimson was actually doing the pushing himself.

"What can I do?" she asked Frame, returning with four more bottles. "I told her what I thought when she raised it with me. I said she shouldn't do it." Anna remembered how misplaced her reasoning had been. Helplessly, she began to work away on her second beer.

They sat together in the loud room until Frame had finished all four of the beers he had bought for himself. The music made further conversation impossible, but there was, in any case, not much to be said. Anna, sick to her stomach, found her body revolting at the thought of more beer. She pushed her two remaining bottles across the table.

"I don't want to drink!" he shouted above the noise. "I don't even like beer. But it seems to help."

Anna nodded. This year has been a disaster for all the nice people I know, she reflected. We're all going to become alcoholics. She wondered briefly whether she should include herself in the nice class or in the class of people known to her. She was certainly in the potential alcoholics class, even though the beer did not appeal. The Scotch bottle awaited her at home.

At about 6:00 Frame began to show signs of having had enough, and they left the building together. They stood outside on the path. Anna was feeling awkward.

"Well, goodbye. I'm sorry about all this."

"Won't you—? Can't I—take you out for dinner or something?" stammered Frame, straightening his clothes. The sunset reflecting from his glasses hid his eyes, and Anna noticed again how shy he was.

"I'd like to keep you company," she said, "but I'm not in very good shape myself these days."

"I didn't know." He sounded sympathetic. "All the more reason then . . ."

"No," said Anna. "It doesn't help."

He shifted to his other foot, the sun no longer reflecting off his glasses, and looked at her intelligently.

"I was never her . . . I mean I didn't . . ." he began. "Of course, I wanted . . ."

"You're very nice," said Anna sincerely. "She's lucky to have someone like you who cares about her. She'll see through Jimson in the end."

"Maybe not, though."

"He's just a pig in wolf's clothing," said Anna. "They eat pigs at weddings in the Gaspé."

"Well. Give my best to Fred Michie," he said. He began to walk towards the Chemistry Building.

It began to rain as she walked home, a soft spring rain which seemed to spread through the air rather than to fall. She thought about Francoise and Jimson and Ian and Judith. Her pity for Frame kept getting mixed up with pity for herself. It had certainly been the right decision not to go out to dinner with him. There are various kinds of betrayal, as Anna knew, herself involved in several of them, but the worst is the use of the suffering as an instrument for assuaging one's own grief.

Anna drank a bottle of milk from the refrigerator to quiet her stomach, still in upheaval from the beer and the noise. Then she took up with the Scotch bottle where she had left off. There was no need yet to worry about running out. She was still not doing anything about the landlord or the packing and sorting or the question of her income for the summer. The fifth of May loomed ahead like a doorway through which Anna had to take a lot of luggage.

Chapter 26

On Friday afternoon Helen came to Anna's office to take her home for dinner. Helen had called earlier, but Anna had the idea that she was getting what for Helen was informal treatment, and she took this as a compliment.

Helen sat down in her spring coat in the chair where Ian always sat and looked around at Anna's office fixtures, which included Michie, who had neither spoken nor moved when she came in. Anna had finished writing her paper, and she was involved in the final task of taking out some of the overloaded clauses and excising 'howevers'. Helen watched her in silence as she stowed the paper-clipped bundle of inky ring binder paper under the blotter.

"Are you writing an article, Anna?" she asked.

"Well, yes—I suppose I am," said Anna slowly. "I seem to have done it, whatever it is." She began putting on her coat. A headlight gleam was trained on her from under Michie's half-closed eyelids.

"Work makes life sweet," said Helen. They left the office, Helen nodding ceremoniously to Michie. Outside the building as they began to walk down the path by the Library, Helen said:

"It is good that you do that. You are ambitious?"

"Perhaps," said Anna. "I was just doing it because . . ." Why had she been doing it?

"I myself was interested in philosophy when I was a student," said Helen. "When I married Friedrich I turned towards literature. I did not finish the degree," she added abruptly. "Cybele was born."

"Do you like teaching literature?" Anna asked dubiously. She thought of the tiny German Department with its three offices at the end of the third floor of the Arts Building.

"German for scientists," said Helen distastefully, continuing Anna's thought. "We have examples of the preterite and the use of the subjunctive from Goethe and Schiller in the textbook."

Anna nodded. "Are you sorry you didn't finish, though?" This typical female predicament was very much on her mind.

"I cared then. But not any more." Helen evidently felt she was not being explicit enough. "I am not a real intellectual as Friedrich was. Or Ian," she added.

Anna nodded again. They walked in silence for a while. New grass was beginning to sprout on the lawns of the neighbourhood houses.

"I usually think I'm not a real intellectual myself," Anna said. "But women almost always think that, don't they? We come to it sooner or later, anyhow."

"Do you think this is simply an inferiority complex?"

"Well, yes I do. Look at Ian. He says he hates thinking."

"That is something only an intellectual could say."

"Yes, but if you or I said it, that would be just because we are women. No one would say that we were being intellectuals."

The afternoon was one of the best they had had that spring. The soft rain of Wednesday evening had finished melting the snow without contributing to the water in the streets. Tulip and daffodil bulbs were poking up bright green spikes under Helen's spruce trees.

"Do you still have Lucy?" asked Anna.

Helen stopped with her hand on the gate.

"Yes. The mother does not visit her," she said, adding, "You need not fear to meet her here."

"Does Ian . . . ? I'm not asking because of me."

"He comes. But the mother disagrees that Lucy should be here. And Lucy is now worse with him than she was with the mother."

"What does she do exactly?" Anna thought of Ian's pain.

"With the mother she would not speak. With Ian it is the reverse. She cries and cries." Helen opened the gate and held it for Anna. "Have you seen him lately?"

"No, not at all."

They went into the house. Helen's house was warm and elegantly comfortable. The heavy woodwork in the front hall had been painted in cream and ivory. There was pleasant, subtly patterned wallpaper on the walls. As Anna followed Helen to the kitchen, she glanced through the glass door into the sitting room where Celeste and Lucy were squatting on the blue Persian carpet playing with a bean-bag frog.

In the kitchen Helen tied on her apron and silently poured the vermouth. Anna took it, looking around her again. Helen had a lot of good, expensive cooking equipment. A row of brightly polished copper saucepans hung over the stove. A mahogany rack revealed a collection of magnificent steel knives. Through the doorway Anna looked directly in at the dining room as she sat down on her stool. A low teak table surrounded by teak chairs stood in the middle of another Persian carpet. The ruddy light came in through a west window.

Anna began to tell Helen about Francoise and Michael Jimson as they drank their vermouth. Anna was peeling potatoes tonight. She was glad to see that Helen sometimes resorted to this homely vegetable.

"I have sometimes seen this Francoise. But the language departments are not very friendly with one another." Helen was putting a casserole into the oven.

"A good thing for you," said Anna. "The French Department is . . ."

"Yes," said Helen. Anna made Francoise's pouf! gesture. Helen went on. "So here is another woman who will not finish her degree then?"

"It's much worse than that," explained Anna. "Jimson is trying to make a marriage of convenience. He wants the job in the History Department, you see, but he is an American. The university has a preferential hiring policy these days. They will only hire Americans on a temporary basis."

"Why does he not become a Canadian?" asked Helen. "I have done this myself long ago. It was not difficult."

"Yes, but he's not even a landed immigrant," said Anna, surprised to hear that Helen was a Canadian. She was finding Helen more and more unexpected. "He is going to marry Francoise (divorcing his present wife first, of course) in order to become a landed immigrant. It's difficult to enter Canada except that way now, you know."

"So you think he does this entirely to gain the job?" said Helen, frowning. "This woman, Francoise, is willing to marry him to help him like this?"

"I don't think she knows that that's why he wants to marry her," said Anna. "Or if she knows, she doesn't think it's the main reason."

"I see." Helen sat down beside Anna. "You must tell her your opinion, no? I have never liked this Jimson, but I did not realize . . ."

"Someone else already has told her. A geologist called Frame. She is not speaking to Frame any more." Celeste and Lucy had begun to set the table. "He's very sad. I think he's in love with her himself."

"What is this world in which we are living!" cried Helen angrily. She got up to pass Celeste the warmed plates.

"Marriage should be made illegal," said Anna. "Or at least only the right people should be permitted to do it," she qualified, thinking of Helen's dead husband.

Anna had made a niche for herself in the Bertelsmann household. She discovered this from Cybele. They were sitting outside on the steps of the back porch since there was no homework to be done on Friday night. Inside, Celeste was doing the dishes and getting a subsidiary French lesson from Helen.

"I shall never go to graduate school," said Cybele, looking up at the sky. "The academic life is not for me."

"Why not?"

"Look at my mother. She goes on teaching in this squalid little town without anyone to talk to from one year to the next. It's not a life."

"She has friends," suggested Anna, thinking of the Bloom's party and her picture of settled academic life.

"What friends?"

"The MacGregors, for instance."

"There's you, I suppose." Cybele paid no attention to the suggestion that the unfortunate MacGregors could be friends.

"Me?"

"Well, she's taking an interest in you, anyway. Things have got a bit better around here lately. You're supposed to be a role model for me."

"Good heavens. How nice. I hope you don't mind about the role model part, though."

"No, no. I just ignore it."

They sat outside as long as they could in the mild air. A mosquito appeared and was welcomed by Anna, swatted by Cybele.

Anna looked around her apartment that night. Packing won't take long, she comforted herself, pouring a glass of Scotch. Almost all of the possessions that moved with Anna were made of paper or cloth. The table, the bed, and the armchair would go back to the Salvation Army. She looked in the cupboards, and decided to take the cake pan. Then she sat down at the table with her drink.

Anna had never before experienced the kind of jealousy she was enduring now. In the past, what she had felt was the mortal insult of being interchangeable with or replaceable by another woman. In this case, she herself was the usurper.

In spite of what she said about marriage, Anna felt a superstitious awe of it. As a legal form it conferred an inadequate and poorly defined set of rights and privileges. But it also brought with it an emotional commitment, a vow of enduring love and respect, that gave Judith MacGregor an indisputable prior claim.

What Ian did and said with her was on an entirely different plane from what he had done and said with Anna. Anna ached at the thought of their talking about the housekeeping, the affairs of the children, Lucy, all the trivial events of life. Even if he did not really love Judith . . .

Here Anna picked up her glass and began to walk back and forth with it between the sink and the table.

Even if Ian did not really love Judith, or did not love her as he loved Anna, they were sharing a house, a kind of life that Anna had not known since her childhood.

Anna began to count backwards from one thousand in time with her slow steps across the kitchen floor. At the same time some part of her mind which was detached from this process began taking her on a tour of Ian's house. The house, identical in its exterior to Helen's, unsurprisingly had the same interior plan. Anna had never been inside.

She entered the shabby front door with its oval, lace-curtained window over the shambling veranda and began to walk down the red Turkey runner inside the hall. The dark wainscoting of the staircase rose beside her right shoulder. Passing the glass door to the living room on her left, she glanced in at the dark, wooden mantel with the tall vase and the clock. It was furnished parlour-fashion, and Anna reprovingly took in the condition of three poorly sprung chairs in brown velours disposed around the gas fire.

The kitchen floor, scrupulously cleaned by the housekeeper, in black, red, and yellow linoleum, met her at the end of the passage. The kitchen cupboards, in glossy eggshell blue and again clean to institutional standards, hung over an oddly modern stainless steel sink. Tulle curtains completed the kitchen, and Anna took a look at the dining room.

The round oak table, now surrounded by five chairs—sternly she counted them—in an odd mixture of ancient and modern, stood under a high window with a criss-cross lattice. A set of lead alloy robins appeared on the window sill, but Anna recalled that they came from her grandparents' house and deleted them. Above the sideboard, she placed a picture of Cutty Sark under full sail.

Anna went back out into the hall and began to climb the

stairs, running her left hand over the cracked newell post and up the bannister rail. Up the opposite wall, parallel with the pitch of the stairs, a long dirty streak against the turquoise green paint on the wall broke into isolated finger prints as she approached the landing. She paused there and looked out the stained-glass window with its two clear panes which interrupted the pattern. The blank wall of the next house, in grey, greeted her eyes, with a glimpse of spruce tree below.

At the top of the stairs, Anna sat down briefly, wishing she did not have to go on.

". . . 799, 798, 797 . . . ," her voluntary thought process continued. Anna poured herself another dram of Scotch and walked, still counting, to the sink for water.

Anna peeked in at the sleeping Jane, cuddled on her bed next to the flowered wall in a room containing a white-painted rocking chair with a worn pink cushion. In the next room Gregor still slept in a crib, with the bars gapped like an old comb. Lucy's room, which was the largest yet and contained most of the toys, was empty-bedded. Two aged bears looked at Anna glassily from the bed.

The smallest room was on the moonlit side of the house, and Anna entered stealthily. Ian was there, asleep on his back with the covers rucked around his knees, his legs curled slightly to one side. The bed was a cot, and the room was otherwise full of cleaning paraphernalia, including a vacuum cleaner whose hoses dangled from hooks on the wall opposite the bed. Anna knelt down beside him with the windowsill at her elbow, praying that he would wake up. But he rolled over onto his other side with his face to the wall, giving vent to a slight moan and a snuffle from some disturbance in his sleep.

Anna went out into the uncarpeted hall again and stood before the last door, the one to the room at the back of the house. She stood there uncertainly, not wanting to open the door but knowing that she was going to. A photograph of Queen Victoria on a Highland pony with her ghilly at its head caught her attention, and she distracted herself by looking to see if it was really there.

". . . 586, 585, 584 . . ."

There had been no traces of Judith yet in the house, Anna realized, still standing with her hand on the knob of the door to the back room. Casting her mind back over what she had seen so far, she remembered two dying philodendrons in the parlour. But Ian must have contributed those. Surely Judith would not like philodendrons?

Ian had undecorated the house after Judith left him; Anna now realized this positively. He had taken all Judith's possessions and sold them, given them away, made presents of them to charity. She looked up at John Brown, the ghilly, staring dourly into the camera and took courage. There was probably nothing to fear in this room. She began to turn the knob of the door slowly, silently.

". . . 441, 440, 439 . . ."

Anna pulled herself together.

"This is absurd," she said sensibly to herself and noticed a slight slur of Scotch in her voice. "I have never even been inside the house. It's probably not like that at all."

Trying not to count now, she poured herself another slug of whisky and took the glass into her bedroom. Setting it down on the orange crate by the bed, she resolutely shed her clothes and settled herself under the sheet.

Presently, so as to prevent herself from counting, she began to sing.

" 'With a ring in the end of his nose, his nose, his nose.
With a ring in the end of his nose.' "

Chapter 27

Anna spent the weekend marking term papers, keeping the Scotch bottle tucked away in its burrow under the sink. Systematically she rewarded herself for achievement: the marking of three papers merited a cigarette. After five papers she drank a cup of tea or a glass of milk, staring vacantly out a window. At ten paper intervals she went outside and walked around the block.

By 4:00 in the afternoon on Sunday, she was seeing spots before her eyes. Certain phrases—"Nowadays, in the modern world . . . ," " ". . . just the product of socialization," "true for me"— gave these spots a purplish tinge. She made a vicious X over a misspelled word and went over to the sink. Her face looked back, ravaged, out of the mirror.

She went into the bedroom and found her favourite hat, which she had not yet worn that spring, a luscious black thing with a drooping feather. Under it her small, pale face looked mysterious and charming rather than fatigued and sad.

She left the house and began to walk towards the river.

The deeply cut riverbank was overgrown as it had always been, since the pre-history of the prairies, with poplar and willow scrub. A maze of paths and skiing trails penetrated this dense bush, breaking out periodically into clearings of scraggly grass and wild-rose bushes. Anna plunged into the labyrinth and came out at last on a little lawn immediately above the river. The day was warm and summery, and the westering sun fell favourably over this place, casting long shadows back from the dead reeds at the water's edge. Careless of damp, Anna took off her hat and lay down on the sun-warmed ground. She closed her eyes. She lay still there on her back, feeling the sun on her eyelids and listening to the bird calls, her arms at her sides. After a time it seemed as though she were drifting in a warm medium between earth and air, and her whole consciousness was focussed on the surface of her skin.

She opened her eyes suddenly. Someone was humming in a rather aimless way right beside her ear. Simultaneously turning her head and curling up her legs, Anna found that it was Gregor squatting on the grass beside her.

"Gregor MacGregor," said Anna, not very loudly. "What are you doing here?"

Ignoring the question, he said "Hi" very casually, and continued to hum. He was putting together the stems of a few early dandelions, covering his small hands with sticky sap.

Anna leaned up on her elbow and looked cautiously around the clearing. No one was in sight.

"Did you come here by yourself?" At this instant she heard adult feet crackling through the undergrowth and the voice of Ian calling, "Gregor! Gregor!"

Gregor got to his feet at once and began to trot away in the other direction. Anna lunged after him.

"Hey, wait a minute," she cried, getting a good grip. Gregor wriggled, and Anna began to tickle him to distract his attention.

Ian plunged into the clearing from a path and stopped short, seeing Anna wrestling on the grass with Gregor, who was giggling and trying to return the tickles.

"I'm not kidnapping him!" Anna gasped, laughing wildly herself as Gregor plunged his feet into her midriff. "I'm trying to catch him for you!" She got a better grip on Gregor, holding him at arm's length.

Ian came closer and sat down a few feet away, taking Gregor into a professional hold between his knees.

Anna straightened her clothes and pulled a twig out of her hair. Gregor went back to his dandelions, his interest in Anna terminated.

"I've been marking papers all afternoon," she said conversationally.

"Here?" He looked around the clearing.

"No. At home. I was beginning to feel like the Lady of Shallott, so I came down here to have a look at the river. You and Gregor are taking a walk?"

He was smiling down at her hat as it lay on the grass. He ran his fingers lightly over the feather. Anna shivered.

"How are things?" she asked, trying to keep it mundane. "Lucy is still with Helen, I gather?"

"Yes," he said, ceasing to stroke the feather at once.

"She's all right there. I've been seeing a lot of Helen recently. Lucy and Helen and Celeste and Cybele and I played Hearts together on Wednesday. She seemed to be having a good time with Celeste on Friday."

"Helen told me."

"Helen is the secret of life's happiness."

"No," he said.

Anna opened her mouth to add something to her claim, and then saw that she was being minutely inspected. She closed her eyes. A light breeze was blowing now off the water, and the sun, lowering over the city skyline, shone squarely in her face and on her ruffled hair.

He took her hand gently from her lap. "Gregor," said Anna, not opening her eyes.

"He's over there," said Ian. Anna looked. Gregor was picking reeds, some distance away.

"Do you still imagine things, sometimes?" asked Anna.

"Constantly."

"Not constantly," she replied at once, looking away. "You can't."

"What about you?"

"Yes." She looked into his eyes. He gazed back, smiling faintly.

"Do you think this will really work, Ian?" asked Anna with sudden energy. "I don't mean because of me. I'm going to have to—go away, anyhow. But can you really pick up the pieces and go on?"

"I don't know. It depends on Lucy." He was looking miserable again.

"It depends on your wife too. Helen says that she was not altogether happy in the past with . . . just with domestic life."

"Judith is going to take a job."

"Oh. That will probably make a difference."

"I don't know. It doesn't seem to be up to me. Nothing seems to be up to me."

"Where's Gregor?" asked Anna suddenly.

"Oh Christ!" He got to his feet and looked around.

"You'd better go after him. I won't come. I should be marking." Anna could not imagine helping Ian find Gregor to deliver him back to Judith.

"I'll see you tomorrow," he said, looking down at her seriously, then he ran across the clearing and disappeared into the bushes.

The Philosophy Department was like a mausoleum on Monday morning. Anna had finished with the term papers on Sunday evening. She went into her office and got out her grade book to enter the marks. Michie was not in. Final exams had begun. Holding the term papers in her lap, Anna began to tabulate, throwing the papers down one by one onto an untidy heap on the floor as she finished with each of them.

Her grading done, Anna read over the paper she had completed on Friday. It struck her as terrible.

"Self-conscious and boring," she muttered, but stayed her hand from the wastebasket. In her present uncaring mood, it was neither here nor there to her what anyone thought of her work. She went downstairs and borrowed the Dean's secretary's typewriter.

A passel of department heads and administrators were meeting in the Dean's office, an oak-panelled chamber large enough to seat an audience and a medium-sized orchestra. Anna caught a glimpse of Scandinavian furniture and oil paintings as they filed out for lunch. O'Toole made a subtle grimace for her benefit as he passed by, wearing his Army jacket in the grey-clad, sober-tied conclave. He passed on quickly and her answering smile was caught by Ian, looking over to see what she was doing there. He smiled back, catching sight of the typewriter in front of her, reassured.

When she had finished typing, something she did slowly and laboriously, getting a good deal of white erasing liquid all over everything, she borrowed a manila envelope from the secretary and, selecting the name of a professional journal at random, sat down again to write an accompanying letter.

The members of the meeting returned.

"Budget Committee," whispered the secretary.

Anna dropped the bottle of erasing fluid. Ian was standing right beside her chair. He picked it up for her. O'Toole was watching them with lively interest from the Dean's door. Reluctantly, Ian walked across the room and disappeared last through the doorway.

Anna went to the mailroom and dropped her manila envelope into the half-full bag of mail on the floor.

In her mailbox were the two remaining letters of rejection that Anna had been waiting upon. She walked slowly back to the Philosophy Department, not bothering to open them. Jimson was quite right. The mail never brought letters of acceptance. There was no such thing.

Eddy was in his office down the hall, and Anna went to talk to him, pathetically wishing for company. A knot of historians stood whispering together by the window at their end of the corridor. Crystal waved briefly at Anna. She realized that he was someone whom she would now never have time to know.

Leaning on Eddy's doorjamb, Anna said, "May I come in for a chat?"

He looked up from his marking. "Sure. Make yourself at home." He turned down the radio on which he was listening to an opera.

"Marking," said Anna, sighing. She continued to stand in the doorway. There was no room to sit down in Eddy's office because of the piles and stacks of books, all his own, on every surface. Eddy did not bother with the Library.

"I've been at it for seventy-two hours," he said, glancing at his watch. "I figure it'll take me about the same amount of time to do these." He gestured towards a small pile. Anna guiltily thought of her short shrift over the weekend.

"You must take time off, though," she said hopefully. "One can't do it day and night."

"I do, but it wrecks my concentration. Can't be helped. There's always some jackass of an administrator wanting a form filled out at this time of year."

"Oh yes, the cheat sheets." Permanent staff were supposed to make progress reports to the Dean and the Vice-President.

"The thing that gets my goat is that those jackasses get paid for looking at how I do my work. I merely get paid for doing my work!"

"Pay is proportional to office size," murmured Anna.

"It's a mug's game! I slave away here, writing three pages of comments on every paper, while—"

". . . downstairs they're scanning your dossier for content—" Anna went on helpfully, familiar with the theme.

". . . and then they write 'Grammar and spelling could use improvement' at the bottom, and that's that!"

"Did they ever really do that?" asked Anna, convulsed. "Probably they should have."

"It was rumoured," said Eddy darkly. "The dossier of some jackass in Education, of course."

"In the Typing and Manual Skills Division, I expect," said Anna, wishing to prolong her pleasure at Eddy's powers.

Something was happening in the hall. The ranks of the historians had closed around the elevator door. A graceful, fine-boned, blond-haired woman wearing very bright red lipstick and big city clothes was getting off the elevator. She began to shake hands all around. The History Department moved back down the hall towards Anna, the woman chatting vivaciously in their midst.

Eddy, attracted by Anna's interest, appeared by her elbow in the doorway. "Mrs. MacGregor," he whispered in her ear. "She's MacGregor's wife."

Anna shrank back into the office against the door, but Eddy stepped forward and said bluffly, "Nice to see you again, Judith."

"Oh, Eddy," she said, taking his hand. Up close she was even more beautiful, with flawless, transparent skin and very blue eyes.

"What are you all doing here?" said Eddy affably to the historians and Judith MacGregor. "It's a working day. I'm surprised to see you."

"I'm being interviewed, my dear," said Judith with a chuckle that dismissed any seriousness in this reply. She had a husky voice, with a slight southern accent.

"We are lucky enough to have an opening in our department," said Crystal, looking at Judith with naive admiration.

"Perhaps we have an opening," corrected the department chairman doubtfully.

"Well—swell," said Eddy enthusiastically. "So we'll have a MacGregor team!" He watched them go on up the hall and into the History seminar room.

"Sorry I didn't introduce you," he said, suddenly noticing Anna in the doorway behind him. "You know MacGregor, right?"

"It's all right," said Anna. "Too late in the year to meet new people anyhow."

"She's a lucky woman," muttered Eddy, going back to his desk. "A bit wild in the past, but she'll settle down now."

"Give my love to your rabbit, Eddy." Anna went back to her office and sat down dully at her desk.

So this was the job that Judith MacGregor was going to get. Without giving it much thought, Anna knew that she would certainly get it. Lucky woman, said Eddy. She had everything behind her: beauty, wit, intelligence, a Harvard Ph.D., Ian's influence, and the whole force of middle class approval for her return.

The thought of Jimson struck Anna with a flash of malicious glee, instantly suppressed. Anna began to think about what she could do for Francoise once Jimson had deserted her. Francoise would need a Helen. Anna wondered if she could be half as kind as Helen. She was desperately keeping her mind off the memory of Judith MacGregor's beautiful face.

Somewhat later, Michie came in and silently trod across the floor to his desk. Anna was now avoiding Michie on an entirely different basis. She hoped that he would never say anything to her again. She picked up a book and went out on the lawn with it.

Sitting on an artificial hummock beside the campus pond, now newly refreshed with water and a few ducks, Anna wondered whether she would see Ian again that day. As usual, she was trying to make herself visible. I did see him, of course, she said to herself, but he could hardly have predicted that. On Sunday he said . . .

Not thinking of something you want is a sure recipe for getting it. Trying to create again her unexpectant mood of Sunday afternoon, Anna lay down flat on the grass with her arms at her sides and, to clear her mind, began like Descartes systematically to doubt all her beliefs.

"I do not know that I am Anna," she said under her breath. "I do not know that I am here, how can I be sure that this is grass, I doubt that I am even saying this, I do not—"

"What are you doing, Anna?" said Helen, standing beside her on the grassy hill.

"Trying to cast a spell," said Anna, sitting up.

"The sun is warm." Helen sat down beside her, feeling the grass carefully first. "Was it an evil spell, such as said the witch in 'Schneewittchen'?"

"No, no. I'm not trifling with black magic. Heavens no!" said Anna, superstitiously taking the allusion. "I saw Judith MacGregor going for a job interview this afternoon," she said, continuing her thought.

Helen looked at her in surprise.

"In the History Department," said Anna impatiently. Surely Helen knew about this. "I told you about them firing Michie. So . . ."

Helen's eyes had begun to sparkle with anger.

"Do you know this?" she asked, her voice dangerously high pitched.

"I saw her," repeated Anna, not knowing what to make of this. "I was talking with Eddy in his office when they all came down the hall with her. She told Eddy she was being interviewed."

"So this is why she has returned," cried Helen, banging her fist against Anna's book which lay between them on the ground.

"Oh come now, Helen," said Anna, thinking their roles oddly reversed. "You were telling me about bondage the other day. Surely this is a good thing. She has a career."

"She returns to get herself employment. That is all." Helen was furious. Tears were running down her cheeks.

"Helen, that's a wild conspiracy theory." Ann put her hand on Helen's shoulder.

"She will destroy him. The child too. But she will have a

career." Helen was trying to prevent Anna from seeing her tears.

"Maybe that's so. Maybe she will hurt them terribly. But do you think she sees that?"

"We have not here to do with stupid people," said Helen shortly, keeping her head turned aside.

"Very intelligent people often deceive themselves," said Anna, adding in a lower voice, "whatever that means."

"She knows what she is doing," said Helen positively.

"You really think she came back because of the job?"

"That is why she came." Helen gave Anna an angry glance.

"But—but it isn't so easy for her. Why go back to Ian? Why didn't she just apply?" Anna realized that she knew the answer to this already.

"Because she would not get it without Ian!" cried Helen explosively.

"What about Ian?" Anna asked, beginning to wring her hands.

"Ian is acting like a fool. He allows her to use him."

"He loves her." Anna was feeling sick.

"He does not. He thinks he should."

Anna lay down and covered her eyes.

"You do not know how ambitious Judith is," said Helen more quietly. "This is why she went with Geoffrey Bateson to Harvard."

"Like Jimson, only worse," said Anna, starting to laugh and instantly beginning to cry. She rolled over face down in the grass, and Helen patted her gently in turn.

"You have not been long in the academic world," said Helen slowly. "I will tell you, there are people who would kill to get ahead in their careers."

"What you said the other day made me admire her," said Anna, rubbing her nose against the ground. "She made a decision."

"Now she has made another decision. I do not admire her for this."

Chapter 28

There could be no doubt that Helen was right. Anna redoubled the pillows behind her head and propped her glass of Scotch on her stomach. She had spent the rest of the afternoon and evening with Helen, playing croquet after supper with the children.

They had said nothing more about it, but Anna and Helen had by now had enough experience with each other's gesture language to convey certain thoughts and feelings. When Anna left, Helen had still been deeply angry.

Anna was now thinking only about Ian. Helen had said he was being a fool. But Anna was in a state of uncertainty and fear about this. If he came to know what Judith wanted of him, it would hurt him much more than if he remained in ignorance, even self-imposed ignorance. Perhaps Helen would try to talk to him.

I am not going to do anything about this, thought Anna. It has passed entirely out of my hands. I am a woman without a future, just passing through. She thought of May the fifth and took another draught of Scotch.

There was a quiet sound in the kitchen as of someone trying to open a door or window without making much noise, and Anna, in the dark with her Scotch, sat up in bed, the hair on the back of her neck pricking. Had she remembered to lock the back door? The sound was repeated; this time it was slightly different, the sound of someone closing a door or window stealthily. Anna hopped noiselessly out of bed and stood behind the bedroom door.

Furtive footsteps came through the living room. Anna, her heart beating, prepared to use her Scotch glass as a weapon. The footsteps stopped short outside the door. The intruder looked in for a long, doubtful moment.

"Not here?" inquired Ian, apparently of himself.

"I'm behind the door!" Anna was limp with relief. She came out, spilling Scotch down her nightgown, and felt for his dim figure outside the doorway.

"You smell delicious," he murmured, catching her. "Why were you behind the door with this?" He took the glass out of her hand.

"I was going to clout you on the ear with it. Before you came in I was in bed with a drink. How was I to know that you weren't a jewel thief?"

"I told you yesterday I was going to see you today." He put the glass down on the floor and began to remove her nightgown.

"You saw me in the Dean's office." Anna put her arms up above her head to help. She was not going to ask any questions.

"Yes. I've been coming around here every fifteen minutes or so since that dread meeting was over."

"I was at Helen's."

He put her down on the bed and turned on the light.

"You're always so much better than I can imagine." He sat on the side of the bed and put one hand on each side of her, looking down. "So much whiter and pinker."

"Let me see, too." Anna reached up and began to unbutton his shirt. The words "Your wife is lovely" arose behind the defensive portcullis of her teeth, but she did not utter them. He had not come here to talk about his wife. She felt a wild recklessness rising in her.

"I'll do it," he said mildly, standing up and beginning to shed his clothes. Anna stood up too, and clung to him, shuddering, hampering the undressing.

"I want to."

"So this is adultery," said Anna presently. "It is wicked."

"This is not wicked," said Ian rolling over and immobilizing her. "This cannot be wicked."

"We've done it before. I suppose one gets used to it."

"I shall never get used to this."

Anna's bones were melting. "Neither shall I," she whispered.

"Do I hurt you?" He was crushing her.

"No. Yes. Yes."

When Anna woke up again it was mid-morning. Ian had left, but there was some evidence that it had not been long before. The air still smelt faintly of him. The towel was wet. Anna repressed all guilt. If he had been indiscreet she did not care.

"Just passing through," she said defiantly and, shivering deliciously at certain thoughts of the night, began to make some toast.

A woman of leisure, she went in to the university. There was now no need to go to the mail. She sauntered to the Library, took a

long look around the stacks and went back to the Arts Building
with a novel. Scribbling a note, indicating that she would be
holding office hours in the mornings only from now on and
posting it on her door for the benefit of students and curious
passers-by, she went to the coffee room and lay down on one of the
sofas that could not be seen from the doorway. It was now noon.

She read steadily through the afternoon, ignoring the
lunchers, who could not see her on her secluded sofa. She lay in all
the best postures of a habitual reader, most often on her stomach
with the book comfortably propped in front of her against the arm
of the sofa. At about 3:30 she fell asleep briefly and woke up to the
sound of Jimson's voice.

"I'm a political scientist. History is politics and economics, as
I'm sure you are aware."

"If you're in the History Department, though, why didn't I
meet you yesterday?" It was the same low-pitched, southern voice
that Anna had heard saying, "I'm being interviewed, my dear."

"There are a number of ways of being 'in' a department," said
Jimson. "I'm replacing Morley this year although, God knows, I
hope I'm more than replacing him."

There was the same husky chuckle. Anna looked around for
an unobtrusive means of escape. There was none. Judith was
saying, "Perhaps you applied for the same job as I did. How
funny."

"Do have some of this coffee." Jimson was being suave. "Yes,
I didn't realize until Speer told me this morning that I had any
competition for it."

"Well, they didn't mention you yesterday, so I just assumed . . .
I came in to see about getting an office for the summer."

"Doing some research?" Jimson was completely cool, Anna
observed with grudging admiration. This must be a blow. The
history faction must have offered her the job on the spot. "You
have a Ph.D. from Harvard, I'm told."

"Yes. Bunny Gibson was my supervisor." Anna recognized
the nickname ploy. Jimson would get a run for his money from
this lady. "I'm surprised you hadn't heard of me. My husband is in
the English Department here."

"Should I have? I'd always thought that Professor MacGregor
was—oh—widowed, or divorced, or something."

"Here I'd been thinking my departure for Harvard would
have been a well-known scandal."

"I'm not much of a one for gossip, I'm afraid." Anna curled
her toes and lifted her eyebrows several times. "I've heard stories
about your husband, of course."

Anna froze.

Judith gave her deep chuckle again. "He's such an old stick-in-the-mud. What stories?" she asked warily. "About his drinking?"

Anna took advantage of a time warp to resent this throwaway. If she knew about the drinking, she should be taking it more seriously.

"Does he have a drinking problem? I wasn't aware . . ."

"What stories have you heard?" The fish was taking the line.

"Perhaps I oughtn't to say. It's none of my business, of course."

"What stories?" Her voice had hardened.

"Really, Mrs. MacGregor, I'm sure you know much more about your husband's aff- . . . I'm not the person to tell you things like this."

"Go on," she said quietly. "I see your game. But I happen to be interested in what you have to say."

Anna wondered whether it would be possible to interrupt this tête-à-tête by rising from the sofa and stalking from the room. Jimson would tell anyway, she realized, and perhaps her appearance would precipitate things in a way which would be even more unpleasant.

"Well, if you insist. He's been having a torrid affair with someone since the beginning of the year. I don't listen to gossip, as I said before, but one can hardly help noticing in this case. Sex scenes all over the Arts Building. Our friend Michie shares an office with the lady, and he was telling me he never knew when it was safe to go in."

"I suppose you think this is going to make some difference as far as my plans go?" The husky chuckle was long gone.

"Well, of course not. I'm glad you don't take it seriously. Marriages are much looser, freer things than they used to be. Even so, I think you're being awfully broad-minded."

There was a silence. Anna began to wonder whether perhaps they had both noiselessly departed, but this seemed so unlikely that she remained motionless on the sofa, one hand still on her book.

"So it's still going on?"

"Oh, I think so. You can find out all about it from Michie if you want."

"Is it that small, pale girl with long hair? The one in the Philosophy Department?"

"Have you met? Anna Callaghan is the name."

"She's only a lecturer, isn't she?"

"It's not a permanent job, no. But I expect she'll be staying around here. I've heard she hasn't got anything for next year."

"How funny," said Judith slowly. She seemed to reflect for a moment, for she added, "I hadn't thought of that."

"I'm sorry if this has been a shock to you, Mrs. MacGregor. Still, truth is better than lies, isn't it?"

"That's very profound, Mr. Jimson. Of course I couldn't have expected my colleagues in this little hell hole to do me such a favour. Thanks a lot."

"I'm sure you'll be able to make your husband see reason sooner or later."

"I think you don't know my husband, Mr. Jimson." She spoke grimly.

There was another silence. Anna wondered whether they were each waiting for the other to leave first.

At last Judith said, "Well, I'll be on my way."

"Going home? Too bad you have to rush like this."

"As I probably won't be seeing you again, *one way or another*—," Judith gave heavy emphasis to these words, "let me say now that I think you're a rotten bastard!"

Jimson may have been taken aback by this. He did not reply. Anna heard Judith leaving the room and going down the hall. Half a minute later the elevator made a ping, and she heard the doors open and shut.

Anna gave a convulsive yawn.

In the next instant, Jimson was looking down at her over the back of the sofa. A malicious smile crossed his face at once.

"Eavesdroppers never hear good of themselves."

Anna got up and straightened her skirt. She went over to the coffee urn and turned the tap, holding a styrofoam cup carefully underneath. It was late in the day, and there was hardly any coffee left. She tilted the urn to catch the last few drops and carefully put her finger into the cup to feel for warmth. It was tepid.

Jimson had followed her over and was sitting on the arm of a chair, looking very sophisticated in his well-cut clothing. When she turned around, he opened his mouth to speak again.

Anna threw the coffee at him with an underhand softball pitch, retaining the cup. It landed with a satisfactory splash in the middle of his face and began to drip down his shirt front, over his jacket, onto grey flanneled knees.

Without pausing longer than the time it took to notice how well she had done her work, Anna left the room and took to the stairs.

When she came off the stairs onto the seventh floor, she found Ian outside her office door, smoking and frowning at the note she had posted.

"Ian! What are you doing here!" Anna cried in agitation.

"I came to get you. The Budget meeting is over for today, thank God." He put his arms around her and looked down, smiling.

"Ian!" Anna was trying to express all by the intonation of her voice, at the same time looking with anxious X-ray eyes at her office door for signs of Michie's presence within.

"What is it?" he asked placidly.

"Ian! We'll be seen!" Anna pushed his arms down. "Jimson has told your wife all about us."

"He has?" Ian did not seem particularly upset to hear this. He locked his hands together behind her back. "I went home this morning intending to tell her myself but she wasn't there."

"You left very late this morning."

"Yes." He smiled again.

"You decided to tell her?" Anna was slowly taking this in. "So then, you've decided . . . ?"

"I've decided to take matters into my own hands for a change. I decided to do that on Sunday, in fact, but I haven't had a chance to talk to you. We had other things to say to one another last night." He gave her a happy, significant look.

"Ian! For heaven's sake! What do you mean, take matters into your own hands?"

"I'm going to leave Judith. Or really I should say she is going to leave me."

"Has she agreed?"

"We haven't discussed it yet. I told you, she wasn't at home this morning."

My God!—So this business of Jimson telling her about us . . ."

"How do you know he did?" Ian asked curiously.

"I was there—inadvertently. I was asleep on the sofa by the far window in the coffee room when they came in." Anna spoke in a rush. "When I realized what was going to happen, it was too late to do anything. Jimson was trying to winkle her out of the History Department job. She called him a rotten bastard."

"So he is."

"When she left, I threw a cup of coffee at him. Too bad it was cold." Anna began to laugh in her agitation.

"A woman of action," he murmured, hugging her.

"But Ian! You haven't told her! You haven't talked to her . . . !

You must find her and explain. If only you'd told her before."

"You're always sending me off after other women," he said, continuing to hug.

"Please? This is awful!" Anna choked on a laugh.

"I suppose I should." He did not move. Anna began to push him backwards towards the stairwell door. "Don't be upset."

"No, no! Just go and talk to her."

"Helen has invited you to dinner, incidentally." He took a reluctant step backwards.

"Go, please!"

"You'll go over there by yourself?"

"Yes, yes!"

"Just remain there quietly, and I'll see you later." Anna opened the stairwell door, and pushed him through, her hands flat against his chest.

"There's nothing to worry about, Anna."

"Goodbye."

"Oh all right." The door dropped shut.

Suddenly smitten by doubt, Anna flung it open again and ran down the stairs after him.

"You're really sure?" she panted, overtaking him two floors down. "This is not just a quick decision because of last night?"

"I decided on Sunday," he said patiently. "After I saw you. While I was catching Gregor."

"But—you still didn't tell her? On Sunday night?"

"I had to talk to Lucy first."

"Oh Ian! I think you are doing the right thing!" She began to run back up the stairs.

Chapter 29

Helen took Anna out on her back lawn, now thickly sprinkled with dandelions, and interrogated her. Anna was incoherent.

"On Sunday Ian spent the night here with Lucy, yes," said Helen.

"Well, he decided to leave Judith. He decided before—in the afternoon. Then he came to talk to Lucy about it."

"So on Monday, why didn't he . . . ?"

"Judith was being interviewed by the History Department."

"It would be like him to help her get the job first. Idiot!" said Helen impatiently.

"Well, good luck to her! Although, after this Jimson business this afternoon . . ."

"What are you talking about, Anna?"

Anna told Helen about the conversation between Jimson and Judith, ending with a graphic description of Judith's parting remark and the coffee throwing. Helen was laughing in a Teutonic sort of way.

"After I threw the coffee, I went to my office," Anna continued. "Ian was there waiting for me. I made him go home to explain. He told me you had invited me to dinner. Did you actually invite me to dinner?" she asked suddenly.

"You are always welcome. I have told Ian this."

"Helen, you're sweet."

"I am sour," said Helen reflectively. "I laugh at what is really very serious."

"You think he's made the right decision, don't you?"

"Yes. I have told you. I think he should not have let her return."

"And then, the job in the History Department. Do you think she'll still take it?"

Helen looked down at her apron thoughtfully. "She would like to, perhaps. But how can she?"

"But if she really just came back for that?"

"How can she accept his help?"

"But she doesn't care about Ian, does she? Besides, he's helped her already. It sounded as though she had pretty well landed the job."

"You were telling me about Professor Jimson the other day. Judith is also an American."

"Good heavens, Helen," said Anna slowly. "So it is exactly the same. In order to stay here she has to—"

"Stay married to him, at least for a while, like your Mr. Jimson and that poor Francoise."

Anna sat down beside a croquet wicket. "Do you think Ian knows anything about all this?" she asked Helen.

"This part you have explained to me yourself. It was not so when we came to this university. I did not know. It has only become clear to me yesterday that Judith needed Ian for this."

They had a spring dinner of steamed salmon and strawberries. Anna, deep in her own thoughts, was unable to make much headway with the general conversation. Occasionally she looked over at Lucy, who was being egged on by Celeste to tell a very long and complicated joke about someone called Nobody. Helen was listening patiently to this with a complete lack of comprehension. It was a relief to see that Lucy was really only nine.

Anna tried to help with the dishes after supper, but this was not permitted.

"I haven't dropped a plate since I was twelve. I swear it, Helen."

"Celeste prefers the washing up to her homework. You will enjoy a game of chess with Cybele."

"You hear that?" muttered Cybele. " 'You will enjoy'—and that's an order!" They went out into the garden with the chess board.

Anna lost three times almost at once.

"My brains are addled," she said, adding quickly, "Of course, you are a much better player."

"What is it like to have an unhappy love affair?" asked Cybele. "I always imagine it as involving a lot of lying around sobbing by the telephone."

"Um," replied Anna.

"You seem to spend all your time over here telling jokes to my mother. Of course he's old. I suppose that makes a difference."

"Not so very old."

"I don't want to hurt your feelings," said Cybele, at once. "I expect I'll like old ones too, not having had a living male parent in the pubescent years."

"I have a perfectly good father."

"Of course old people can still have sex," Cybele went on, taking no notice of Anna. "But I don't know whether my mother is aware of that. Celeste told her the facts of life only a few years ago."

"What are you discussing?" asked Helen, coming across the grass towards them, her quick eyes taking in the disposition of the chess pieces from the end of the last game. "When I was young, I have had such serious intellectual conversation with my friends as you are having now with Anna, Cybele."

Ian came at about 9:00. He could not stay long. Judith was going to a hotel. While she remained with Gregor and Jane, he had come to collect Lucy.

"Have you eaten anything?" asked Helen, looking at him critically.

"Dread lunch downstairs at the Faculty Club with the Budget Committee and the deans," he said, taking Anna's hand under the kitchen table.

"Chicken cutlets and canned peas," said Anna promptly, squeezing gently.

"Tapioca pudding."

"Judith can wait while you have tea. Lucy will butter the toast, Anna. She likes to. Go into the other room, and we'll bring it."

In the living room Anna said, "That must have been awful."

"Not as awful as all last week and the week before." He sat down in the chair by the fireplace, pulling her down with him.

"Did she mind—a lot?" Anna had accepted Helen's interpretation of Judith, but she was worried.

"She said you are pretty," said Ian. "She will not try to take the children. She is going back to Harvard."

"What about the job in the History Department?"

"She said it was a pity to let Jimson have it."

"I agree with her about that!"

"She thinks she would be taking charity from me if she accepted it." He frowned. "Although I don't really see what I have to do with it."

Anna pressed her nose against his shoulder thoughtfully. Helen would probably tell him. She hoped he would not entirely believe it.

"What about you?" she asked into his jacket.

"Lucy and Gregor and Jane," he said, stroking her hair. "And you."

Anna remained silent. She wanted him to explain more fully but knew he could not.

Anna gave two exams at the end of the week. The Budget Committee continued to meet. The Arts Building was in a state of museum-like emptiness. O'Toole and Ian, wrestling the Administration for higher salaries, would appear only in the late afternoon. From under Eddy's door a continuous drift of opera music betokened profound devotion to his work.

Anna, too, was marking examination papers and, as this went on, found that her habits were becoming more and more eccentric.

"What are you doing?" asked Ian, coming out into her kitchen at 3:00 in the morning to find her hunched over the table in her nightgown and shawl with a red pencil.

"I remembered a punctuation error in the comments I wrote on this paper."

"Why are you writing comments? After you mark these, they will be put in a locked vault in the Registrar's office," he said, taking away the pencil.

"What about posterity?" she asked. "Someday they'll open the vault and . . ."

"No one will be able to read 100 years from now. I shouldn't worry about that."

Anna and Ian were drifting placidly through these days on the surface of their love affair. In the spring evenings they walked home together, sometimes crossing the bridges several times for the pleasure of prolonging a conversation. The river poured pellucid beneath their feet, sparkling in sunshine, smug and glossy in rain.

He was spending all his evenings and spare afternoons with the children. This was no longer problematical for Anna.

"I will take Gregor for a walk tomorrow while you go with Lucy and Jane to the pool," she announced one Friday evening as they were coming reluctantly off a bridge towards home.

"There's no need for you to do a thing like that," he said.

"But I'd like to."

"You don't know what you're saying, woman. Going for a walk with Gregor is all running. Then there's 'Can I have some candy?' ('May I have some candy,' really, but he doesn't speak the language yet) and breaking up fights with stray children, and making him spit out pebbles."

"I like non-organized outdoor sports."

"Do you remember that day by the river when—?"

"I do," said Anna firmly. "Gregor and I were having a marvellous time until you appeared."

"He was kicking when I showed up."

"Well, before that he was humming and getting on with some dandelions."

"Do you think it's possible for someone not related by blood to like a child like Gregor?"

"What kind of a question is that?" asked Anna, breathless, as they breasted the riverbank. She sat down on a convenient park bench at an outlook and watched contentedly as he lit two cigarettes.

"Blood has nothing to do with it, I suppose," he said slowly, frowning, and passing her one of them. He took her other hand.

"Contiguity is more imortant than consanguinity. I'm getting to know him."

"I decided to leave Judith because of seeing you that day with Gregor."

"Oh dear," she said taking her hand away from him.

"You cannot hold yourself responsible for that." He retrieved the hand. Anna looked up at the tree above their heads. The shiny, sticky buds glistened in the late afternoon light.

"It would not have worked—with Judith," she remarked, to reassure herself.

"Yes. I realized that sooner than I otherwise would have because I was throwing away something that was working."

"Something different." Anna smoked, gazing stubbornly ahead.

"Better."

"Can you compare apples and oranges? This is not like being married, you said, almost the first time . . ."

"That was then."

" 'That was in *there*,' " mocked Anna. " '*Then* I would have said anything.' Don't you know that men almost never marry their mistresses? And when they do, it's invariably a mistake."

"What are you intending to do when this is over," he asked abruptly. He meant, as all the academic community did, the end of the term.

"I haven't been thinking about it." Anna had done none of the things necessary for her departure on May the fifth except for the notice she had given her landlord at the first of the month. "I'm going to have to go away, Ian."

"You could just as well get a job here for next year." He looked up hesitantly. "In a bookstore—or something." He trained his eyes back down on his knees.

"Perhaps I could."

"Helen thinks . . ."

"What does Helen think?" Anna wanted to know.

"She thinks you should not leave here. She is sure you won't be happy if you go away. Even if you go back to . . ." he named Anna's old university town.

"Why not? I have friends there. I could find a job and get on with philosophy in spare moments. It's not so far away. We could visit each other."

"Post cards," he said bitterly.

Anna felt the tide of anxiety rising in her chest.

"I'm trying to spare us both something," she said quietly. "It's not because I don't love you. It's because I do. What do you think it would be like to have me around all the time . . ."

"I want that."

". . . moaning about having to work in a bookstore or something worse, and . . ."

"You wouldn't have to."

". . . being envious of you and Helen and everybody else having something real to do—not just collecting a paycheck."

"But it wouldn't be different if you were somewhere else. You would be all alone, too."

"At least I wouldn't be oppressing people I care about. Better to be alone."

He smoked in silence.

"It's not just ambition and pride," she said pleadingly. The effort she had been making all spring to say and think nothing about this was being breached like a dyke. "I have to have time to sort things out. Everything will be so different, you see."

"You'll get it all wrong, brooding about it by yourself," he said urgently.

"But I can't let you think about it for me."

"I don't need to think."

"There, you see? I care about you." Anna got up, stamping her cigarette underfoot. "But one cannot just say, Now that he's got rid of that dread wife of his, I'm going to . . ."

"Marry him," he finished, getting up as well. "Why not?"

"Because not," said Anna, horrified that she had finally let this be said. "It's nothing to do with you. I love you. I am fond of your children. But I won't. If we could go on as before, it would be different. But we can't go on as before, or at least we don't have much time left."

"How much time then?"

"May the fifth," said Anna, still not really believing it herself. "If only we could go on as before."

"We need time," he said despairingly. He took her arm and they continued their walk in silence, heedless now of lace curtains, each wrapped in sad, private reflections.

Chapter 30

On Saturday Anna took Gregor back from their walk to Helen's house. She stopped at her apartment briefly to pick up a bunch of asparagus which was her contribution to supper.

Like most children of his age and educational advantages, Gregor was fascinated by the sound of words.

"Sparegrass," he said.

" 'Sparrowgrass' is good," said Anna, who shared this interest.

"Aspergas."

"A stomach ache."

"Peargasp."

"Too much green fruit."

"What are you talking about?" asked Ian, meeting them at the gate.

" 'S aspargas," cried Gregor, flourishing the paper bag.

"A kind of tea drunk by Sarasote Indians."

"Are you having a good time?" Ian looked at her quizzically as Gregor ran into the house.

"Very good. It was fun, except for the part when the Newfoundland dog glopped all over Gregor. He didn't enjoy that. Unlike you, I never have a handkerchief."

"I see that he lets you hold his hand. He doesn't like me to do that. He regards me as a kind of ball and chain."

"Children should be separated from their parents at birth," said Anna sternly. "That way no one would expect anything more than physical similarity. When they are of an age to be content with that—the parents, I mean—they could be allowed to see their offspring."

"It's true that Gregor and I are very different." He led her up the porch steps.

"You both like body contact," Anna replied, getting an intent look from Ian in response.

They wallowed in asparagus. Helen had bought some as well, in the same neighbourhood market as Anna.

"Why couldn't it always be spring?" asked Celeste dreamily, pouring cream on her strawberries. "No hideous winter clothes, no ugly grey snow, no cabbage salad every day for weeks . . ."

"In Scotland at this time of year—" said Ian, clearing his throat. They all looked at him attentively. The only other male at the table was constructing a log house of asparagus stalk-ends. "—we would be eating nettles."

"What about the sting?" cried his listeners.

"No sting. They are boiled—"

"But how do you pick them?"

"—sometimes with oatmeal and sometimes without."

"Ugh," said Celeste.

"Like Mama's stomach soup," said Cybele. "I'm glad I didn't grow up in Europe."

"Tripe is both cheap and delicious," said Helen severely. "Tripe soup is good for the digestion and for the nervous system. *Tripe à la mode de Caen*—listen to me, Cybele, for you will eat tripe in France very often . . ."

"Poor Cybele," said Celeste. "Too bad for her she is an intellectual." She dodged a sharp nudge from her sister's elbow.

After the dishes were done, they played croquet with all eight balls. Ian was not permitted to help with the dishes either, but he hung around to assist in the French lesson to Anna's admiration; his rolled Scottish 'r's' contrasting oddly with Helen's inability to say the letter.

"Did you play croquet in Scotland, Daddy?" asked Lucy. Scotland was still a myth to Ian's children. Unlike Cybele and Celeste they did not yet have to face the awful reality of going there.

"We played golf," he said, testing the balance of his mallet.

"You never play golf here."

"They can't play the game on this continent."

The croquet game became hilarious. Gregor and Jane hid the balls, and the players stumbled around in Helen's rose hedges looking for them in the half-dusk.

"Gregor and Jane count as natural obstacles."

"Like a sand trap."

It was obvious from the beginning that Helen was going to win. She played a steady, even game, always taking advantage of the extra shot when she hit someone's ball.

"What is this, a vendetta?" cried Anna, as Ian knocked her ball away around the side of the house for the third time. "Why are you always picking on me?"

"This is why," he said, coming up behind her quietly, as she went to retrieve it, "as you very well know."

"Everyone is noticing. Your children . . . Lucy."

"They know about kissing."

Afterwards they had tea as usual. It was not a school night for the children, so they were staying very late. Helen had Lucy working on buttered toast. Jane was sleepily sucking her thumb on Ian's knee. To Anna's surprise Gregor climbed up on her own lap and fell into a doze.

"Is he putting your foot to sleep?" asked Celeste solicitously. "He always does mine."

"It's all right, I think," said Anna, cuddling cautiously. Gregor's warm, childish bulk against her chest was very pleasant, even though her foot was asleep. Self-consciously she avoided glancing at Ian.

They walked home together, Ian carrying the sleeping Gregor.

Wasn't it fun?" murmured Anna, happily. "Helen and Cybele are so much alike, only Cybele is the North American version."

"Why won't either of those two children speak German?" asked Ian. "It is an ideal opportunity. They understand it perfectly well."

"Have you tried Lucy out on Gaelic?"

"He's tried," said Lucy darkly.

"I go in here," said Anna, pointing to her dark fire escape. She detached her hand from Lucy's.

"Can't she come with us?" asked Lucy.

"Yes, come with us," said Ian, stock still on the sidewalk.

"All right, if . . ." Anna paused, surveying them. "I'll have to see whether it's okay with my cat."

"Can I come with you while you tell him?" asked Lucy.

Anna sat quietly in one of the brown velours unsprung chairs in the parlour while Ian put the children to bed. She had been quite wrong about the philodendrons. There were none. The mantel, however, was as she had imagined it. She began to examine the bookcase, which she had not noticed before.

He came downstairs at length and stood in front of the mantel looking down at her with an entirely new kind of gaze.

"You look just right there," she said, curling her legs underneath her and lying back in the chair, which was surprisingly comfortable.

"Why do you say that?" He continued to give her this new look.

"I think I am a sort of house-detective. It's a form of

clairvoyance no one seems to talk about. This is all just as I imagined it."

He looked around at the large, barren room.

"It's not very comfortable," he began, clearing his throat.

"It's exactly right. It's perfect." Anna sprang to her feet and went up to him. "You don't mind my being here? It must seem strange." She thought of Judith. It had been an entirely different kind of look he'd been giving her.

"Mind?" he said. Anna gave him an anxious kiss. She realized that it had been less than two weeks since Judith had been here, probably standing where she was now standing and sitting in the same chair. She looked around nervously. There was no sign of Judith's ever having been there.

"Mind?" he repeated more forcefully. "How should I mind? This is just what I wanted." He followed her eyes around the room. "I never noticed how hideous it all is. You stand out against it," he added helplessly.

Anna's perception of the room sharpened. This really was what it was like to be Ian. House-detection equals knowledge of character. She thought of her own apartment. So that is what I am like, she thought. An iron bedstead, an orange crate, a winter chrysanthemum.

Ian was saying hesitantly, "Everything could be different, of course, if you lived here."

"With my talent for house decoration?" Anna parried. "Look closely at me. Look into my eyes. Do you see any furniture there?" She gave him the opportunity to take a good look.

"Bed," he said. "I see bed in your eyes." He began to draw her gently towards the door.

"Is everyone asleep?" Anna was feeling a certain reluctance. He nodded. They were in the hall now, the dark wooden wainscoting below the stairs on Anna's left. She thought of the room at the back of the house whose door she had never opened.

"I can't . . . I mean, I wouldn't like . . ."

"That's all right. We won't," he said, divining her thought with quick intuition. Anna found this eerie.

They began to mount the stairs. The homely familiarity of the house no longer seemed amusing to Anna. She was overpowered by it. The whole house was giving her Ian's new kind of glance. It was a proprietary glance, a married glance, a settled glance.

"Bathroom." He pointed to the room on the left at the top of the stairs.

She nodded. "I know."

They went down the hall to the little room on the moonlit side of the house. Anna was slightly paralysed. He opened the door, and she entered first.

"The bed is not very large," he said dubiously. Anna wrapped her arms around her chest. She had her eyes closed. She was feeling terror now. The house cried, Love me, wash me, paint me, make curtains! The room sighed, Cure my loneliness, give me a child.

"Anna."

Anna made an inarticulate sound and opened her eyes.

"Don't be frightened. Why are you afraid?" He was standing by the window in the moonlight, looking worried.

"Vacuum cleaner hoses. They make me think of snakes." She gasped and tried to laugh. She looked around. There were no vacuum cleaner hoses on the wall. The bed was much larger than she had imagined it. There was nothing else in the room but a tall, gloomy bureau. Ian's clothing hung in the closet.

"I just imagined it," she said weakly, letting him take her in his arms.

Some time later, Anna struggled out of sleep and gently wriggled away from his side. Kneeling beside him, she watched his sleeping face, smoothed by moonlight. Anna wondered whether she was really awake.

He said suddenly, "Was I snoring?"

"You snuffled."

"You're being polite. I snored." He sat up, rubbing his forehead.

"Do you always sleep here?"

"Yes. Not always," he corrected himself. "This room is where I thought about you all winter."

"And now I am here."

"And now you are here." They smiled at one another. "But why are you over there?"

Anna thought of something. She got to her feet and looked around for one of the larger pieces of her clothing.

"Where are you going?" he asked in alarm.

"Just a moment. There's something I have to see."

"Take my dressing gown," he said. "It's in the closet."

"Thanks." She put it on and went out into the hall. There was no picture of Queen Victoria and John Brown outside the door to the room at the back of the house. A map of Scotland detailing the clan territories and associated tartans hung there instead. She took this in and, with a sigh of relief, began to go back to Ian's bedroom.

He was watching her from the doorway.

"Did you see it?"

"It's not really as I imagined it," she murmured. "In fact, I got it all wrong."

"Come here immediately."

She woke up the next morning to the sound of bathwater running. Ian was standing over her in his shirtsleeves holding a cup of tea. A fresh, spring breeze was blowing through the striped curtains around the open window.

"Is it late?" She sat up. The sun was shining brightly.

He gave her the teacup and straightened the pillows behind her.

"Half a minute," he said and went out. The bathwater noise stopped.

"Good heavens," she said, moving her legs so that he could sit down. "The maid at home never does this sort of thing. Union regulations forbid tea in bed. Is the bath for me, too?"

"Yes."

"This is so nice." Anna looked around. Everything in the room was illuminated by the cheerful, spring sun. "Did you have tea in bed in Scotland?"

"My mother liked it," he said.

"I've never done anything like this for you," said Anna remorsefully. "Just glasses of water in the morning at my house."

"Lucy seems to be organizing breakfast. Mostly toast, I think."

"And you never get anything to eat."

"You cannot cook," he said austerely.

"No, of course not." Anna began to laugh. "I forgot."

"You'll spill your tea." He took the cup away and put it on the bureau.

"Is the bath next?"

"Bath, and then there's some sort of a picnic in plan. First, however . . ."

"But the water will get cold!"

"It is much too hot at the moment."

Chapter 31

Anna gave her last examination on April 27th, two days before the end of the exam period. The examination was being held in the skating rink. She rode in from her apartment on her bicycle in the early morning, remembering with nostalgia her 8:30 walks of the winter before. The sun was well up at this hour now, while during the winter it had been pitch dark. It was hard to believe, looking around at the budding trees and the green grass, that she was still in the same part of the world.

ffrench was the Head Proctor, according to her timetable. Anna collected her armload of examinations from the Registrar and waited with the other proctors before the locked door to the arena for ffrench to come with the key and the seating disposition of the students. He did not show up.

At ten to nine a chemist took charge. Selecting a credit card from the fistfuls offered by those around him, he jimmied the lock on the door and began hurriedly making up a seating plan.

Anna distributed her papers and then, as the students filed in, bethought herself and ran back to the Registrar's office to collect ffrench's exams.

"Are you Professor ffrench?" asked the factotum, an efficient woman, tales of whose arbitrary decision-making powers were whispered around campfires in distant Africa.

"He may have slept in," Anna said, starting her story at the wrong end.

"Every professor is to collect his own examinations and distribute them himself."

"But the students are waiting."

"We cannot give examinations out to students."

"Who else should we give them to, then?" asked Anna stupidly.

"I'm afraid you and the rest of the class will just have to wait until we contact Professor ffrench."

After a great deal of argument, Anna was able to convince the woman, whose name was Mrs. Bartlett, that she was not a nameless student pretending to be ffrench, nor a student named Anna Callaghan deputizing for ffrench, nor a student pretending to be an unknown faculty member named Anna Callaghan, nor a student at all. The second, more difficult part of the discussion was about whether Anna Callaghan was a professor. After consulting several directories, they determined that this was so but ran at once into the difficulty of whether she could be identified conclusively as the Anna Callaghan of the directories.

Anna ran back to the skating rink with ffrench's exams and distributed them hurriedly to the angry students. Her own students were also upset, and Anna spent most of the second half of the first hour of the examination walking the aisles to answer more than the usual number of nervous questions.

About half way through the examination period Anna went out for a cigarette. Finding a pay phone in the porch of the Rink, she hesitantly dialed ffrench's number. Her impulse was to cover for him.

After a great many rings, someone answered the phone.

"Classical Guitar Incorporated," said a female voice. "Nelson is wearing the earphones just now. At the end of the long dash, state your name, your problem, and a number where you can be reached." As the woman began to produce a nasal hum, Anna slammed the phone down on the hook. She went back to the exam room, thinking of ffrench's fingernails.

In the huge, sterile arena which smelt now not of sweat but of ink, the students poured their hearts out into the blue booklets. Anna sat down with an existentialist novel lent her by Helen but was unable to concentrate, her being filled with empathetic terror as she looked over the serried ranks of bent backs before her.

She went back to the Arts Building with the chemist, her papers tucked together with ffrench's in her bicycle basket.

"ffrench must be a real nincompoop," said the chemist. Anna had confided to him the result of her telephone call.

"No, no. He's very smart. It's just that he goes all out for things, like Toad: canary-coloured caravans, red motor cars . . ."

"Really?"

"Well, classical guitar at the moment, anyhow."

"I'm glad you agree he's a toad. Care for a cup of coffee?"

Anna considered. At the beginning of the year she would have accepted gladly. But her horizon was closing in now; it seemed hardly worthwhile to try to get to know someone when she would be leaving so soon.

"I really shouldn't," she said, gesturing at the stack of papers.

"Oh well. See you next term." He waved, turning towards the cafeteria.

Dumping her papers in her office, Anna went down to the mailroom and stuffed ffrench's examinations into his box. Looking into her own she found and discarded two circulars. There was also a letter from the journal to which she had sent her paper.

The letter began doubtfully, describing the difficulties the journal was having in meeting its present publishing commitments, which extended well into the late 1980s. The last two sentences expressed an interest in her "short paper" and added that she would receive referee's comments under separate cover.

Anna dashed back up to the Philosophy Department, looking for someone to pour this news out to. Not even Eddy was present and so she ran on up to the coffee room. There was a tiny colloquy of people who had given examinations that morning having lunch there. O'Toole was standing by the coffee urn.

"Peter!" cried Anna. "What do you make of this?" She thrust the letter at him, panting.

"Right here?" he asked, taking it tenderly and looking around him at the little gathering, hunched over their sandwich papers. "In public like this?"

Grimacing, he read the first paragraph. Anna watched his face, her heart in her mouth. "What do you think?" she asked.

"B," he replied thoughtfully. "Perhaps a B+."

"Surely it's yes or no?"

"Not no. I'd say it's 'pending pending approval approval'." He looked up. "When did you make this magnificent effort?"

"About three weeks ago. I had nothing better to do, so I just—"

"It got into the mailbag accidentally when you were going for the wastebasket." He nodded. "Your hand slipped. I know how these things happen."

"What's this?" asked Eddy, coming into the room with one of his enormous bottles of Coca-Cola. "What's up, Callaghan?"

"Perhaps Anna will have a paper published," said O'Toole, showing the letter.

"Perhaps, perhaps," said Anna pensively.

"Well, at least they admit you wrote one," said O'Toole. "What more do you want?"

"That's swell, Callaghan!" cried Eddy enthusiastically. "You must be happy! How do you feel about it? Is it worth anything?"

"I thought it was awful when I sent it in, but now that they say almost yes, I think it must be sort of good."

"There, you see!" Eddy was shouting earnestly. "That's what gets my goat! If some jackass can really shovel the—pardon my French, Anna—if some jackass can put out a lot of garbage and get it across, then it doesn't matter to anybody, least of all the guy who wrote it, whether it's worth a plugged nickel! Where's the integrity in that?"

"There, there," whispered O'Toole. "He doesn't mean a thing by it."

"Now you take a fellow like Peter, here—" Eddy grasped O'Toole's lapel like an ear. "Slaving away eight years on his dissertation! It's as thick as *The Critique of Pure Reason*. Can he find a publisher? Not on your life! It's a mug's game!"

O'Toole made a number of gestures throughout this along Alfred E. Neuman lines: What, me worry? Don't know a thing about this. Nothing to say to that! Shrugging, lifting his eyebrows and extending his hands palm outwards at shoulder height.

The others present looked on with pleasure during the continuation of Eddy's speech. Anna recognized the at-least-we-don't-have-this-sort-of-thing-in-our-department reaction. She rescued her letter and slunk away with it, reading it over several times in the elevator and outside her office door.

Michie was within.

Anna sat down at her desk and lit a cigarette. She put her feet up on the wastebasket and hummed a few bars. Then, carefully balancing the burning cigarette on the edge of her desk, she got out her powder compact and gazed at her face in the little mirror.

"I'll be going to see Ian MacGregor shortly," she said to the mirror. "Don't bother to get up."

"They offered his wife my job," said Michie expressionlessly. "I suppose you know."

Anna had not known this for sure. She dabbed a bit of powder on her nose.

"She turned it down," said Michie.

Anna continued to gaze silently at her face in the mirror. It was impossible not to feel sorry for him at this juncture, whatever he had said about her to Jimson.

"I suppose you think they gave it to Jimson," Michie went on.

"Why do you care, Fred?" she said, stubbing out her cigarette in the wastebasket. "What does it matter, really?"

"Wait. Don't you know any of this?" He scraped back his chair abruptly and walked around the desk. Anna swivelled about, alarmed. "They've cut it out altogether. When the MacGregor woman said no, there was a big to-do in the Department. History and Politics—"

"They've cut out the job?" Anna was dazed.

"They went for each other's throats, don't you understand? They couldn't agree on Jimson. Then the Dean got into it, and—"

"There is no job in the History Department now?" Anna was desperate to get this straight, suddenly.

"The reviewers' report was very bad. So when the Dean found out that they couldn't make a decision about hiring someone because they all hate each other so much . . ."

"So Michael . . . ?"

"The Dean went straight to the Vice President, and they took away the funds. There's no job at all any longer. Jimson's out on his ear!"

Anna stared at Michie who had been hissing these last words at her, bent forward over a corner of her desk. He reached for an old cigarette package on the blotter and withdrew the single, stale cigarette from it. Anna silently pushed the match book towards him and he fumbled inexpertly with the paper match.

So Francoise was saved. Anna realized with guilt that she had given no thought to Francoise for nearly three weeks. Not that there was anything I could have done, she comforted herself.

"When did all this happen, Fred?"

"After the MacGregor woman left. You ought to know when that was." Michie was getting on with his cigarette very well. He must have been a born-again non-smoker, Anna thought.

Ignoring his last implication, she asked, "What is Michael doing these days?"

"He won't get anything now. It's too late," said Michie with relish, puffing away.

"There's always Sierra Leone," murmured Anna.

"He ditched Sierra Leone."

"How careless of him. No thought for the future."

"Mrs. MacGregor took that one!" Michie put down his burning cigarette and burst into sudden laughter.

"You can't be serious!"

"Oh yes I am!"

Anna looked up. He was standing over her chair with a glazed look in his eyes. Revenge and nicotine were stirring his blood.

"You mustn't let it get to you like this, Fred." Anna pushed back her chair carefully and stood up.

"Get to me?" There was something almost sinister in his expression.

Anna began to back away towards the door.

"Get to me? I've never felt better in my life! This is nemesis! God is good!"

Anna pulled the door open, reaching behind her, and slipped back through the gap between it and the doorjamb. She was nervously grateful for the first time that her desk was the one next to the door.

Michie followed her to the threshold, his face still showing in the crack as she slowly closed the door on him.

"My whole life has meaning now!"

Chapter 32

Anna had invited Helen to her apartment for tea the next day. Helen had very nearly finished marking all her papers, something she did conscientiously, sitting upright at her desk hour by hour. Estimating that she would be finished by 3:27 that day, she had accepted Anna's invitation.

Anna nervously spent the morning ignoring her fresh pile of examination papers and making a chocolate cake from a recipe in a German cookbook. She had not been spending very much time at home of late. The apartment no longer struck her as a very congenial setting. Going into the living room, she lay experimentally on the floor, pretending to be Helen.

"This will never do." She took the cushion off the single arm chair in which no one but the cat ever sat and placed it experimentally on the floor. The canvas sling of the chair gaped at her, a few pennies from the pockets of Ian's carelessly draped trousers in a dismal pile with a hairpin and some cat fur at the bottom.

Anna put the cushion back. She got the orange crate from beside the bed and put the two pillows in a casual heap beside it. The orange crate was wrong. She took it back and went out to the kitchen to pick out the least broken of the chairs. Sighing with exasperation, she put her keys in her pocket and went out the door to go to the university for a few hours.

"I like this Bohemianism," said Helen, sitting on Anna's living room floor. "It reminds me of my student days. Of course we had no oven, no hot water . . ."

"It is not that I am poor," said Anna. "I have twice as much money as I had when I was a student. Three times as much, actually. But with this moving from job to job, it seems hardly worthwhile to collect any possessions. 'A move is as good as a fire', you know."

"This we did not have to face," said Helen. "When Friedrich and I came here we knew it would be to stay."

"Your house is so pleasant," said Anna. "It is a haven of civilization. Ian's is rather more—Scottish." She thought with love of the dark, wooden mantel with the clock. She went out into the kitchen to fetch the cake. Helen was pensively stroking the cat when she came back.

"So what do you do now?" asked Helen, waving her hand around to indicate Anna's way of life. "Will you hear further from any employers?"

"That's still possible," said Anna beginning to cut the cake. "There's an open market for casual labour—part-time sessional appointments and research assistantships. I won't be staying here, anyhow. I've given notice on this place for May fifth."

"What if you hear nothing? You will have no place to live."

"I had to give notice at the first of the month," said Anna. "People who own houses forget how awkward that is."

"Yes, I had forgotten." Helen was suddenly agitated. "But you must plan. You will stay here for the summer at least."

"I could take back my notice, I suppose. It's the time of year when no one is renting anything in a university town. But what good would it do? I'll have to leave in the end anyhow."

Helen was not eating her cake. "You will leave on May fifth? You have told Ian this?"

"He knows."

"What will he do? What will you do?" She was staring at Anna angrily. "You cannot . . ."

"I will see him again. I'll probably go home to my parents for a while." Anna felt as though Helen's stare was pushing her against the wall.

"Helen, Ian wants to marry me. He wants it and wants it, and you know why that is. It's getting worse too. I barely spend any time here at all. The cat is miserable."

"You need not marry him. But you should not . . ."

"I should not marry him. You know that very well. He's still all confused about that, even though on the surface . . ."

"He is very happy," said Helen, still staring.

"Yes he is, and so am I, but it's no good, don't you see?"

"Like Judith, you are ambitious."

"Like Judith and not like Judith. I want to pursue my profession if I can, yes; but if I can't, I won't use Ian as a vehicle for economic and social security. Especially not now when he wants to be married so much."

Anna got up and went out to the kitchen. She stood by the table at the window looking out, her back to the living room.

After a moment Helen followed her.

"The cake is delicious," she said. "But in Germany we would have walnuts, not pecans."

"Oh Helen!" said Anna, laughing and giving her a brief hug. "It is right. I see that. If you could go on as before it would be different."

"If I had got a job here for next year we could have. But as it is, I'd just end up living on him. I'd make him horribly unhappy in the end."

They went back into the living room.

"You have so little time left," said Helen, frowning. "If only you had more time."

"If only we had time," Anna wailed.

On the afternoon of the twenty-ninth of April, the Faculty met to approve the new contracts with the University. Anna went to the meeting out of some sort of herd instinct and because she wanted to hear Ian and O'Toole do battle with the Administration for one last time over the Budget. The issue over which the battle was pitched was parking.

"Why do you care about parking?" Anna had asked Ian the night before. "If it costs more to get a parking place, more people will just walk. It's a small city. You always walk."

"It's part of an overall policy." He replaced the dishtowel in her hands with a glass of sherry and began himself to wipe some plates. "Every time we give way on one of these issues, we lose a bit more out of our salaries. We have no unified basis for negotiation. It's a piecemeal business."

"O'Toole thinks we—you should have a union."

"The pension fund is a disgrace," went on Ian. "There won't be anything in it by the time I retire."

He put a small stack of plates into the cupboard, which was painted pale institutional green, not eggshell blue, as Anna had imagined it.

"There aren't any poorhouses on this continent—not like in Scotland," said Anna in imitation. He still had nineteen years of teaching ahead of him.

Today, as they filed into the huge meeting room, O'Toole tapped her on the shoulder urgently. "Where have you been all my life? I've got something to tell you. No time to talk now. Coming to the party tonight?"

"What party?" asked Anna vaguely.

"The same one as last year. We always have one."

"I didn't get an invitation."

"We never bother with the things. Too much talk. Got to get the right people. Can't do that with invitations.." He pushed his way through the crowd, and Anna caught a glimpse of him up ahead, tapping people's shoulders.

She took her usual place towards the back of the theatre and catching sight of Frame nearby, went over to sit beside him. "How are things?" she asked. The hall was still filling up. "I haven't had a chance to see anyone lately. Is Francoise . . . ?" She meant to ask whether Francoise was speaking to him yet but decided that this would not be a tactful way to begin.

Guilt arose in Anna again. She had not even called Francoise. The woman had tried to befriend Anna when she was in trouble. Why am I such a heartless, selfish person, Anna asked herself.

"I'd love to have got my hands on that rat, but he left quite a while ago," the gentle Frame was confiding to her through his teeth.

"He just left, without even saying goodbye?" Anna controlled her levity. She repeated, "Is Francoise . . . ?"

"Francoise is getting better now," said Frame. "I don't think she'll ever really trust anyone again," he added sadly.

Anna felt sad, too. "She's not here, is she?" she asked, looking around. Perhaps they could have a talk after the meeting. Anna would tell her some comforting lies about Jimson.

"She decided not to come. She's still quite self-conscious about it all. I told her she should stay at home."

At home? "You're seeing a lot of her then, I hope?"

Frame was smiling tenderly at his hands. "She's staying with me," he whispered confidentially. "Her apartment still reminds her . . ."

Anna felt a surge of joy for Frame. Maybe life did have meaning after all, as Michie said. She turned to pass on part of her thought to Frame, but he was now gazing down at the demonstration table with intense concentration. The meeting was beginning. The President had arisen.

Throughout the President's opening remarks, some of Anna's joyful sympathy for Frame began to subside. If Francoise was a woman who could be attracted by Jimson, was she right for the timid Frame? She remembered Francoise's masterful way of getting a table in the crowded cafeteria. Anna recalled her own association with Jimson at the beginning of the first term. There's a bit of Michael in me, too, she confessed to herself sorrowfully.

Anna found herself growing more and more bored as the meeting went on.

She had started to see the faculty through the eyes of a waitress or a truck driver. It was just a pretentious gathering of fortunate, middle-class men and women interested only in increasing their already ample salaries.

Remembering the debate over the special report of the Committee on Teaching Improvement and Evaluation, Anna began to rate them for performance as teachers as they rose to speak. O'Toole got an A for his presentation, although Anna was tempted to lower his grade because of certain correctable defects in his personal appearance. Emily Dowell got an unexpected A- for her presentation. She gave many C's, a few D's. When Ian got up to speak, she gave him an A and then, trying to be fair, lowered it to a B.

All the same, she thought, popular standards are not everything. After Ian's part in the debate was over, she unobtrusively left the hall.

So that was the last Faculty Meeting, thought Anna, reefing her skirts before she got on her bicycle. Tonight, I'll be going to the last party. But before that, I must mark the last papers. She set herself to pedal home quickly. Anna had still done nothing about packing. But she did not think of this.

Ian called her up.

"Why are you there?" he asked. Anna inferred that he was at home.

"I am marking papers."

"You were at the meeting."

"I stayed until I heard you speak. I loved you," she said truthfully.

"But you didn't hear how it came out," he complained. "We won."

"I'm glad. I had to get these things done. Besides, I wasn't feeling like a participant, somehow."

"Ah."

"Peter is giving a party tonight. I expect he told you."

"Yes. In a burst of enthusiasm he even invited the Vice-President. Shall I come and fetch you?"

"It'll have to be late. This is going to take at least three more hours."

"We won't miss anything. O'Toole's parties go on and on."

"I remember. I was hired at one last year."

"I'll fetch you in three hours."

Chapter 33

The O'Tooles' house, more modest than Ian's and in a more distant part of town, was filled to bursting with a crowd of newly freed students and faculty still hysterical from their marking. Anna perceived that she had outdone herself in her efforts to be late. She and Ian were soon swept apart in the drunken crowd. Anna lingered in the kitchen beside Melissa O'Toole, listening to her chat to James about Oxfam, CUSO, Amnesty, IAWF, CASCA, INRO, and a number of other political action groups to which they both belonged. Anna was surprised at James' presence. The whole Philosophy Department seemed to be there. She supposed that this change from last year was due to the fact that there was no candidate for a job present.

The living room and dining room were darkened and crowded with swaying, jostling dancers. The music was filling the rooms like a thick syrup. Anna began to edge around to the living room door, looking for Ian. The front hall was the only remaining refuge for conversationalists. She had already canvassed the kitchen.

Nelson ffrench confronted her in the gloom. He was rooted to the spot right next to the door. Not moving his feet at all but bending his knees slightly, he was moving the whole upper part of his body in time to the syrup like a long, skinny water weed swaying in the shallows of a swamp. Catching sight of Anna, he began to make rhythmic come-hither movements with his arms, moving his shoulders back and forth in such a way as to send reptilian waves down his arms. Anna, seeing no means of escape, began to shift back and forth on her legs, trying to keep her hip movements to the absolute minimum required for classification as dancing.

"Obscene, isn't it?" came ffrench's voice through the syrup. "Utterly, totally dirty. Pornographic. Filthy," he went on dreamily, beginning to make the same waves flow up and down his stalk-like neck from his shoulders.

O'Toole appeared suddenly behind ffrench in the living room door, dancing briskly with the rye bottle under his arm. Seeing Anna, he dodged under one of ffrench's uplifted arms and began to dance her backwards through the living room to the dining room door. Using a combination of a waltz grip and some jive-like turns, he steered her through the dining room and around a constellation of onlookers hanging in the kitchen doorway. Anna was clutching him wildly, her muscles seized from the exertion of trying not to trip as he executed this manoeuvre.

"You don't dance very well," he said reprovingly, giving her the rye bottle to hold.

"She looks like she ought to be better at it," said Gore, taking O'Toole's bottle out of Anna's hand and having a breathy swig. "Time and a place for everything I suppose." He gave the rye back to Anna and let a full bottle of beer gurgle gently down his throat. His estranged wife, Emmy, shot Anna a look of hatred.

"We can't talk here," said O'Toole, looking furtively around the cluttered crowded kitchen. "Step over this way into my office."

He led Anna toward the back door, where a small antechamber contained the O'Toole family winter clothes. O'Toole kicked aside some rubber boots and positioned himself against the back door. Anna leaned her arm on a rack of U.S. Army Surplus fatigue jackets, apparently O'Toole's whole collection, and closed her ears to the claque in the kitchen behind her.

"I wonder if you realize that ffrench is no longer with us," O'Toole began without preamble.

"No longer with us? But I was just dancing with him in the living room."

"I didn't mean dead, woman. Although, now that you mention it, it's a surprise one of his students hasn't got around to murdering him yet. He's resigned."

"Resigned?" Anna repeated.

"It was a surprise to me, too. I never thought he'd have the guts to do it."

"Guts?"

"What are you, an echo? He wants to be alone with his guitar."

"Does that mean . . . ?"

"You've got me. There is an opening for next year in the Philosophy Department."

"Are you sure?" Anna leaned heavily on the swaying rack.

"You're thinking of History's predicament, no doubt. Over-

staffed, that department, very. No, this is a deal. Term
appointment, of course. No promises for later. Couldn't expect to
get that out of them at this late date."

"And I . . . ?"

"You're a shoo-in, my little pending-approvaled one."

Anna stared at him in wild disbelief.

"Faint in this direction!" he shrieked. "Faint this way!" He
grabbed her and jumped up and down several times on her feet.

"Peter," said Anna, catching hold of her voice, which had
gone up an octave. "This isn't some hideous practical joke of
yours?"

"Not at all. Cross my heart and hope to die." He took the rye
bottle out of her hand and ritually made an X over it. "You're
going to apply, I hope."

"Yes!"

"Well, apply then."

"Right now? Here?"

"Yes, of course."

"I apply! I hereby apply!"

"Good. We'll be having a short departmental meeting later
on. Meanwhile, have some of this." He offered the bottle back. "It
allays tension. Understandable in a candidate for a job, of course."

O'Toole began looking over Anna's shoulder, grasping her
by the hip as she applied her lips to the bottle.

"There should be enough of us here," he muttered. "I don't
think Peterson has gone home yet. Whoops!" He let go of her and
began to sing:

    " 'Scots wha hae wi' Wallace bled,
    Scots wham Bruce has aften led,
    Welcome to your gory bed,
    Or . . .' "

Anna did not have to look behind her.

"Ah, MacGregor. You're the very person I wanted to see. I was
singing a song to Professor Callaghan here (you have met, haven't
you? Oh good!), and it occurs to me that I've always been in doubt
over its meaning. Now then . . ."

"Ian!" cried Anna. "Peter's told me . . . Did you know . . . ?
There's a . . . !"

"Now then," went on O'Toole implacably. " 'Scots with
hay'—I understand that. They used hay in their mattresses of
course; the reference to bed in the third line makes that clear
enough. But what is this 'wham' at the beginning of the second
line?"

"Ian!" cried Anna more urgently. "Peter says . . . I've got a . . . !"

" 'Wham' is an onomatopoeic term for the sound made by a musket ball striking the head of a Sassenach or other hard, dense object," replied Ian calmly, putting his arm around Anna's waist.

"Oh really? But now wait—there seems to be some problem with the syntax. 'Scots wham Bruce'—I can't really see . . ."

Anna was no longer trying to communicate. She leaned back against MacGregor's arm dreamily. May the fifth of next year began to come into sight like a tiny black pin prick at the end of a long, well-lit tunnel.

About the author

Susan Haley was born in Wolfville, Nova Scotia in 1949. She has a Ph.D. in Philosophy from the University of Alberta and taught at Calgary and Saskatchewan. She now lives in Fort Norman, a village on the MacKenzie River, where she owns a small charter airline.